DECAY TIME

A Wall Street Murder
and
Morality Tale

SCOTT STEVENSON

IceCold
Crime

Published by
Ice Cold Crime LLC
5780 Providence Curve
Independence, MN 55359

Printed in the United States of America

Cover by Laura Rahinantti

Library of Congress Control Number: 2013936896

ISBN-13: 978-0-9824449-7-9
ISBN-10: 0-9824449-7-4

Contents

Author's Note

Smiling, I tossed my Blackberry to its watery grave in the East River. It was May of 2008, months before what would become the most explosive meltdown in U.S. financial market history. I had had enough of my investment banking career, it was time to ride off into the sunrise of that new life to which I had so often daydreamed. I was exhausted, mentally, physically, and spiritually. That voice inside my head, acting as my compass, was saying "no más."

And so it was that I left my vocational battleground in Manhattan. Feeling unencumbered and with no specific plan—atypical, putting it mildly, for a Type-A banker—I had no intention of becoming an author. After 20 years of communicating in broken English via email, text, and Bloomberg messaging, that prospect could not have been more daunting or further from my mind.

Then, immersed in my detached and blissful new lease on life, watching the financial world crater, the inspiration hit me. With each passing day I grew less able to suppress my intolerance toward the widespread media distortions, mischaracterizations, and political vilification of the "evil bankers on Wall Street." In a relatively short span of time I had gone from scratching and clawing to end my days as an investment banker to developing the urge to tell a story far different than what these portrayals would lead one to conclude. That urge was emboldened by a YouTube video I stumbled upon. The level of economic illiteracy was staggering.

In the video, a starry-eyed college student, joining an Occupy Wall Street protest in New York, was holding up a sign which read "Throw me a bone. Pay my tuition!" When asked why someone should pay his tuition, the student, after citing a number of vacuous comments about taxes, banks, and corporate exploitation, meekly responded, "because that is what I want...I can say what I want. That is my opinion." While, of course, I fully support the First Amendment, we have to do better than this as a country. It's an embarrassment, not of riches but of ignorance. As the father of a college student, I cringe.

It is within this spirit that *Decay Time: A Wall Street Murder and Morality Tale* was conceived. Contrary to what its title suggests (*time decay* being an ingredient in the Black-Scholes Option Pricing Model), it is purposefully intended not to be another academic product exposé on the 2008 meltdown; there are ample books predating this one covering that topic. There is, however, an abridged Glossary for those wishing to better appreciate some of the necessary technical language used sparingly throughout.

A fictional account, the novel uses a murder mystery of a banker both to entertain as well as to inform the reader about what daily life on Wall Street actually resembled in the years immediately preceding, during, and in the aftermath of the 2008 meltdown. In doing so it provides glimpses into a range of topics spanning behavior, lifestyle, compensation, ethics, business culture, and the time immemorial quest for money, power, and control. Through such insights, the novel suggests, as a matter of blunt social commentary, that the frailties observed on Wall Street are no different, in concept, than those acted out, past and present, on the stage of politics, the military complex, athletics, the entertainment industry, and virtually any other American enterprise.

The novel also tacitly acknowledges that no system of enterprise is without its imperfections. There are clear deficiencies—behavioral, regulatory, and otherwise—that need and continue to be addressed on Wall Street. My hope is that these deficiencies will be addressed thoughtfully, rather than in a counterproductive, draconian fashion. Dandruff is not cured by chopping off the head. Wall Street, insofar as it exists to create a "river of money," is inexorably essential to the proper functioning of the global economy. It is much more than a single, narrow street physically located in lower Manhattan.

Finally, *Decay Time: A Wall Street Murder and Morality Tale* stands in tribute to the many I left behind in 2008, an overwhelming majority, to be sure, whose talents, ambition, work ethic, and principles for which I have nothing but respect.

Scott Stevenson
May 2013

DECAY TIME

A Wall Street Murder
and
Morality Tale

Prologue

Tuesday, October 14, 2008
12:32 A.M.

The Peninsula
New York City

Detective Victor Rodriguez counted the steps as he walked into the lobby of The Peninsula New York. There were six in total, all polished marble and partially covered in plush, inviting red carpet. These steps were different, he thought, than the cement steps leading up to his precinct or the 432 steps he used to take from his elementary school to his home in Queens. How or why, for that matter, he remembered that precise number from more than 20 years ago was a mystery to him.

He was met by a uniformed officer, Sergeant Tommy O'Roarke, who was already on the scene. The flashes of siren lights from the half-dozen police cars and the ambulance pierced the building's windows, illuminating the lobby.

"Top of the morning to you, Detective. Sorry to interrupt your coffee break," greeted O'Roarke, smirking.

"What do we got here?" Rodriguez responded, in no mood for sarcasm at the end of his shift. It had been a

remarkably quiet night, until now, with only a couple of petty assaults to handle over the course of the evening. A dead body in a luxury hotel was rarely an easy case.

"A male, dead at the scene with a gunshot wound to the head, approximately 30-40 years of age. Firearm lying next to the body."

"What else?"

"It's in the Presidential Suite," the sergeant said, pushing the PS button on the elevator. "Whoever it was, he must have had some cash."

"Okay. Anyone else there?"

The elevator climbed its way upward as the two continued their conversation.

"The suite was empty when we got there. The female—on call, if you know what I mean—who reported the incident was here in the lobby when we arrived. We checked that the victim was in fact deceased and then came down here to wait for you after sealing off the crime scene. She doesn't know his name."

"A prostitute? Please tell me it's not an Eliot Spitzer celebrity type, one of the Rockefellers, or someone of that ilk... Not in the mood for that kind of case now. I have enough casework without that profile being added to the list."

"She's with Officer Johnson in the hotel manager's office now, more than a bit shaken up by what she walked into."

"I bet she is. Hard enough doing that job without walking into that. Unless of course she had something to do with it. Johnson is keeping her for further questioning, I assume."

"Of course."

"Anything from the hotel manager at this point?"

"The hotel manager confirmed that the deceased was a somewhat frequent guest, always renting the

Presidential Suite and almost always with a different female companion. The manager also said the guy signed in as Jack Jones, in all likelihood an alias. The women always followed a bit later. He paid with wads of hundred-dollar bills. For that reason, the manager thinks the guy might be some high-flying Wall Street type, sports agent, or someone from the Hollywood establishment."

"Great. So much for this not being a high-profile case. I hope to God it's not a Wall Street guy. The media will have a field day with all the shit going on in the markets these days. Nothing better than conducting a homicide investigation in the middle of a media circus."

The elevator arrived at the penthouse floor, which had high ceilings, cavernous hallways, and crystal chandeliers spaced every 10 to 15 feet as evidence of its opulence. Even by Manhattan standards it was impressive, made that much more impressive when both officers realized a month's salary might cover the cost of a two-night stay.

The pair walked past a few more uniformed officers standing by the door to the suite. Rodriguez scanned the suite from the doorway, paying close attention to any and all details that might suggest a forced entry. Across the room on the floor lay a body in a pool of blood. Rodriguez had seen the grisly sight of a gunshot wound to the head plenty of times before, though typically not in the opulence of a $2,400-a-night midtown Manhattan hotel suite with two bedrooms, a giant Jacuzzi, and a living room with a Steinway piano overlooking the city.

"Has anyone else been in there?"

"No, sir, apart from hotel security and me, after I was dispatched following the 911 call. I took vitals—there were none—backed away to the hallway and immediately called Dispatch for backup."

"Good. Presuming Forensics is on the way?"

"Yes, sir."

Adhering to protocol, Rodriguez carefully slipped on plastic gloves and paper shoe covers and started walking over to the body. O'Roarke did the same.

Rodriguez' mind fixated on the hotel manager's conjecture about the victim being a Wall Street guy. At a minimum, the comment, albeit totally unsubstantiated, had some credence given the financial market meltdown that had been unfolding—in spectacular fashion—over the last month. He had seen the talking heads on CNBC, Fox, and seemingly everywhere else obsess over the 3.000-point drop in the Dow, the Federal Reserve brokered private bailout of Bear Stearns, the subsequent decision to let Lehman Brothers file for bankruptcy, and the "too big to fail" taxpayer-backed bailout of AIG.

Each of these events, epic in its own right, occurred within the span of six month's time. Rumors of other global financial titans on the cusp of collapse circulated at dizzying rates. Blood was in the streets, and had now flowed onto the floor of the Presidential Suite. He wondered how many more murders or suicides he would be called in to investigate over the next few weeks and months as the meltdown gained momentum.

In the back of his mind Rodriguez was hoping this was a suicide—at least suicides were easy from his perspective. There would be no need to testify at trials, no nasty questions about procedures from pesky defense lawyers, and no cold case files to worry about. Open and shut cases were always best, but probably wishful thinking on his part.

Why would a guy who could self-indulge like this kill himself? And why didn't he wait to do his business with the prostitute first?

This was going to be interesting.

PART I

The March to Armageddon

August 2007 to September 2008

Decay Time

Chapter 1
Don Pepe, mi amigo

Thursday, August 2, 2007
6:45 P.M.

Outside Penn Station
New York City

Chip and Sasquatch left the office with a mild sense of jubilation, having secured a client order that would enable Michael Feinberg, a superstar trader at Smyth Johnston, to close another deal. In their produce or perish world, however, they each knew they were only as good as the next deal they would close. Today's victory was tomorrow's challenge.

Their day, as did most, began at 7 a.m. and was consumed by a relentless onslaught of conference calls, internal reports, and emails, as well as meetings with clients, lawyers, risk managers, product control, and whomever else was necessary to get deals done on the Wall Street assembly line. The pace was as fast as the stress was high.

The two colleagues lived a few towns apart from one another on Long Island and would often catch the same train, something their wives were convinced was premeditated to give them the opportunity to drink more beer together. Though it was difficult to establish a predictable commuting routine as a Wall Streeter, they had done the best they could.

"We need to do something to memorialize one of these deals. What do you think about Pebble Beach? We gotta tick that box before we call it quits," Sasquatch said.

"I like your thought process. I can see it right now. You and Feinberg getting all cozy together looking out over the Pacific Ocean. With any luck, you may even become his personal boy-toy. Just imagine the upside your career will have then," joked Chip to Sasquatch as they walked through the thundering herd of humanity between them and Penn Station.

"Sounds like the winner's curse to me. How is it that even when you win, you somehow lose in this business?"

"You Brits eventually catch on. Hey, you know what, if we do find ourselves heading to Pebble Beach let's just try to compartmentalize the good in that."

It was 6:45 p.m., yet the Midtown rush hour traffic had not begun to subside as the two descended the escalator on the east side of Madison Square Garden into Penn Station. The summertime heat had overwhelmed the air conditioning, causing the sweat to pour through their clothing including their suit jackets. Continuing toward the main concourse, hoping to avoid the sight of the dreaded "Delayed" posted on the train schedule board, they would spot what had become one of the simple pleasures that defined their commuter existence.

"Don Pepe, mi amigo," either of the two would blurt out instinctively from 30 feet out. Don Pepe was one of the many beer cart vendors abutting the main concourse at Penn Station. Taking his cue, Don Pepe would immediately grab four Foster's Lager 25-ounce "oil cans," which he placed two apiece in brown bags. He would make it his personal challenge to have the bags ready by the time they got to the cart. It was quintessential New York service at its finest.

"Man, I love Don Pepe. He has to be my favorite human being in New York," Sasquatch said. "No doubt he ought to be nominated for some form of humanitarian award. Viva Don Pepe," added Chip as he placed one of the ice-cold cans against his forehead.

"What does the board say? Let me guess we have a delay due to mechanical issues on all Long Island Railroad trains, with no end in sight until the mechanical issues magically resolve themselves. Can't they at least humor us with some other line of bullshit?"

"C'mon man, you don't think the LIRR would bullshit you. Oh yeah, lesson number one: people lie," Sasquatch said, quoting one of Chip's many personal adages.

"It looks like we have a few minutes until boarding. That assumes the miracle of no delays. I gotta take a piss," Chip said, as he headed across the concourse to the bathroom.

The bathroom was yet another joy associated with the Penn Station commuting experience. Walking into the men's room on any day, let alone an oppressively humid summer day, was nothing short of a full assault of the senses. It was a putrid mix of smells that included urine, vomit, foul mop water, body odor, and anything else humanity could possibly create, naturally or otherwise. Chip had grown accustomed to taking a deep breath about 10 feet prior to walking into the bathroom, hoping he could hold his breath long enough to avoid the undignified assault.

As wily veterans of Penn Station, they generally could narrow down the number of potential tracks to one or two. This allowed them the advantage of strategically positioning themselves to minimize the daily stampede that occurred once "Boarding on Track X" appeared on the monitors. No matter how seasoned most New York commuters were, a maniacal sense of panic and urgency would overcome the masses once a track number was posted.

Today was one of those rare commuting days for Chip and Sasquatch. There had been no delays, yet, and they guessed right on the track, ensuring they would get a seat on board. All too often they found themselves in the vortex of the stampede, on some occasions failing to secure a seat. There was nothing like standing in the vestibule between railcars, as if human sardines, for their entire one-hour train ride home.

Pulling out of the station, the oil cans were instantaneously cracked open. How quickly they were emptied became the yardstick for that given day's level of pain. The bar had been set high, having recently finished oil can number two by the time the train pulled into the first station in Queens after reemerging to daylight from the tunnel beneath the East River. Today was more temperate, with each finishing just prior to arriving at their respective stops.

Still under the alcohol legal limit, Sasquatch decided to drive home from the train station. He was tired, hungry, and irritable, his beer buzz having begun to fade. All he could think about as he climbed into his car for the 10-minute drive home was how much he hoped to avoid any discussion of dinner parties or other imminent social activities.

"How was your day, Nigel," dutifully asked Kelly, his wife of seven years (longer than his prior two marriages), as he walked into the house.

A Wall Street Murder and Morality Tale

"Well let's see…it sucked like pretty much all of them," Sasquatch replied, in no mood to celebrate his success of earlier that day. "I'm beat."

"At least you're not stuck in the house with kids screaming 'Mommy' all day. You're out with your buddies, come home drunk half the time, and don't have to do anything when you're here."

"You're right. This is great. I get to live in a snake pit for 12+ hours every day, commute 3+ hours to and from the snake pit, and then come home and have this same asinine conversation every night. Meanwhile, you get to do what you want, when you want, with whom you want, and live in this leafy suburb in your dream house with two kids. You know what, we made this choice of a lifestyle. Believe me, if you are unhappy with it, let's move to a trailer park. It's cheap, and we don't have to worry about all this bullshit. How does that sound to you?"

"Who said anything about a trailer park?"

"I did. That's the alternative right now, and I'd be fine with it. Can I please just have something to eat? Or are you about to spring some great news about an upcoming dinner party or a major expense? Not in the mood for that tonight, please."

It was the usual Sasquatch-style rant, probably shades of the same rant playing out in many Wall Street households that faced similar challenges posed by the stressful lifestyle. Not that those challenges were altogether different than many of the other career paths common to big cities. Where Wall Street arguably differed, however, was in its extreme nature. The stakes were higher, the competition for sustained employment was higher, as were the hours and the endless politics. It was as if you lived life one step away from calamity, on a short fuse, incessantly. All of which led to comparatively higher levels of personal stress, the quid pro quo for the possibility of higher, albeit riskier, compensation.

There were reasons for Wall Street being regarded as a young person's business, with higher divorce rates and early burnout rates.

Sasquatch's rant was, comparatively speaking, mild. Just a few weeks prior he had arrived home drunk, having had a long wait for a taxi at the train station in the rain. Evidently his wife had forgotten to pick him up or lost track of time. After knocking on the door repeatedly, he blew a gasket. He didn't have a key for the front door, and Kelly had locked the door from the garage to the house. After multiple additional attempts to get into his house, he decided—dead tired, wet, and much to his wife's horror—to kick the door down. Kelly, who had been in the basement unable to hear him, witnessed barbaric behavior from her otherwise mild-mannered— at least when at home—husband. This was not the man she had married. He had become a volatile mess, a product of his environment.

Chapter 2
Zeus, Zeus, Zeus

Friday, August 3, 2007
8:02 A.M.

Smyth Johnston Trading Floor
New York City

"Zeus, Zeus, Zeus," exhorted Joey Karros to his troops. As sales manager of a 30-person team, it behooved his direct reports to listen to their boss.

Karros had just returned to Smyth Johnston's trading floor, one of many, from a meeting with senior sales management. It had been a typical management meeting, held without fail at 7:30 on Friday mornings. He and the other managing directors used these meetings in large part to manipulate, or more colloquially, "manage up" their bosses. The art of managing up was a thinly-veiled tactic to make yourself look comparatively better than your peers in hope of currying favor with those senior to you. Whatever the means—petty politics, prevarication, shameless self-promotion—managing up was a means to an end on Wall Street. That end was money, power, and control, in that order.

"We have a new deal coming. Mandatory sales meeting at four," Karros continued.

After recent failures of some well-known hedge funds, there seemed to be cracks in the foundation of what had been a prolonged bull run for Wall Street. Management had begun to stress the need for the entire sales force to start cleaning up the bank's balance sheet. Until recently the bank had been content to hold pieces of deals in inventory, making untold billions over the past decade. The strategy worked flawlessly in a bull market: buy an asset, earn interest on it while it sits on the balance sheet, wait for the price to appreciate, then sell it for a profit.

"Zeus, Zeus, Zeus," responded most of Karros's team. They had gotten used to the drill. Those who weren't enthusiastic enough about whatever Karros wanted to push felt it in the wallet at bonus time. And getting a big bonus was the name of the game. Absent the prospect of a big year-end bonus, typically denominated in the hundreds of thousands to millions of dollars, there really was no justification for enduring the 12-month survival quest that preceded the annual compensation ritual. It was a ritual that made some very happy while leaving many with the feeling of being woefully underappreciated. Regardless of outcome, the bonus was typically large enough to enable recipients to pay down mortgages, buy second homes, new cars—with cash.

"Let's go guys, make those calls. We need to be best in class. Run hard, boys and girls." The list of Karros's clichés seemed endless, if not sophomoric, both to the senior team members—many of whom were 5 to 15 years older than their 35-year-old boss—as well as some of the younger team members who just happened to be cynical enough to see through Karros's cheerleading.

"Hey, chief," a young salesman with slicked back, jet-black hair hollered to Karros over the trading desk. "I just sold 15 million of Isis to an Icelandic bank."

Investment banks always gave names to their deals. This one was Isis and Zeus was next, as if to suggest that a sequence of deals was in the making for their investors.

"Great work. If one Icelandic bank sneezes, the others catch a cold. Call the other ones and tell them they're missing out, and mention that Zeus is coming," Karros responded from his perch in the center of his desk, not taking his eyes off the barrage of emails on any one of his four computer screens.

The *desk* was but a small section of physical floor space among many sections that comprised the jungle-like, territorial setting of a trading floor. It could also refer to a whole department or product group residing on the trading floor. There were Sales desks and Trading desks, scattered in some loosely configured fashion across the expansive, often acre-plus-sized trading floors. Each desk, with roughly 20 to 30 work stations, resembled the high-tech equivalent of a telemarketing office.

Desks were filled with monitors, varying from six per desk for a highly quantitative trader to just one for a lowly secretary or intern, plus phone banks and headsets, with each inhabitant confined to approximately a phone booth's equivalent of personal space. Deal pitch books, prospectuses, and countless other documents cluttered the limited space. There was also the yelling and other chaos that incessantly defined trading floor existence. So many smart, ambitious, and well-educated people, each of whom could likely land a job that would have them comfortably ensconced in a large office with all the trappings that come with it. Yet they chose the trading floor with so little decorum; it was an interesting dichotomy that somehow worked well as a survival of the fittest, money-making machine.

In mid-conversation Karros got up to trek across the trading floor to visit with the New York head of credit trading, Michael Feinberg. Karros would spend much of his day having an *end-cap* with any and all people on the floor with whom he could personally benefit by association. An end-cap was a meeting, generally of an impromptu nature, held at the end of a sales or trading desk for theatrical purposes to elevate your own visibility on the floor. The actual topic of the end-cap need not matter so long as management got the impression that the end-capper was making things happen on the floor. Form over substance, perception driving reality, to be sure.

Looking like a million bucks in his Hugo Boss navy suit, starched white French-cuffed shirt with the standard requisition Wall Street Hermès power tie, Karros could hear the edgy banter on the floor as he passed by the multitude of desks that delineated various businesses on the floor.

"No, fuck you, asshole. That's my side of the trade. You took the other side. Too bad," yelled one trader into the phone, "you knew what the trade was. There is no misunderstanding here. You lose, I win. Thanks for the trade."

Not that this type of exchange was different from any other day. The lexicon of profanities was vast.

Karros continued his walk toward Feinberg's desk.

"You have a big brain and little balls," one salesman chided his trader on the mortgage desk. "You want that fancy new Porsche this year? Can't get it by taking no risk. Do the deal, asshole."

When Karros arrived at Feinberg's desk, he lapsed into spin mode and offered Feinberg an awkward fist pump as if to reaffirm the unspoken alliance of convenience between the two—you scratch my back and

I'll scratch yours. Life on the trading floor, oftentimes the razor thin line separating success from failure, was all about internal alliances, the quid pro quo and other premeditated deposits in the personal favor bank.

"Hey, buddy," speaking just above a whisper as if to ascribe greater importance to what he was about to say, "we just sold another $15 million piece of your deal," said Karros.

"Isis?" asked Feinberg.

"Yes, Isis. You make it, *I* sell it," said Karros. *I am the man*, as if he, not his team, deserved all the credit.

Similar to many sales managers, Karros was well known for taking credit for anything or anyone's work product, something many saw as fueling his ascent to managing director. It was less through pure intellect or actual profit contribution and more by positioning, politicking, and mastering the trade of managing up. Karros's cunning adherence to this tool chest of largely non-value-added tactics enabled him to assemble a team of 30 people who reported directly to him. In many respects, Karros represented the stereotypical story of the boy from Staten Island who had *done good* after seeing, as a youth, stars glimmering on the Manhattan horizon while peering wistfully across the Verrazano Narrows.

He knew he wanted that moneyed life, and, upon graduation from Pace University, was able to secure a low-level administrative position at a Wall Street firm. It was the type of position that offered little opportunity for advancement. But Karros, despite lacking the Harvard-type pedigree or any discernible value proposition to speak of, was a success story insofar as Wall Street success stories went. He mastered the use of buzzwords, made friends with co-workers, traders, and managers indiscriminately, and, importantly, earned the trust of many traders by pushing their deals without asking too many questions. Traders wanted him to advance on the sales side as their partner because of his enthusiastic willingness to push their deals. Karros had also shown uncanny survival skills at avoiding client fallout when one of the deals he sold went bad, typically by having one of his minions take the relationship hit while he retreated into the protective cocoon of management. Karros was a player of the game, a self-promotional, Teflon genius. The formula worked for him, as it did for many others who had successfully figured out how to navigate the path to managing director.

After years of multimillion-dollar bonuses, Karros was eager to flash his newfound wealth and moved, like so many from the New York boroughs, from Staten Island to New Jersey. He built a custom 10,000-square-foot "McMansion" in Monmouth County replete with a grand marble foyer, pool, home movie theater, and the rest of the materialistic trappings that in his way of thinking screamed success.

The house abutted a brand new private golf course, built at the expense of an erstwhile family farm—the typical story of runaway growth, i.e., out with the old, in with the new, bigger is better. A casual observer of Karros's materially-abundant lifestyle could hardly overlook the statuette of Zeus in the roundabout at the end of the long driveway. Karros's face could easily be imagined in place of Zeus's.

"You are the man, Joey," Feinberg said, patronizingly.

"What price did you get rid of it at? Price matters…we have seven other deals behind this, starting with the announcement of Zeus later today, that we have to get done before we'll own it all. This gravy train may not last forever."

Feinberg always seemed to get the joke faster than others.

Feinberg was intimating that he was positioning his book for a market reversal, more specifically the scenario where the long-standing bull market would end, and prices across most asset classes would begin their decline. It was a directional signal he would not offer most salesmen. Feinberg tightly controlled the flow of information about his book, even among his immediate trading colleagues, many of whom felt at times that Karros knew more than they did. Giving Karros a peek in the box cost him nothing, since Feinberg knew Karros either wouldn't quite comprehend it or, more likely, wouldn't care how the book was positioned so long as come year end there was a huge bonus in it for him. Karros could be trusted not to reveal any sensitive information to his team, and, from that standpoint, it was easy to deal with Karros.

"At par," Karros said, responding to Feinberg's question.

Feinberg had been observing over the first half of the year that mortgage delinquencies had started to climb, as did the consequent prospect of heightened foreclosures and defaults. Not everyone in the market agreed, however, that it was an early sign of trouble for the housing market. Some expected, certainly hoped, that the good times would continue; housing prices hadn't fallen since the Great Depression, and they wouldn't start now given the consumption-based economy that had persisted since the end of World War II. Others, including some hedge funds, were convinced that the party may soon be over. Feinberg, ever the contrarian tactician, was in the latter camp. He was now positioning his trades and book to profit if housing prices fell—he was shorting the market.

"Wow… I guess your friends in Iceland will buy anything," Feinberg joked. "Now we only have 50 million more of this to move. Kerr is calling me every hour. He's on the warpath. I'll tell him what great work you're doing. I'm sure he'll remember that at the end of the year. By the way, when we announce Zeus, you can tell your team that I pre-placed five million of it with my dad's asset management firm. I guess you can call that eating your own cooking. Make sure you tell your clients that. I know they think I never own any of the risk myself or only sell them the bad pieces."

"We'll make the calls, believe me. Your deals always get to the top of the heap," Karros assured him. "You really sold this to your dad's firm? Aren't they a bit too conservative for CDOs? That takes some balls…but I presume you're giving me the sales credits for it."

Political animal or not, Karros never missed an opportunity to ask for the money.

"What about Chip and his sidekick…what do they call him? Oh yeah, Sasquatch?"

"Yep. Those guys have the clients who should eat this stuff up, and they know their custies better than anyone on the Street," Karros said. "That's why I hired them in the first place."

"Get them over here. We need them to focus on Zeus," Feinberg barked.

With that not-so-subtle command, Karros retreated to his fiefdom in search of Chip and Sasquatch.

$ $ $

"Get off the phone. Feinberg wants you," Karros said from the door, making no attempt to do so politely. He had found the twosome in a small meeting room on the back of the trading floor.

Rude interruptions were part of life on the trading floor. Those interruptions could take the form of talking to someone knowing full well they were on the phone or, perhaps slightly more polite, by simply taking a seat next to the person on the phone and staring at them until they got so irritated they would drop their call.

With Chip preoccupied on the call, Sasquatch told Karros they were in the midst of pitching to one of their clients, Mal McMahon.

"Tell Feinberg we'll be there in ten minutes. We're trying to sell his Isis deal," Sasquatch said.

"No can do. He needs you guys now. Get off the phone and call him back in thirty minutes."

Chip ended the call, irritated by Karros's senseless urgency. Was it really that important or was it Karros trying to make himself look good by obsequiously serving his master? He had many masters, defined loosely as anyone who could help elevate his footprint within the bank. The bigger his footprint, so his theory went, the bigger his bonus.

"Sorry guys, when Feinberg says jump, we ask him how high. We're all his bitches. You want him to like you guys, or he can *and will* see to it that your bonuses get crushed at year end."

Chip and Sasquatch got their answer. For the removal of all doubt, they, like Karros and so many others in Sales, were in fact riding bitch for Feinberg. Never mind that they were on a call pitching a Feinberg deal to one of their clients, a client who would also be shown the Zeus deal.

As the threesome walked over to Feinberg, Chip reflected on what he had noticed earlier in his career as one of the principal differences between salesmen and traders. It was an innate difference that served as a source of tension between the two breeds and could only

21

hope to be contained, but never fully eliminated. Whereas a salesman would view a trade as part of a longer-term, multitransactional relationship, a trader most often only viewed any particular trade in isolation. In many respects, this philosophical difference represented opposite sides of a behavioral spectrum that, once understood, explained a lot to and about all involved.

Chip, Sasquatch, and Karros reached Feinberg's desk.

"Guys, you need to help out on Zeus and the other deals behind it. It's going to be bad for all of us if the bank winds up swallowing these deals. And with six more coming after them, you have to move fast. The rumor is that more hedge funds might be in trouble, and it'll shock the market again. I know you have the relationships with your clients... It's time to call in favors. By the way, Kerr is ballistic on the slow sales progress so far," Feinberg said.

"Well, the problem," Chip weighed in, "is that Eros—remember that deal we did with you—was a disaster, and our clients are seriously pissed off at the bank. You're now marking it down five points in two months—nobody expected that kind of volatility from our deals. So, that's not something that breeds customer loyalty."

"Pissed off? I've been good to your clients. I paid them a higher-than-market coupon at the time, and I even guaranteed the coupon when nobody else would. It doesn't get any better than that for them. It's not my fault the market has gone down."

"Two things. First, our guys are already five points underwater. It doesn't really matter if you paid them a little bit over market. Second, the guaranteed coupon is so small relative to the principal at risk that it really doesn't matter in the big picture. You might call that a hollow concession, a very generous hollow concession on your part," Chip said facetiously.

"Guys, it just is what it is. Your guys did their own diligence on the deal and knew exactly what they were getting into. Stop being so protective of your clients. Selling Zeus and Isis is a great opportunity for you to show your value to the firm. Sell it, and I'll make sure Kerr hears about it. Make sure you talk to Vasily this afternoon about the Zeus deal structure."

"I already set up a Sales teach-in for 4:00 this afternoon, Michael. All of my team will be there. Afterwards, they'll be working the phones," Karros assured Feinberg. The teach-in, as most of Feinberg's meetings with Sales, would be led by Vasily Bure, his second in command. Feinberg turned to his screens—the meeting was over. Karros, Chip, and Sasquatch walked back to their desk on the other side of the jungle.

The sartorial contrast among the three was striking. While Karros was dressed to the nines, Sasquatch was wearing a poorly fitting gray suit from a cheap outlet store. His pants were hanging low around his waist, and a blue shirt was not doing a satisfactory job of hiding his protruding, beer-belly stomach. Chip, though not looking quite as dapper as Karros, certainly looked the part of a banker more so than his East London sidekick.

"What an asshole that guy is. He screws our clients and claims he was good to them. You have to be kidding me," Chip said to Karros. "The ink hadn't even dried on the contract before the first loss happened. Mal feels duped and wants to come in and talk to Kerr about it."

"MIGA."

"What?"

"Make It Go Away. You have to manage your client. One trade gone bad does not define a relationship. And besides, Feinberg is the king. You can't get into it with him. Kerr will never buy your story—heads Feinberg wins, tails you lose. Trust me. You gotta figure out how to work with him. Now make the calls. Keep running strong, buddy," Karros said dismissively.

He knew how to work both sides of the fence as well as anyone.

After Karros was out of earshot, Sasquatch chimed in.

"Dude, Karros and Feinberg are such assholes. One of them rips off our client and the other makes us the bad guys. Of course we ought to be used to this by now: same shit, different day with these guys. You ever wonder where these guys come from or how they get to be the way they are?"

"You're telling me. We'll have no clients left if it really works like this. Hopefully we'll get paid at least something before our franchise gets destroyed," quipped Chip. "Yeah, great business model and career strategy."

"Yep," Sasquatch nervously replied. "This is great alright, really, really great," already developing a thirst for the multiple beers he would consume after work to numb the madness of another day. Drinking, often heavily if not in binge fashion, was one of many survival tactics used on Wall Street.

$ $ $

The four o'clock Sales teach-in on the Zeus transaction was still a couple of hours away. Michael Feinberg sat in one of the many conference rooms around the periphery of Smyth Johnston's trading floor. He was joined by Vasily Bure.

Bure, true to the melting pot culture that now defined the business, was an interesting cultural amalgam of Middle Eastern parents who had raised him in Moscow where they changed their names in an effort to appear more of Russian descent. After the fall of Communism, the family emigrated to Brooklyn in search of the proverbial better American life. Bure was to have the opportunity to go to a top university and, upon graduation, venture out into the world to make money—lots of money if all went as planned. At the ripe age of 19, Bure had graduated from the University of Chicago with a major in math, deciding immediately afterwards to enroll in the JD/MBA program, which he completed in a startling three years. He was soon discovered by Wall Street, and recruited heavily by nearly every marquee firm.

Bure was in many respects tailor-made for the Wall Street life. Highly quantitative, aggressive, hungry, willing to work around the clock, he kept score in a one-dimensional framework: money. Like so many who had landed on Wall Street from non-American cultures, it was less about broadly assimilating oneself into the traditional business norms and more about the chase for a better life where success was measured overwhelmingly in monetary terms.

Across from the two of them sat Bob Lancer of 14th Street Asset Management, wearing reading glasses while perusing his deal papers. The trio was finalizing details on Zeus.

"Bob, are we on the same page here?" Feinberg asked.

14th Street was a newcomer to the CDO business, having recently been founded by Lancer and two of his former banker colleagues. Perhaps born out of deal fatigue or outright investor distrust from less than stellar results on some of his recent deals, Feinberg felt the need to add a new twist to this deal offering: a third-party manager, whose responsibility it was to select the assets and manage the deal in the best interest of investors. A third-party manager would add an air of legitimacy and diminish investor sentiment of once again becoming the victim of Feinberg's "sharp elbows."

For Feinberg, Zeus would ostensibly be heralded as the first of its kind in a new category of credit derivative deals called a managed synthetic ABS CDO. He and Bure were already planning to submit it to *Derivatives Week* for Deal of the Year consideration. Such an accolade was similar to winning an Oscar in the credit derivatives world. It was also great for internal perception—or bonuses—something Feinberg would exploit to the fullest extent.

Feinberg and Bure had chosen 14th Street Asset Management, a new firm, because of its willingness to be aggressive and flexible, while looking to build a track record and assets under management. Another benefit in dealing with 14th Street was that Lancer wasn't currently covered by Karros's sales desk. This allowed him direct access to Feinberg and Bure, which ensured that none of their deal structuring discussions would be leaked to the sales organization.

"Yep, it's all good," Lancer said.

"Okay, Bob, here's the list of assets you can choose to build the Zeus portfolio," Feinberg said, handing over a piece of paper.

"Isn't that what I'm supposed to do? I'm the portfolio manager, right? We can pick any assets that fit the portfolio criteria, on the list as well as off, right?"

"We can have that discussion later, but I want you to focus on the spreadsheet first and foremost. You understand what's going on with our partnership? After all, you're piggybacking on my desk's credit analytics and trading record. No offense, Bob, but you guys are getting a huge benefit by being in bed with us on this deal. Not to mention the kudos you'll get as the manager on a potential deal of the year."

What Feinberg failed to disclose was that his desk had carefully chosen assets that they believed would perform poorly in a housing meltdown.

"Sure, I understand what's in it for 14th Street as a new manager, but I also need to make sure we get it right. We don't want to ruin our reputation at the outset with one bad deal, especially if it's our first."

"Bob, we have a lot of guys who will do this deal with us. No one has a gun to your head. If you want to pass on it, no hard feelings. We can regroup another time. I know you get it—we all need partners in this business, and we can be great partners in Zeus." Feinberg paused, before continuing, "And, needless to say, you'll execute all the trades through me. No sense in giving away the bid-ask spread to the competition."

Feinberg never missed an opportunity to make money.

Lancer nodded. He realized he had no choice—a deal of the year candidate with Smyth Johnston could really launch their firm. "Sure, that's all good. This is going to be a great deal for both of our firms. We'll get back to you tomorrow with the first cut of the portfolio."

There was no doubt as to who had the upper hand in the deal. Lancer knew it wasn't him.

Feinberg and Bure exited, leaving Lancer behind to gather up his things. Zeus had become a reality. The pieces had been put in place. Now they just needed to sell it to the sales force, something Bure was soon to begin in the meeting room across the hallway.

"The rating agencies are okay with this, right?" Feinberg asked as the two walked back to the desk.

"I don't know how but Jorge and Peter got them to adopt our standard correlation models on this."

"Good, so it's mostly triple-A?"

"Yep, 94 percent of the capital structure."

"Wow. So you know what to tell the Sales guys, right?"

"C'mon, Michael. I get it. Truth well told."

Feinberg was pleased that his guys had somehow managed to convince the rating agencies, three in the case of Zeus, that bundling various tranches from diversified pools of mortgages passed muster despite the concentration risk of subprime mortgages in California, Nevada, and Florida. It wasn't his fault if the agencies were lazy, greedy, or stupid. Though he was surprised by 94 percent being triple-A, it wasn't his job to second guess their methodologies. His job was to make money—for himself and for the firm. The rating agencies, much like the investors, were big boys capable of making their own risk assessments.

$ $ $

Sasquatch was something of an enigma on the trading floor. How was it that he was still doing this at age 47? It would be one thing to be sitting in the ivory tower of senior management at that age, but an entirely different one to be sitting in his three-foot-by-three-foot personal space with most people half his age making twice what he's making. He should be *done* by now, with enough money in the bank to do something other than this. That was the Wall Street dream for most. It couldn't be that he liked doing this to himself, as very few actually did. Many bankers rationalized it away—the lifestyle was a risky investment in a better future.

His colleagues wondered whether Sasquatch had somehow screwed himself through his two divorces, bad investments, lavish lifestyle, or a combination of all of the above. No one really knew the answer, left only to hope they would avoid the same fate. Wall Street was a crass means to an end for most, an opportunity, similar to professional athletics, in effect to cram an entire career into a shorter span of time. The goal was to go ugly early and get out before the lifestyle wreaked indelible damage on your physical or mental state or, for that matter, your soul.

Sasquatch was sitting at his desk typing a follow-up email to one of his clients on Isis, before Tracy Maxwell, the team's 22-year-old analyst interrupted, "Hey, Sasquatch."

"Yep," he answered, without looking up.

"You goin' to this Zeus meeting?"

"Yep, wouldn't miss this party. So, are you ready? You know all there is to know about ABS CDOs?"

"Of course."

"Alright... Here's a pop quiz on CDOs: get them all right, and I'll let you join us on Monday at the Whiskey Bar with Mal. We gotta make you streetable one of these days."

Tracy was tough enough to handle the military-like indoctrination into Wall Street culture. Equal opportunity—the opportunity to be treated like shit—presented itself to everyone in her newly-hired capacity. Wall Street, as Sasquatch often reminded her, was not a place for feelings.

"Okay, let's start with...do you know what CDO stands for?"

"Ha, easy one...collateralized debt obligation."

"Good, that's a start. What about ABS?"

"Asset-backed securities."

"Two-for-two. How do CDOs work?"

"How much time do I have?"

"Sixty-seconds, 30,000-foot version."

The pretty, stylishly-attired blonde drew in some air and gathered her thoughts. A single-digit handicapper and recent graduate of the University of Virginia, she imagined herself sitting over a three-foot putt—easy enough, she thought. It was actually her golf experience that had drawn Chip's attention to her résumé. Chip had been impressed with her intelligence, ambition, and her ability to be friendly with the alpha males of Wall Street, without allowing them to cross the line.

"Okay, you put together a pool of assets, say a portfolio of loans, and then slice and dice them into different pieces, each having varying degrees of risk. Some investors, like hedge funds, prefer a lot of risk, while others, like insurance companies, want less risk. Hedge funds will buy the riskiest piece, meaning they will get big returns if no companies go belly up, but can lose all their money if enough of them do. The insurance company gets smaller returns, but for them to lose money, a big chunk of the companies in the pool will need to default, something very unlikely in a diversified portfolio."

"Good so far."

"One way to think about it is like one of those champagne pyramids at weddings. So the glass on top is the senior tranche, the safest one that the insurance company buys. It gets all the cash flow first, and when it's full, then the next tranche gets the money, all the way down the line. The glass on the bottom is equity that the hedge funds like. So it doesn't get any money until all the glasses, or tranches above it, are filled."

"Okay good. Well done. So what about an ABS CDO like Zeus?"

"The underlying assets are mortgage-backed assets, not corporate loans, but the idea is the same. In this case, if mortgages default the underlying mortgage-backed securities won't be able to pay, and the losses ultimately flow to Zeus investors, starting with the equity first."

"Now for the most important question. How does the bank make money? By the way, if you don't know this you're fired."

"Bad news, you won't be firing me. If the bank owns the assets in the underlying portfolio, then the idea is that the income from the portfolio is greater than the cost of selling the risk pieces to the various investors."

"In simpler terms you might call that buying low and selling high, no different than buying a whole cake for $20, slicing it up into 8 pieces at $4 each and pocketing the $12 difference. A fancier term is securitization. How do we make money when the bank is not the manager?"

"That's easy as well. When someone else owns the risk, the bank gets paid a fee for helping to structure and distribute the deal."

Chip interrupted, "Okay you two geniuses, let's go."

"Thanks, Sasquatch," Tracy said and hurried ahead to the meeting. She wanted to get a front-row seat.

Sasquatch got up slower, "Why do we have to go to this meeting, I have too much shit to do."

"And miss all the fun and feel Karros's wrath? You know he sends emails to management about how his sales team was the only one with 100 percent attendance at sales meetings. He wants it for his own political purposes. Also, you remember what Feinberg said? We have to appear to be helpful. While our guys still remember what happened on Eros, we still have to show it to them. If not, we'll get screwed come bonus time.

"What's up with this guy Bure? He seems like a total jackass, the type of guy who's in it for himself and wants it all and wants it all now."

"Well, I'd put it to you this way… What does it start to sound like when you say 'Vasily' 10 times fast?" Chip laughed as he asked the question.

"Huh?" Sasquatch was puzzled.

"Seriously dude, say 'Vasily' 10 times fast. By the tenth time it starts sounding like 'Vaseline', as in get ready to get lubed up."

Chip broke out into laughter and then delivered another line that Sasquatch didn't see coming, "Yeah, good thing his name's not Anatoly... There used to be a guy around here with that name. He and Bure would have made for quite a pair. Say that 10 times fast."

"Anal-Toy! That is absolutely brutal. Whoa."

"Yep."

"I hate my life," Sasquatch reactively blurted out as he felt his anxiety pulse rise at the grim reality of a work life he so badly wanted to leave behind, but couldn't.

"So much pain, so little time." Chip was once again taking some pleasure while commiserating with Sasquatch's personal anguish.

This was the new Wall Street, no longer a bunch of clubby prep school boys in some old-world, unspoken white glove business society. Hardly. To the contrary, Wall Street, more specifically the Sales and Trading division, had become the epitome of the multicultural melting pot of languages, values, ethics, and business philosophies, among many other interpersonal differences. It was no small wonder that the trading floor seemed to be in a state of perpetual chaos.

Chip, Sasquatch, and Tracy found seats at the perimeter of the conference room, closest to the door. At the front of the room, in addition to Bure, were Peter Baum and Jorge Soto, two of the many structuring experts Feinberg had sitting on his desk. Feinberg made it a practice to delegate sales meetings to his people.

"Well, well, well, if it isn't the rest of the Hitler youth," Chip whispered to Sasquatch.

"Who? Baum and Soto?"

"You mean the A-Bauminator and the Sotomizer," relished Chip, once again laughing at the madness and irreverence of it all.

"That sounds about as bad as Anal-Toy."

"And it's not even my bitter and twisted material. We'll chat more after the meeting. Warning, beer needs to be involved," Chip said.

Bure began his spiel on Zeus, making every effort to keep the deal description in as simplistic terms as possible for Sales.

"Okay, Zeus is a managed synthetic ABS CDO. Our previous deals have been static, i.e., the portfolio is fixed at the outset. Here we've added the advantage of a third-party asset manager to oversee the portfolio selection process, akin to loan deals where having managers is market standard. This is the first managed ABS CDO, and we believe the manager feature should appeal to a number of your clients across the capital structure. It's a great opportunity for clients to access the risk profile they want on a managed basis and gain leveraged access to the mortgage market."

Bure continued his high-level deal description for a few more minutes. "Let me turn it over to Peter and Jorge to provide a specific breakdown of the capital structure, ratings, and target pricing. After that we can answer any questions you may have."

Peter Baum, the "A-Bauminator," began his techno speak on the deal structure. "Zeus is structured into five tranches in order to achieve ratings efficiency. At the bottom of the cap structure we offer $10 million of equity with expected case returns of 18 percent. Next is $30 million of junior mezz piece rated BBB with a coupon of LIBOR + 150bps; $20 million of AA senior mezz piece at LIBOR + 80bps, $40 million of junior

AAA piece at LIBOR + 50bps, and then $900 million of AAA super senior at TBD pricing," he droned.

"Really, shoot me, why do I have to sit here and listen to this," Sasquatch texted to Chip from his Blackberry.

It was common for sales people to be constantly checking their Blackberries during meetings. Chip felt the buzz from the incoming text and gave an acknowledging smirk to Sasquatch.

While feigning attentiveness to the techno spiel, Chip's mind began to drift. Maybe it was prompted by the A-Bauminator's use of "ratings efficiency," a euphemism for how the deal was structured to provide maximum benefit to the desk and most likely not the clients. Or was it the rapid, make that *rabid*, development of credit derivatives. The product had enjoyed a meteoric rise from its advent in the mid-1990s. By 2007, credit derivatives had become measured in the multitrillions, with vast innovations in products, ranging from standard to more exotic types of collateral upon which a deal's performance was based.

Much like prior derivative products involving interest rate risk, credit derivatives emerged to play an invaluable role in enabling risk to be more efficiently hedged, transferred, and traded between buyers and sellers. This hedging, risk transfer, and trading added vitally important market liquidity that in the end result creates a "river of money"; in essence, the funding flows from capital market investors to companies, and, eventually, well downstream to individuals. Economic growth and general prosperity follow on the back of this river of money.

These enormous positives notwithstanding, Chip pondered whether credit derivatives had grown too fast, in too many directions, with too much complexity, and without ample market and regulatory constraints or, for that matter, internal risk management controls. There were trillions of dollars of risk at play using these relatively new instruments, as witnessed by a market that had grown from about $1 trillion in notional size in 2001 to $34 trillion in '06. And there appeared to be no signs of decelerated growth anytime soon.

Chip wondered whether the market participants really understood what was going on, or whether they actually cared. The gravy train was firing on all cylinders: banks were making money, investors were making money, everyone involved was making money as the river of money gained current. Was it really his job to scream *Fire!* in a crowded theater? Don't fix it if it ain't broken, so the conventional wisdom had it. Besides, his bonus was being paid out of the same river of money.

$ $ $

Charles Smith III, aka "Chip," was no exception to the innumerable Wall Streeters who had arrived at the beacon of capitalism brimming with positive expectations of what was to lie ahead, only to soon discover that life on the "Street" was, in reality, a volatile cocktail of pain with less frequent pleasure. Business culture shock, both good and bad, guaranteed that volatile ride and offered a sound explanation as to why Wall Streeters got paid more for the incremental risk they were taking, not only in their professional lives but also their personal lives. It was a brutally fair proposition, with those in the seats knowing they would be taking roughly the same amount of career pain—in absolute terms—as those in other industries, albeit compressed into a smaller capsule of time.

Raised in the affluent suburb of New Canaan, Connecticut, Chip attended Dartmouth after graduating from high school. There, like many of his classmates, he decided he needed to turbocharge his academic pedigree by attending business school, in his case Yale. Chip felt he had the near perfect pedigree to make it in the New York investment banking business. Little did he know that the largely waspy, white glove clubby world of the past had evolved into something far different.

He found out just how different a mere two weeks into his Wall Street existence when he walked into the office one day, and was shocked to find no one, literally, in his entire section of the trading floor. The lights were on but no one was home. They had all been fired— vaporized overnight—following a major market disruption event that forced banks into a form of corporate bulimia to disengorge whole armies of people. After discovering that he was unable to log in on his computer and panicking that somehow, after a mere two weeks at the firm, he, too, was part of the bloodletting, Chip called down to the IT department. Soon an IT staffer arrived at his desk, poked around for serial numbers, and called downstairs to ask "if today was a sunny or a rainy day" for Smith.

Welcome to the big leagues—feast or famine, sink or swim, business Darwinism.

The incident served as an important early lesson of how circumstances far beyond any individual's control could quickly shape one's career trajectory. All of the positive expectations and preconceptions of what may lie ahead were erased. No one knew what to expect in the world order that characterized the new Wall Street. It was, to borrow a phrase from finance theory, a random walk.

After working his way up through the sales ranks for more than five years as a vice president, Chip was considered a seasoned veteran in Wall Street terms and an expert with deep client relationships covering life insurance companies. Rather than continue to peddle corporate bonds, he took a career risk and moved to the credit derivative world where he assembled a team of people including Sasquatch and Tracy.

Chip and his team faced inordinate hurdles on a daily basis. There was the perfunctory political infighting, internal competition with other groups (who for turf-grabbing purposes would baselessly claim to be covering the same clients), management's lack of understanding of his clients, constant transactional conflicts with Trading—often with Feinberg who wielded far more power than he—and a mountain of other unnecessary stress that added to the volatile cocktail. Deal stress was the least of it.

It's no small wonder that very few days would pass without the use of beer for attitude adjustment purposes.

$ $ $

"Any questions about the structure, pricing, specific names, anything else?" Bure asked of those in the room.

"In these ABS CDOs, how do you actually price the tranches?" asked one of the associates in the front of the room.

"Jorge, can you take them through the modeling."

Jorge Soto, the Sotomizer, eager to display his quantitative brilliance, stepped up to discuss the model and how pricing was derived from the models.

"Okay, we rely on our proprietary model that uses Gaussian Copula to figure out the default correlation of the portfolio. Based on the price of each name in the pool…"

"Jorge, that's probably a bit beyond the scope of this meeting," Bure interrupted.

"Okay, sorry. So based on portfolio default probabilities, we incorporate recovery value and calculate a probability of default and expected loss for each piece of Zeus. When comparing this pricing basis to comparable instruments, we feel Zeus offers great relative value. Of course, we build in margin for origination of the deal, portfolio selection, deal structuring, as well as the overall position of the book."

Chip decided it was time for him to chime in. "That sounds great, but stepping back, this isn't one of the deals where you guys have picked the most efficient names, is it? Most efficient as in screws my client most efficiently? I've seen that play before and didn't like it the first time."

Chip asked the loaded question to see the A-Bauminator squirm and, tacitly, to send notice to other salespeople that they may want to be careful with this new type of deal. Chip had become a hardened, Machiavellian actor on the Wall Street stage.

The A-Bauminator hesitated, somewhat stunned by the question, but recovered quickly. "Absolutely not. As Vasily mentioned, we've engaged an independent, third-party asset manager to watch out for the investor's interests."

"Why would you do that?" Chip pressed.

"One of the criticisms from clients is that we stack the deck or rig the portfolio to our advantage in these deals. Having a third-party manager pick the assets alleviates that concern, albeit a baseless concern. And the manager will look after the asset performance throughout the deal and make any changes as necessary."

"So who is this manager? What are we supposed to tell the client when they ask who the mystery man is? The Wizard of Oz, Superman, or Batman?"

The room burst into laughter, nervous laughter at the clear disdain felt between Chip and the A-Bauminator. There must be some bad history, people thought, which of course there was.

"I assume," Chip continued, "this manager has a name."

"Of course. Feinberg and Bure just met with the manager and are finalizing the details of their involvement. We'll be in a position to disclose the name later today or over the weekend at the latest."

"All our clients are going ask why you brought in a manager after all the static deals we've shown them," continued Chip, ever suspect of the trading desk.

"First you tell me the clients don't like it when the trading desk selects the names, and now you're telling me they may not like it when a professional third-party manager selects the names. Not sure what else you want us to do? I guess your clients can build their own credit infrastructure and do it themselves. Good luck to them on that megamillion dollar task. We put these deals together because investors have demand for product and yield. They don't have to do it through us if they don't want to."

"Look, I'm just asking questions we need answers for. Zeus will be the first time for this type of deal to have a managed component."

"Correct, and we're doing that to give your clients more comfort with the deal," concluded the A-Bauminator.

There were no other questions.

As the meeting adjourned and the attendees scurried back to their desks, Ben Cook, a member of Feinberg's desk, caught up with Chip.

"The deal seems pretty good, no? Our guys have been working on it day and night. We'll have preliminary marketing materials to you over the weekend, and I'm working on the offering circular now. This is pretty interesting stuff, and the manager involved is good. But anyway, the clients can do their own analysis, quiz the manager, and see if they think it's good value for them. Seems fair to me."

"All of which is fine except for Bure and you guys know a lot more about individual names than our clients. That's why I pressed the question on 'efficient names' in the portfolio," Chip said. "And what's the manager doing relative to Feinberg? Who produced the portfolio, how was it selected, etc.? Who is really doing what here? But in any case, let's face it, Ben, you traders are always one step ahead of the rating agencies and clients. It's not you I'm worried about. It's the monster that lurks behind you, the zero-sum mentality."

"A-ha. So what's the story with Baum...you two don't seem to be best of friends."

"You would be correct in making that astute observation, Ben. I can give you the background, but we need to have beer in our hands—it's 5:30 anyway... To the Stone we go."

"Really? This early?"

"Yep. That's what we do. Go tell your boss you're going to a meeting with me. See you down there," Chip said and walked off.

$ $ $

Irish connotation aside, the similarities between the Blarney Stone on 3rd Avenue and 44th Street and most other Irish pubs in Manhattan were few. It was Happy Hour, a daily occurrence for the construction workers and other blue collar patrons drinking harmoniously among themselves with the occasional neighborhood drunk passed out at the end of the bar. The hope was that the cheap aluminum bottles of Budweiser, consumed in large quantity, and the Mets game on TV would mask the pungent scent of ammonia and dirty mop water emanating from the bathroom.

Chip and Sasquatch were sitting at the end of the bar. Few bankers, apart from the two of them, would dare be seen at this unmistakably down-market establishment. For the two of them, it was, oddly, a haven away from the trading floor madness, a place that could not possibly be more different than the expensive, trendy places that most herd-mentality bankers frequented for image and personal benchmarking. Paradoxically, the Blarney Stone had a special appeal to both Chip and Sasquatch. To Sasquatch it was the next best thing to some of his old pubs back in East London, while for Chip it was the perfect counterweight to the Wall Street high life, reminding him in some respects of his fraternity house back at Dartmouth.

Soon after settling in to their first beer, Ben Cook arrived. Chip and Sasquatch had befriended Ben in his prior role in the legal department where he had helped them set up the necessary documents for transactions with their clients. Ben was a perfect example of a middle- or back-office person getting noticed by someone in the front office and given the opportunity to get involved on the deal side. If Ben performed as planned, he could substantially increase his financial upside. Chip had tried to recruit Ben to his team until

Feinberg all but stole him away to become a junior attorney on his trading desk.

"Nice bar, you boys come here often? Just like back home in Ohio," Ben said, while pulling up a bar stool.

Early on in his tenure with Feinberg's team there had been a flurry of losses to clients, and it had been Ben's job to deliver the bad news to the salespeople. Chip had good-naturedly bequeathed him the nickname "Grim Reaper," since any time he came by, he brought nothing but bad news that led to more relationship-damaging conversations with clients who had participated on that deal.

Being referred to as the Grim Reaper, the Triggerman, or any of the other unflattering nicknames was a serious departure from his Ohio farm boy background. Seldom a day would go by that Ben didn't question his role, wondering if he had made a mistake. Was the potential for a lot more money worth it? Was this incremental money enough to compensate him for the utter disdain from those around him? Was he just a puppet, collateral damage, in an increasingly volatile business environment? Was there something more nefarious at work in terms of business ethics, having noticed soon after arriving on the desk it seemed to be winning a lot more than the clients? He, like most young people on Wall Street, had to live with these and other vexing existential questions as they climbed aboard the credit derivative money train.

"So, tell me about Baum. After all, I have to sit three feet from the guy all day, every day. He never talks about anything but work. Never goes out, seems like he lives in the office."

Chip ordered another round of beers, hoping that Ben would fall victim to the truth serum and cough up any useful information about Feinberg, Zeus, or anything else of interest. All fair game.

"Baum came to New York from Frankfurt by way of London. He is scary smart, and even more frighteningly cold as a trader. Many Sales people have felt betrayed by the guy for his having all but terminated relationships with their clients," Chip said.

Sasquatch chimed in, "Since the 'Terminator' was already taken, someone came up with the 'A-Bauminator' instead. And he sort of looks the part, too, as a German. As to Soto, most feel he is a good guy but under Baum's thumb. In other words he, too, will torch, or 'Sotomize' your client at the ready command of the A-Bauminator."

"So Ben, you work with some great guys: Feinberg, Bure, the A-Bauminator, and the Sotomizer. Have fun with that...you should have joined us in Sales," added Sasquatch.

Ben could resort to nothing other than downing his beer.

"I have to get back to the desk, and can't show up hammered."

"Too bad—we call this work. Before you go, what's up on Zeus? Is Feinberg up to something we should know about?"

"Not that I know of. All he tells us is that he wants to get these deals done because Kerr is putting lots of pressure on him to get his book cleaned up. Not sure I can tell you any more than that," Ben said as he stood up to head back to the office.

Sasquatch watched the Cropduster walk toward the green door and said to Chip, "That must suck: work from 7 in the morning until 10 at night. At least we get away from the desk occasionally, and we don't have to deal with Feinberg and his guys 24/7 like he does."

"Yep, you got a point there… No such thing as a free lunch. But don't think of all traders as necessarily bad guys."

Both knew that the traders simply took orders from Feinberg, and that Feinberg had been minting money while senior management had become tone-deaf to his reign of terror tactics. He had hotwired the system, as long as the money printing machine continued.

Chip paused, "Sure, we can find plenty of other deals to work on, but don't underestimate Feinberg's power and ability to help screw us at comp time if we don't try to help him out. It's a razor's edge. All we can do is present his deals to our clients and give them whatever color we can. We play the role of translator or bridge-builder between our clients and the traders. Think of it as the Gaza Strip of business: our clients and Feinberg have fundamentally different transaction cultures, accounting and tax regimes, risk perspectives, margins, you name it as the list goes on. That's why we get paid a lot more than the guys peddling Swiss francs."

Sasquatch ordered another round of beers. Chip willingly partook in one of many "Okay, but just one more" rounds. He wondered what Feinberg and Bure might have up their sleeves on Zeus. Should he pitch the deal to his clients knowing he didn't feel altogether comfortable about the deal's motivation? Was he being too protective of his clients as Feinberg had just told him? His level of trust, suspicion, and skepticism of Team Feinberg had recently gone from bad to worse.

In the past, he was always confident that the deals he showed his clients were, in a manner of speaking, as advertised. That didn't mean those deals always worked out well for his clients. The clients were big boys, sophisticated investors (Qualified Institutional Buyers or QUIBs for short) fully capable of assessing the inherent risks. But recently the complexity and lack of transparency in the deals had grown discernibly.

The pace of innovation, often manifested by the use of obfuscating Greek Alphabet language, had begun to overwhelm his and many other market participants' ability to fully understand what was actually going on with a given deal. Deal risk had become multiplied. It was no longer adequate to simply understand the credit risk associated with a particular loan; it was now about understanding the risk of that loan times the risk of it being in a portfolio times the risk of the portfolio being within other portfolios. Had the risk of doing deals with Feinberg or any credit derivative trader become less about understanding the actual risk and more about the risk of the unknown, more specifically about the deal's motivation? Had behavioral risk become a nontrivial factor alongside the more obvious credit, correlation, and contagion risk?

Whatever the case, something felt different with Zeus and the other deals taking flight off the innovation runway. Did the business Gaza Strip, as he had described it to Sasquatch minutes before, include an ethical component to it? No one really knew. All he knew was that he needed to show the deal to his clients and would have to live with the lack of understanding that gnawed at him. The dilemma was picking the lesser of two evils: don't show the deal to his clients and get screwed by Feinberg or show it to his clients and run the relationship risk of having the unknown screw them.

Sasquatch returned with the beers, nodding toward the TV showing the Mets losing to the Reds. The pair decided it was time to talk about baseball. After 15 minutes, Sasquatch looked at his watch only to remember that he had promised—whatever that meant—

his wife that he'd be home before she fell asleep, typically about 10:30.

"Yep, leave me stranded here with nothing but my beer," Chip replied, realizing that in 45 minutes he'd be able to take a car service home per company policy. It was a nice perk for a Wall Street salesman who often found himself out late at night with clients, tired and wanting nothing to do with the hassle of a train commute.

Alone, staring at his Budweiser, Chip drifted back to the "salesman's dilemma" notion

His thoughts were shortly interrupted by another patron. Chip was startled that this patron was someone else wearing a suit—most people here were blue collar and dressed so. After all, the Blarney Stone was his oasis of virtual anonymity. No one knew him, and no one, apart from his colleagues, bothered to talk with him when there.

"Hey, I'm Jack. I couldn't help but hear some of your conversation with the other guys who were here with you earlier."

"So you were eavesdropping, in other words?" Chip replied reflexively, and a little more aggressively than he had intended.

"If you thought so, I'm sorry. But I found some of the stuff you were saying very interesting. And for that matter relevant to my job," Jack added demurely, perhaps disingenuously. "Can I get you another beer?"

Chip was curious. Was the guy a headhunter, or what? He decided to see what the man had to say. "Sure, but I need to be out of here in 30 minutes. You're not from the press, are you?"

"No, no need to worry. You're not going to find yourself on the cover of the *Wall Street Journal* tomorrow."

"On the cover and unemployed, that is."

"You don't strike me as someone in love with what they do for a living. Not that disliking your job is unusual. How long have you been doing the Wall Street bit?"

"Too long. Fifteen plus years, and that's in human time. In dog years, which is probably a better measure of time on Wall Street, make that 90 years."

"Cry me a river. You guys make a shitload of money," Jack laughed.

"We make good money, as long as we perform. As I tell all my friends and family, the money is good and I don't regret being in this business. But there is a reason people call this a young man's business. I tell them it's hard to say just how good this business really is when adjusted for pain or stress, which is felt through all facets of your life."

"I gather you're in Sales and the blond-haired guy was a trader?"

Chip wondered how closely Jack had listened to his conversation. Being cautious, there was nothing that seemed dangerous about the guy.

"Correct, in something they call credit derivatives; most people have never heard of them."

Jack sipped his beer with a smile. "So, tell me, in a nutshell, why this business causes you so much stress."

"We could be here all night. But in a nutshell, spoken after a bunch of beers, the number of assholes in this business has been on the rise in recent years."

"Like who? Everyone?"

"Definitely not everyone. For the most part the people on Wall Street are decent, very smart, highly ambitious, and goal-oriented people who've worked hard to be in their seats. But in the last five to seven years, it just seems like the number of assholes rising to power has changed Wall Street. It's become a tyranny of the few. The more money these assholes make, the more power they amass and the more control over the outcome they assume. You'd think these large banks would have enough management oversight and accountability in place to make sure these guys don't run wild, but I wonder. As long as they're making big money, they seem able to do whatever they want and act however they want, with senior management along for the ride. Why wouldn't they be along for the ride? They benefit directly from it all."

"Hey, I'm no expert on corporate life, but it sounds like most large companies."

"I suppose it does, except that the big money seems to poison the water a lot more here. The level of behavioral decay that has emerged as of late, within the limited accountability I mentioned, needs to change. What's the expression…oh yeah, the lunatics run the asylum. That's a bad recipe."

Chip said he had to go.

"Fine. I enjoyed talking with you. Perhaps we can figure out another time to talk again," Jack said as he handed Chip his business card.

Glancing at the business card while walking to the car service line outside of Smyth Johnston's office, Chip took immediate note at what it said: Jack Bonfiglio, Investigator, Securities and Exchange Commission.

Soon climbing into his town car, he was left to wonder about his brief conversation with Jack. Was it a coincidence? Or was he being investigated? Or was he being sized up as a potential informant on some financial crimes investigation?

"Dude, you're not going to believe what just happened after you left the Blarney," he texted Sasquatch, as the car rumbled east over the Queensboro Bridge to Long Island.

Chapter 3
La Banque, c'est Moi

Monday, August 13, 2007
6:05 A.M.

The Hamptons
Long Island, New York

The alarm clock sounded, interrupting another night of restless sleep for Michael Feinberg. Thoughts of new trades, P&L, and office-related bullshit crept into his mind throughout the night, as they did almost every night. As he arose from bed and walked into the bathroom for a shower, he could see the sun rising in tandem as he glanced east across the horizon on the Atlantic Ocean.

He dried himself off with a checkered, plush towel that matched the rest of the bathroom's décor. As he finished his Monday morning bathroom ritual, he tried, in vain, to keep his thoughts away from what lay in store for him. There was no time to daydream, and in fact he sometimes wondered if he even had any dreams. It was all about the here and now as a trader; dreams were for a future date, after he had amassed an even greater fortune. Mortgage the present for that future date.

Almost on perfect cue, he could hear the helicopter hovering on his helipad a mere 100 yards away from where he was standing. Clad in his custom-made attire, he made his way downstairs to the kitchen where his juice, Danish, and a double espresso awaited him—all courtesy of their maid, Rosa.

Swallowing a final shot of espresso, he put his cup in the sink and walked outside. He loved the early morning smell of the ocean, a scent that would soon be replaced by the helicopter's exhaust fumes. As he approached the helicopter steps and looked back at his Southampton home, he wondered how many more hours Franny and Deborah would lie asleep negating the ill effects of the expensive Bordeaux and cognac from last night.

Feinberg lowered his head instinctively and seated himself up front next to the pilot. He preferred being up front, despite the back seat having considerably more space. Within minutes of taking flight, Feinberg could see that the Long Island Expressway was already a congested mess. No chance he would put himself through that pain, even at the $500 one-way cost of the private helicopter. In his world, time really was money, and the 45-minute flight was far better than what could range anywhere from one and a half hours to two and a half hours or more by car—especially on a Monday morning when the summer crush of bankers migrated back into Manhattan.

He pulled out his Blackberry to check in on the European markets and any email traffic of note. Forty-five minutes was just the right amount of time for Feinberg to get a handle on what might be in store for him as he began a new week of trading. Digesting the content of one email in particular, he again glanced below at Long Island, aptly named for its 120-mile east-to-west expanse. As had become a force of habit, he would always try to spot his elementary school in the Woodside section of Queens as the helicopter approached the western end of Long Island. He had recently endowed a scholarship in his name, given annually to the school's top math student, as he had once been. Maybe he'd step up even more this year, and have the school named after him. Whether this philanthropy was self-serving or genuine didn't matter—it felt good either way to him. He wondered whether the sports-crazed, dumb jocks from his class had ever given back, or could.

$ $ $

Despite being 32 years old, Feinberg was advanced beyond his years. He was regarded by many as a "Six Sigma" intellectual event. Borrowed from Jack Welch and General Electric, this became parlance for a level of intelligence that was far, far above the norm even by Wall Street standards. His astrophysics degree from MIT was testimony to this uncommon intelligence. Unlike many of his colleagues he had chosen to begin his career working for the Department of Defense, only to decide after three years that he wanted to make more money than government work. He never felt the need to go back for his MBA. It wouldn't have provided any value to him.

Since joining the firm as a junior trader seven years ago, his track record of making a boatload of money—high margin, high velocity money—in credit derivatives was also a Six Sigma event.

All of senior management loved his money-making prowess, conferring on him virtual carte blanche to pursue his business as he saw fit—at least until he was proven otherwise. Feinberg knew he had little if any adult supervision and behaved accordingly with anyone who interfered with his money-making pursuits.

Soon after being hired as a junior trader, and recognizing the momentum of credit derivatives (which began in earnest in the mid-'90s), Feinberg convinced his managers that credit derivatives was an explosive growth area and he was just the man to spearhead this new product initiative. Initially, trading was slow, maybe a few deals a month with select investors. As commercial banks grew more sophisticated and sought to limit their risk profiles by buying insurance on their loan books, global investors had simultaneously recognized the inherent return potential as well as the many other benefits credit derivative products offered.

Feinberg was more than happy to stand in the middle as market maker, with a money printing machine at his disposal.

Profitability of Feinberg's book grew from virtually zero in its first year to closer to $400 million in 2006, his seventh year in charge of the group. That's serious money, which his compensation of more than $15 million reflected. It seemed like an absurd amount of money for a 32-year-old to make, but it was really no different from athletes, rock stars, or actors at the top of their game. If the market bears it, then so be it.

Feinberg put his Blackberry down, sensing he was getting close, and approaching the lower Manhattan skyline on what appeared to be a gorgeous sunny day with vivid blue skies. The morning's beauty, however, was immediately transformed as he saw below the lingering, gaping wound of Ground Zero. Each time he flew over the somber reminder, he thought back on that day, with varying emotions.

Like almost every New Yorker who had been in the city on 9/11, he felt tremendous sorrow when seeing

Ground Zero. Professionally, however, he often recalled the market circumstances surrounding that tragic event with pangs of guilt, as having been a catalyst for his rapid ascension on Wall Street. Immense volatility and illiquidity were at all-time peaks, making the theoretical arguments for credit derivatives even greater. Not only had he survived the worst tragedy in American history, he had thrived in its aftermath. In some respects, 9/11 created a business climate of fear, a need for heightened risk management and new products, all of which played into Feinberg's hands as he capitalized on the market opportunity. It had propelled him and the world of credit derivatives to the forefront.

$ $ $

As the helicopter began its descent to the 34th Street helipad on the East River, he spotted his office building. He reflected on the significant change that had occurred there for its occupants, largely financial firms, over the years. Smyth Johnston was no exception to this significant change, never more so than in recent years following the advent and widespread acceptance of derivative products.

Feinberg and his credit derivative brethren viewed retail and commercial banking as low-margin dinosaurs fossilizing before their very eyes. Business extinction was nothing new on Wall Street, particularly over the last 10 years of rapid innovation: businesses were continually lost to commoditization (where transactions went from being executed by people to electronic auctions on faceless computer screens) or disintermediation (where the people standing between buyers and sellers were eliminated). They also saw their own investment banking counterparts in the once-venerable, fee-based advisory corporate finance businesses get swallowed up in the same vortex. The 1950s clubby gentlemen of Wall Street lore had been replaced by the 1980s leveraged buyout "masters of the universe," who were in turn replaced by the 1990s mortgage-backed securities "big swinging dicks."

Now, Feinberg was replacing all of them as the center of the Wall Street universe. Feinberg knew his world within Sales and Trading had unmistakably revolutionized the traditional pecking order on Wall Street, almost in a 180-degree fashion over their rivals in corporate finance. It wasn't that long ago that Sales and Trading was viewed as the distant stepchild. Now, thanks to the explosive growth of new products across a seemingly endless array of asset classes that lent themselves to vast innovation and financial engineering, Sales and Trading was the dog rather than the tail—the big dog.

A new-age system of finance had emerged. The shadow banking system was comprised of financial institutions, including the likes of hedge funds, money market funds, repurchase agreement markets, structured investment vehicles, special purpose entities, and other non-bank financial institutions whose legal status and business practices orbited outside the boundaries of most regulatory monitoring. The investment banks, technically speaking, were not part of the shadow banking system given that they were subject to the regulatory monitoring of central banks and various other governmental institutions, the Securities and Exchange Commission being but one example. Though technically not considered a part of it, the investment banks were in practice the heart and soul of the shadow banking system, originating and structuring many of their transactions in an off-balance sheet accounting framework so as not to fall under their otherwise onerous regulatory scrutiny. By 2007, the volume of transactions comprising the global shadow banking system had grown to roughly $50 trillion.

Shadow banking in effect bypassed the traditional financing mechanisms of commercial banks and other regulated lending institutions by allowing its institutions to act as intermediaries between investors (the money source) and borrowers. No longer did a borrower need to go to their commercial loan officers for money. Instead, a special-purpose company could readily be established to lend directly to the borrowers with money that had been funded by the capital markets. Of course, Feinberg or other de facto operating entities within the shadow banking system would pocket handsome fees for their efforts in structuring the transaction. No more need for the neighborhood bank branch which relied on deposits as its funding source. While both a traditional bank and shadow bank provide credit and essential liquidity into the financial system, shadow banks arguably do so more efficiently, since the likes of hedge funds and other boutique, more nimble capital market investors are able to absorb risks that traditional banks are either unwilling or unable to absorb. In short, shadow banks, by their customized, transaction-specific nature can provide credit to more entities who might otherwise have limited access to credit.

On the face of it, the shadow banking system seemed overwhelmingly positive. After all, the extension of credit and liquidity, both hallmarks of a smoothly functioning market (much like oil is to an engine), deepen the river of money. Lurking in its midst, however, was a host of operational frailties that, if overlooked or underestimated, posed significant risk to the global financial system. Among those frailties—most stemming from the lesser regulation from not being depositary institutions—was the potential for excessive risk-taking through the use of leverage, funding mismatches (the use of short-term funding to invest in long-term risk), and the interrelationship shadow banks had with traditional banks and with one another as a form of potential contagion.

Feinberg and its many other active participants could use shadow banking to securitize mortgages, credit card receivables, auto loans, or all the above, while hedging any unwanted risk vis-à-vis credit-default swaps.

With the financial revolution ushered in by the shadow banking system came an accompanying behavioral revolution.

As Feinberg walked onto the trading floor he smirked as he passed by those "poor bastards" from corporate finance toiling away on yet another deal that would span months to complete for a "paltry" $2 million fee. What a joke, he thought. He could make multiples of that on one trade today. These guys are fucking dinosaurs. The manufacturing of money was all that mattered in the final result. It wasn't about the fancy suits, the Ivy League required pedigree, or the long-term, multitransactional client relationships anymore. It was all about making money in this brash new Wall Street culture.

Feinberg was feeling the nature of his unbridled success; he was in the right place at the right time, with the right trading aptitude and intellectual firepower to do no wrong. He knew he had the world of finance at his disposal, so much so that he began to ascribe a royalty-like quality to himself by paraphrasing Louis XIV, "La Banque, c'est Moi."

All was good for Feinberg. With each passing day, his star power grew to juggernaut proportion, as did his ability to leverage the system to his advantage. Settling into his chair, a steaming cup of espresso and a fresh bagel with lox awaited his arrival. It was time to turn on the money machine again.

$ $ $

Joey Karros arrived on the floor at seven as usual. He wanted to set a good example for his team, be one of the first ones there. On his dance card were many items for what lay in store: he had deals to cheerlead, politics to play, and lots of good old-fashioned ass-kissing to do.

Soon after his arrival the rest of his troops came to fill out the desk. Those who arrived later than 7:30 were greeted coldly by Karros. He wanted everyone in their seats by 7:30, likely as a show of force for management to observe.

"Zeus is the game today. Get it done. Run do not walk. We need to sell more than any other Sales desk. Baum is seeing everyone in Sales, and the other guys will be calling your clients on this deal. So get on it. I'm talking to Feinberg today to see if we can get double sales credits on it. He needs our help."

Karros knew to mention the magic words: sales credits.

Sales credits were a sort of monopoly money that sales management used as a proxy measure of how much value sales people were adding. As the actual profit of each transaction stayed in the trader's book, sales credits were claims, of sorts, on that profit that became the currency for year-end bonus discussions. Theoretically, they were supposed to equate to the profit from a particular transaction. In reality, Trading used them as carrot-and-stick tools to motivate salespeople to work on transactions that were most important to them.

Karros proceeded to take inventory of his team and to whom each person was showing the deal, starting with Chip.

"Okay, Chip, besides the usual suspects, who's on your target list? We have to focus on the upper end of the capital structure—it has the largest dollar amount of bonds to sell. Your guys should be all over this deal. Don't let the amateurs from the mortgage desk make you look bad. It's a jump ball on this deal and the flow sales guys want some of our high margin business."

It was the typical Karros ploy—create the impression that there was internal competition for one of his salesman's clients. He had learned that management tactic from the master himself, Duncan Kerr, head of the Debt Markets Worldwide division, who referred to the competing internal factions approach as "management by creative chaos." Under this management theory, Kerr believed that if his people got comfortable in their jobs, they wouldn't perform as well. Having competition for every deal, every task, every client, every trade, every phone call kept the firm's performance at its peak. The troops needed to be kept uneasy, hungry, and fearing for their jobs at all times. If someone couldn't handle the pressure, there were jobs in other industries. Wall Street was for the best and the brightest, for those who were able to work 24/7 at peak performance.

Rather than take the bait, Chip chose to ignore the thinly-veiled ploy of Karros.

"I have a bunch of guys looking at this. I think Mallory McMahon will be my next call. Sasquatch is making calls, so is Tracy."

"Make the calls, now," replied Karros as he marched down the row to find out what the others on the team were doing to sell Zeus.

"Hey, Sasquatch, are you hungry, need more coffee?" Chip asked, hoping to take a break from Karros's "rah rah" bullshit as he was wading through the nearly 300 new messages in his inbox. Sadly, he knew that 90 percent of the emails were useless market updates or price level updates on deals he was not involved with.

"Sure. I drank a bunch of beers last night, surprise, surprise, I need a breakfast sandwich to soak up the stomach acid. Want me to get my *bitch* on it?"

"That's the most important thing she can do today. Tell her she's on the clock and that I'll take the usual."

And with that Sasquatch turned to his immediate right, where Tracy was awaiting the breakfast orders. She knew it was part of the job and actually thought it was an amusing part of her job at that, an essential rite of passage as a newly-hired associate at an investment bank. She didn't even mind being referred to as Sasquatch's bitch, as the term was doled out regardless of gender to anyone in an entry level position.

$ $ $

Sasquatch, or Nigel Woodley as was his given name back in the East End of London, had come to New York to reinvent his banking career after multiple positions at various firms in London. He lacked the Oxford or Cambridge pedigree, instead obtaining his university degree at the City of London Polytechnic Institute at night while working in a clerical capacity at a bank during the day. Though he was considered by some to be lacking the intangibles necessary to run a client interfacing business himself, he demonstrated keen street smarts, tenacity, and a work ethic that got him noticed.

Following 12 years in London in various positions, Sasquatch, coming off of a failed marriage, felt it was time for a new life and decided to accept a position at Smyth Johnston in New York. It was an opportunity for a fresh start, professionally and personally, and he hoped the change would alter the trajectory of both facets of his life.

In many ways, Sasquatch was the London equivalent of the Brooklyn, Bronx, or Queens "BBQer" who found himself, against all odds, grinding away on Wall Street in hope of one day punching his lottery ticket as a salesman or trader. Examples of that human drama had unfolded countless times before; he wanted to be one of them, and with each passing year when seeing it fail to materialize, his anxiety level increased.

Soon after arriving in New York he received the nickname of Sasquatch. The nickname was in part due to his large, imposing stature, but also in part due to his fair but aggressive-once-provoked demeanor. One incident, particularly befitting of the nickname, occurred when an internal lawyer had failed to get him a critical, time-sensitive answer on a deal document. He began patiently reminding the lawyer that he needed the feedback as soon as possible. But the lawyer played tone-deaf and failed to respond, placing the deal's completion at risk. Soon enough, Nigel decided it was time to stalk the lawyer outside his office door. The tactic proved effective, obtaining an answer just in time to save the lucrative deal he had worked on for months.

Sometime after the incident Nigel's boss at the time ran into the lawyer, who said that Nigel reminded him of an angry Sasquatch lumbering back and forth outside his office prepared to attack at any given moment. Not seeking to allay the lawyer's fears the boss responded by telling him that Nigel might well have made the attack had the lawyer not soon coughed up the answer.

No holds barred—get it done. It became a defining moment for Nigel, as Sasquatch became synonymous with someone who knew how to get things done in a kill-or-be-killed fashion. There was arguably no greater attribute in the jungle of a trading floor. Years after the event, Chip, aware of the story behind Sasquatch, had recruited him to his team. The two shared a strong commonality. Both were on edge, anxious, and tired, coming to the end of the line, somewhat like cats that had exhausted nearly all their nine lives.

$ $ $

"Tracy, you're in luck today. I'll walk over to the deli with you. Need some air anyway," Sasquatch said.

"Sounds good, big night last night, eh? There's a couple of things I wanted to talk to you about anyway," she replied.

As they left the building and walked to their go-to deli within a block of the office, Tracy broached the first topic she wanted to bring up with Sasquatch.

"So, I've been in this associate position for more than a year now. When will I start running deals? I know I still need to provide support for you and Chip, but you guys should know that I want to progress beyond that sooner rather than later."

"Believe me," Sasquatch replied, "Chip and I would like that to be sooner than later also. We've been doing this a long time and want to get out of this game. I can't speak for Chip, but in my case I need a few more bonuses at least. Chip is probably done with one more bonus, maybe two."

"So Chip is close to the finish line. What happens when he leaves?"

"I'd have crossed the finish line if I hadn't been divorced two times already—very painful from a financial standpoint. When he leaves, the hope is that I take over the business, keep it running for a few years, then turn it over to you, when you're ready. You're still too green to take it over in the next year or two. If Chip and I flew the coop, they'd go outside to find someone to head the group. That could be a good thing for you, or it could be a bad thing for you. My guess is it would be bad, as most outside hires want to bring in their own people. I've seen that play a million times in this business."

"So the best near-term scenario is Chip leaves in a year or so, you step into his role, and I step into yours—does that mean I get to hire my own bitch?" Tracy joked.

"Yep, and I'll even let you do the hiring. Believe me, I want that day to be yesterday. In case you haven't noticed, we don't really love this game anymore," Sasquatch said.

"Yes, I have noticed. Both of you guys are fairly clear about your love of the game at this point."

"Tracy, you actually have it pretty good. In a few years, this business can be yours, your own client base delivered on a silver platter. That's a much better deal than being one of a number of associates sitting on a larger desk competing against one another for the next raise."

"It's true. I just wanted to let you know what I'm thinking. Can I ask about something else?"

"Sure," said Sasquatch, as they ordered their breakfast items to go.

"I heard you have some real estate business or investments on the side. I'm interested in getting involved with that. Seems like the New York market just keeps going up, it's up something like 50 percent in the last three years."

"I can help you with that. So what do you make now, 150 grand, maybe 200, including your bonus? You can get plenty of leverage with that... The market's been good for me, a 'can't lose proposition' thus far. Basically what I do is buy an apartment for a million bucks. The bank will give me a $950,000 mortgage, and then another bank will lend me $50,000 home equity line of credit."

"So, no money down?"

"Well, yeah, you need to pay something like 25 grand in closing costs. Then, you rent it out at six grand a month. And that basically covers your interest cost too."

"But you're not making any money?"

"In a year, you can sell the apartment for 1.2, and pocket 150 grand in profit after expenses. Or if you want, wait two years and sell it for 1.4. The story just keeps getting better."

"Will you introduce me to your people?"

"Sure, as long as you promise not to bid on the same properties I do. Maybe you should start somewhere in the 500s or some price range like that. Let's talk about this sometime over beers. Better get back to the office before Chip's bacon, egg, and cheese gets cold. Believe it or not, he can become an even bigger asshole if he gets a cold sandwich," Sasquatch laughed, as he and Tracy headed back to the office.

Tracy liked the idea of supplementing her income, particularly by using *OPM*—other people's money. She also liked the idea of piggybacking on Sasquatch's real estate experience. By all appearances it seemed like a smart approach and at the very least served as a useful career hedge that would enable her to keep the lights on if she, as happens to many Wall Streeters young and old, walked onto the trading floor one day only to be told that her business was being shut down. She trusted Sasquatch and respected the wisdom, although harsh at times, that he could impart to her.

$ $ $

Franny Goodman, or Feinberg as it would have been had she accepted her husband's surname when they married, leisurely strolled through ever-so-trendy SoHo to Nobu, one of her favorite restaurants. Located at the corner of Franklin and Hudson Streets, the place was arguably the top sushi restaurant in New York, and among the best in the world. It was all too easy to sample a variety of sushi and sashimi ranging from the standard yellowfin tuna and California rolls to the more exotic Pacific sea urchin, and walk out with a sinfully eye-popping bill, excluding wine, something Franny never suffered without. As with the many other patrons crowded into the restaurant each day, she thought nothing of the expense. It was how one lived in New York in 2007; it was the best of the best, a by-product of Michael's meteoric success on Wall Street.

Clad in fashionable black, Franny was with her mother, Deborah Goodman. Both were carrying shopping bags loaded with items from the several SoHo boutiques they had just visited. SoHo, once a somewhat downtrodden bohemian bastion for starving artist types, had rapidly been transformed over the course of the last decade into *the* place to live and shop in Manhattan. Luminaries such as JFK Jr., Robert DeNiro, and the like once called or still called SoHo home. Untold millions had been invested in commodious loft space, former factories or warehouses that had been artfully converted into beautiful homes. Old brick-laid streets had been reawakened by open air gourmet markets, cafés, and world-class art and clothing boutiques. Franny loved SoHo; it fit her lifestyle to a tee.

As the two walked through the restaurant's front door they immediately spotted Michael sitting at Franny's favorite table. It was highly unusual for her to get him to leave the desk for lunch. Only Franny's constant begging had gotten him out of the office. Usually he wolfed down his sandwich at his desk as he stared at the numbers on any one of his four computer screens, occasionally barking orders at his minions in between bites.

But today was her birthday, and she had insisted on having lunch at Nobu with her husband, who agreed, not knowing Deborah would be part of the celebration.

Feinberg couldn't help but notice the multiple shopping bags.

"Michael, sorry we're late, but Mother and I had a great morning out together. Can you believe she had never been to Foravi?"

"Yes, I am surprised to hear that, but it looks like you made up for lost time. Anyway, Happy Birthday," he replied, feigning interest in the conversation.

"I bought a pair of Jimmy Choos. They had the pair I've been looking for since last season. In fact, I liked them so much I bought Mother her own pair. Don't they look great?"

Michael, much like any other male when confronted with this great news, struggled to muster any visible enthusiasm for Franny's conspicuous consumption. It was one thing for his wife to be on the gravy train, but the mother-in-law, the lecherous one incarnate, tagging along for the free ride was another issue altogether. Hadn't he had this conversation with Franny earlier?

"Okay. Let's order. I need to get back to the office shortly," said Michael, as his wife and mother-in-law proceeded to order hundreds of dollars of sushi and wine. Not that it really mattered financially. Whether it was a $5,000 or a $10,000 shopping spree plus another grand for lunch, it was nothing more than a rounding error. As a matter of principle, however, it had become a source of irritation in their young marriage.

Striving to take his mind off his mother-in-law, Michael had hoped to have a nice birthday lunch with his wife. No such luck.

"I'm glad the two of you had a nice morning on the shopping circuit. I assume there's something in one of those bags for me," Michael said wryly.

"Oh," as Deborah Goodman sipped her expensive celebratory champagne that Michael could not partake in, "I knew we forgot something, Franny. Maybe we can pick out something for him when we go to the Hamptons tomorrow."

"Good idea. I'm sure you'll appreciate it, honey," Franny said as she smiled at her husband. It was an attempt to mask the fact that she had not told him she was retreating to their beach house tomorrow to spend the balance of the week as well as the upcoming weekend with her mother.

Detecting that Michael was suitably unimpressed, Franny tactfully changed the subject.

"So did I tell you the Schwartzes will also be out at the Hamptons this weekend? They're looking to buy that house; then they can finally get some use out of that new Range Rover."

"It's about time they got with the program," he said.

"Maybe you can catch a ride with them on Friday afternoon. It'd be so much more social of you than that helicopter you take. Anyway, I invited them to come by the house for some afternoon cocktails and dinner." Franny went on, making her plans with little or no regard for Michael and his schedule or desires for the weekend. It was as if he was irrelevant in the discussion, so long as the money was there to bankroll it all.

Michael decided that he had no upside in the conversation, so he decided to stay quiet. The conversation meandered back and forth between Franny and her mother for what seemed an eternity. Reaching his tolerance threshold, he eventually asked for the check, said he was sorry he needed to get back to the office, and kissed his wife as he left the table.

As lunch ended, Franny and Deborah decided to walk back to Franny and Feinberg's nearby loft. She was happy. It had been a nice birthday so far.

As she greeted the doorman at her building, her reflections on the day's events were further indulged by the abundance in her loft. She had spared nothing decorating their multimillion-dollar marital nest. The beach house was no different.

In fact, the beach house, certainly to Franny, was the quintessence of the *good life,* serving as a staging ground by which to display her New York riches. Seldom a summer week would pass when Franny didn't host friends or acquaintances, many from Vassar College, her alma mater. They would gladly spend the week at the beach with her, leaving behind their European nannies to deal with the child-rearing duties. The daily regimen generally included mimosas to get the day started, a trip into town to shop at the many boutiques, then back to the house for some beach or pool time. Later in the afternoon, generally after some pampering by the masseuse or beautician, it was off to dinner and whatever might be the social function du jour. Franny's $20,000 monthly credit card bill summed up the materialistic   trappings   of   her   Manhattan-to-Southampton, glamour-drenched lifestyle.

The two decided to open a bottle of dessert wine after settling into the loft. The conversation quickly took a less jubilant turn when Deborah, with her maternal antenna up, asked her daughter a question.

"Is everything okay between you two?"

"Sure."

"Sure?"

Franny hesitated, "Sure."

Deborah raised her eyebrows, leaving Franny with no choice. There was no use hiding it any longer.

"I wish I knew. I think he's too busy at work. He has a lot of responsibility, and markets have been crazy lately. He's been distant, never home, and really hasn't cared about what I do or say. We really don't talk much. I can tell he doesn't seem to care. He's married more to making money than to me," proclaimed Franny.

"I thought you two were in counseling and things were going along fine. You know, Franny, marriage is not easy. Why don't you two take a long vacation together? Maybe Paris, St. Maarten, or some other place to collect yourselves and talk, a kind of second honeymoon."

"I'd like to, and of course our counselor suggested we do that as well. But Michael tells me he can't leave the desk now. Of course, he can never leave the desk. He's too important and his business is volatile. He knows too much to leave...blah, blah, blah. Even if we went to Paris, he'd be on his Blackberry the whole time."

Deborah Goodman was hoping for a better life for her daughter. Her husband had been a mid-level manager at a pharmaceutical company, which afforded her daughter and her a decent home in suburban New Jersey as well as ample pay to cover the cost of Vassar but not much more, as he travelled constantly. With her husband deceased from cancer four years ago, she collected the proceeds of the life insurance policy and moved to a small but nice apartment on Park Avenue. It pained her to see Franny's marital turmoil.

In many respects Franny was singing the same tune as many Wall Street spouses. The story of her marriage was par for the course as far as life on Wall Street went. With the good came the bad, proving there really was no *free lunch*.

There was a price to pay for money, power, and the high life. That price was spousal absenteeism, preoccupation, restlessness, irritability, limited intimacy, and, sadly all too often, divorce. Certainly it was no different than most marriages among other highly-compensated professionals. It was, as her mother said, not easy to be married. It had never been easy, but today's marital institution seemed to face increased difficulties.

"Maybe I have to accept my marriage and its imperfections. Maybe it is just a marriage of convenience, something that 'works' for Michael and me on terms very different than for your generation. One guy in Michael's office I was talking to at some boring cocktail party was laughing about one of his clients who was on his ninth marriage. Another guy was heading to divorce court for the fourth time. And he joked that this marriage lasted so little time they could at least return their wedding gifts within the six-month refund policy. I guess that's why we, like most of our friends, have a pre-nup in place."

"Well, Franny," Deborah maternally advised her daughter with a tone of consternation, "that seems a terrible commentary on marriage. You and only you have the choice as to what you find acceptable in your marriage. More wine? This Chateau d'Yquem is really good. Worth every penny for it."

$ $ $

Chip, Sasquatch, and Tracy began their second shift as they departed the trading floor for a meeting with their favorite client and potential Zeus investor, Mal McMahon of Broadway Life Insurance Company. The chosen meeting place was one of Mal's long-standing favorite places, the Whiskey Bar on 57th Street and Central Park South. It was among a multitude of popular places to convene for some high quality cocktails and local scenery. That scenery alternated between the natural beauty of the park across the street and the scantily clothed waitress staff. They settled into a nice comfortable leather booth where they could be assured of prime viewing.

Whiskey Bar could be summarized in three words: elegant, macho, and sexy. Elegant due to its décor, macho due to its patrons, and sexy due to its waitresses.

After the usual banter about the families, sports, or other non-work topics of interest, Mal wasted no time jumping right into the business at hand: Zeus. The sooner he took care of that, the sooner he could begin drinking more freely and staring at the stunning waitresses. Both were far more interesting than talking about credit derivatives deals.

"So, I've been looking at Zeus, and on the face of it looks like a deal I can get involved with. What's the latest on your end? Where do you need help, or is it spoken for?" Mal said, sipping his Maker's Mark.

"Tracy, you just spoke with Structuring an hour or two ago. What's the status? What tranches do we need help on, if any?" Chip said.

"Bure told me they need help on the equity and is willing to upsize someone's participation elsewhere in the structure if they help him there. Not a big surprise, there's always a horse trade to do."

"There is no way I'm doing a piece of the equity, no matter what the deal looks like or how Feinberg sweetens it for me. My company is new to the credit derivatives game, and I have limited powder for these deals. In the interest of self-preservation, my job ceases to exist if I get burned early in my tenure. I'm already getting enough shit about Eros and the five-point drop in price. Luckily, we're so far removed from any losses that I've been able to convince my guys that the risk-reward on these deals is still better than our alternatives. But make no mistake, these guys are conservative, to put it mildly. You'll have to find a home for the equity with the go-go hedge fund crowd. After all, those guys are smarter than everyone else—just ask them."

Mal continued, "So who is this asset manager, 14th Street? I've never really heard of them, and find it interesting how they've gotten into bed with Feinberg."

"We just had the Sales teach-in with Feinberg's team on Friday, as a matter of fact. The spin they're putting on it is that the manager, as an independent third party, adds more credibility to the portfolio selection process. Feinberg says he's cognizant that some of his recent deals have generated greater losses to investors than was expected. The job of 14th Street is to mitigate those fears."

"Come on, are you suggesting Feinberg might have motivations that aren't in the best interest of his investors. Really?"

Another sip.

McMahon was among a growing universe of investors who had grown wary of this new generation of traders. While traders had always been perceived to have sharp elbows, something seemed to be different with this new breed. In the past, client interests had usually been part of the discussion, with most traders recognizing their long-term value in the equation. This new breed seemed much more short-term oriented, focusing mostly on how to maximize short-term profits, much like a proprietary trader would do.

Mal's instincts were strikingly similar to Chip's. What the foursome at the table didn't know with certainty was that Zeus was designed as a naked short. In effect, Feinberg was paying the customers a small fee to take the risk of mortgage defaults. If mortgages defaulted at a higher than expected rate, their investment would decline in value, with the corresponding gain going into Feinberg's pocket. It was the ultimate zero-sum proposition.

What Mal and the sales guys believed, as was the case with all of their previous deals, was that Feinberg was intermediating the transaction, or buying from one customer and selling to another. Typically Feinberg or other traders amassed a pool of assets, then sliced and diced them into pieces to sell to various clients and took a fee for the service. Now, Feinberg was just selling the deal without anyone on the other side. So if the value of the portfolio dropped to 50 cents on the dollar, he would keep all that gain. If the portfolio kept its value, Feinberg would only lose the amount being paid to the clients. He had little downside and massive upside.

"What are you thinking, apart from Feinberg being an asshole?" Sasquatch asked Mal.

"Well, Nigel, my quant guys tell me we could possibly consider a piece of the senior-most tranche. You know that as a life insurance company we have issues with the capital charges on the riskier tranches.

Keep in mind we don't have a lot of powder for any of these deals. Our investment committee is extremely conservative and, as I have told you before, has allocated only a small percentage of the portfolio to alternative assets. But at the same time, they think the economy will continue to grow and want to beat their return benchmarks. These credit derivatives deals offer a nice kicker to help with that."

"What kind of size were you thinking?"

"Probably a hundred." Mal replied, meaning $100 million.

"That'll work. We'll take it back to the desk and see what they say. Can I call it a soft circle? That would be very helpful in getting their attention."

"Yes, you can call it a soft circle, subject to Investment Committee approval as always. We also need to finalize price, but your indication wasn't that far off from what I think our models will tell us. Also, you can tell them I want an early look at Zeus II. That will help me get approval rather than have my committee think this is just a one-off deal. In new asset classes it's always better to be one in a series of deals, so we don't do all the work solely for one deal. My guys see things as multitransactional where relationships, like ours, matter and make a difference."

Mal lifted his high ball, and the foursome clinked their glasses. Tracy got the waitress's attention, circling her finger in the air for another round to celebrate the soft circle order.

The horse carriages carrying tourists around Central Park clopped outside.

She then said eagerly, "Anything else we can tell you?"

Mal paused, then asked, "Now that we've had a few cocktails, and gotten the details out of the way, what do you guys really think about these deals? To me, I understand the regular CDOs: take a bunch of corporate loans, slice them into various pieces by risk level to segment the investors, so on and so forth. But with underlying assets in the pool being mortgages, inherently more complex than loans, and putting them into the framework of a CDO. That can get really hairy. Hey, I like the extra yield pickup, but is it worth the trouble?"

Chip chose to field this one.

"I hear you, man. I don't know. This stuff is complicated, I give you that, but maybe that's where the extra kicker comes in as compensation for the added complexity. You remember Fabozzi's textbook with the description of different kinds of risks from interest rates, credit, prepayment, et cetera. Then there was the notion of *risk risk,* where you haven't thought of everything intrinsically risky in the deal. In the Sales teach-in this afternoon a lot of questions were asked about the deal, its structure, the collateral, how it gets priced, and so on, and it all seemed to hold together pretty well. But ultimately, these deals are bets on the economy. If the economy holds up, people can afford to pay their mortgages and you'll get your return on Zeus; but if the economy tanks, then well... none of us sitting on this side of the table," as he gestured at Sasquatch, Tracy, and himself, "are smart enough to figure out the complexities of these deals. Our job is to match our client's risk appetite with the bank's needs and make business happen. In our opinion, subject to the caveats already discussed, there seems to be a decent match here."

Mal chimed in. "Yeah, but speaking of the caveats, what is Feinberg really doing here? Is he keeping any of the deal for himself? The fact that he isn't willing to take some of the equity is concerning. As an insurance company we see the world in terms of risk sharing, you know, an alignment of interests where both parties win or lose together. I've been around the block enough to know that trading savages don't always see it that way. It means we have to be very cautious with new structures like this rather than become helpless prey."

"You know, Tracy," Mal said, turning his eyes to her, "I used to be on the sell side of the business where I had enough exposure to predators like Feinberg who are all about what's in it for them. They don't care about you as a salesperson, they don't care about your client, and they don't even care about their own bank. They care about themselves and how much they can take from the system in the current bonus cycle. Chip and I have talked about this for years now—how can so few assholes, which I'd say are roughly 10 percent of the industry, wind up controlling as much as they have lately. Someday there will be classes on this topic in the halls of business schools around the world. Sorry to get on my soapbox, but you need to be aware of the world you've entered into."

Mal paused, "But, the fact of the matter is that my company needs Wall Street to source assets. So we have to deal with guys like Feinberg to make any money in our investment portfolios. The hard part is trying to figure out which ones are trying to screw you the most."

Chip, sensing the gravity of his client's sermon while not necessarily disagreeing with it, attempted to mollify his concerns as best he could.

"Well, Tracy, there you have it. It seems like you've heard that sermon before. Mal, if you were to ask me whether I know exactly what the desk is doing in terms of how this deal fits with the rest of their book, I would tell you I don't know. And as a sales guy, I will never know. Light has a better chance of leaving a black hole than truthful info leaving Feinberg's lips about his book position."

"I appreciate your honesty; it's a lot more than we get from most of our coverage guys. We know Feinberg's reputation—the sharp elbows, win-at-all-cost bit. No, we don't trust his type but we like doing business with you guys, especially when you host me here."

$ $ $

It had gotten late. Mal chugged his cocktail, took one last look at the Whiskey Bar waitress staff, and then walked out onto Central Park South where he promptly hailed a cab to Grand Central. He was shooting for the 10:34 train to Rye, an affluent suburb in New York's Westchester County, where he had just purchased a large home for his family. After apartment living in the city, they had decided to move to the suburbs. With Mal's new job, the hours weren't as bad as they were during his sell-side banker days. And the 40-minute train commute wasn't all that bad. Tonight, as had been the case over the course of most of his career, he would in all likelihood arrive to a house of sleeping family members. At least that was happening less since joining the more lifestyle-friendly side of the Wall Street game.

He wished he could order a car, as he had been readily able to do in his sell-side days. It was a downside of being on the buy-side. Broadway Life didn't pay for car services.

After he departed, Tracy wanted to recap what had transpired with their client. "Pretty good. Looks like we have an order."

"It's not done until it's done. Trust me, they will ask for a million different default scenarios. And LifeCos are notoriously slow to confirm anything. But, yes, it's promising and we can at a minimum promote the hell out of a soft circle."

"That commentary on the trading savages and Feinberg wasn't the nicest thing I've heard," faintly slurring as the amount of alcohol she had consumed was more than typical. Tracy had a lot to learn, all part of the seasoning process.

"No, it wasn't, but it's probably true."

"Do you think there's something going on here?"

"That's the billion-dollar question. All we can do is speak frankly with Mal or any of our clients. If we don't trust what the traders are doing, we just need to tell the client they need to go in as big boys with their eyes open. They have to do their own analysis and come to their own conclusions about the deal. Frankly, I worry more about Feinberg here than the complexity of the product."

"Do you really think Feinberg knows that much more about the underlying names, more specifically if one of the mortgage pools has a higher probability of default than its rating may indicate?"

"Let's just say I think Feinberg and his people have spent a lot more time studying this than most clients ever would. I think there is some informational asymmetry going on, but how much, I don't know. Legally speaking, there is nothing wrong with him knowing more than the clients, but the clients just need to understand what they're getting into. By the way, no one has ever suggested these deals are risk-free. All we can do is hope that if the portfolio begins to degrade, it doesn't degrade faster than advertised because that's when clients get angry and feel duped, rightly or wrongly. What I know for sure, and you should take this as mentoring advice, is that a Wall Street salesperson is only as good as the trust they have with their clients."

Chip always felt uneasy, queasy at times, when pitching a new deal type to his long-standing clients. Did he really know what the trading desk's actual motivation was, or was he becoming yet another soundbite salesperson, much like a politician, relying on talking points with no conviction. As the evening's libations had taken hold, he mused that doing his job was not unlike a form of career Russian roulette. Not because of what he knew, but rather for what he didn't know. He always remembered a fellow salesman's description of a particular trader as "someone who would slit his mother's throat for another nickel."

In a changed business culture, steroids, drugs, rampant infidelity, media manipulation, half-truths, ethical malaise, all had become seemingly accepted parts of a toxic culture that often turned a blind eye to such behavior. Wall Street was in its own way a microcosm of a broader toxic culture that had come to define modern-day life globally. It was hard to reconcile how such corrosive behavior could lead to astoundingly positive financial results for its perpetrators. The scum had risen to the top.

No doubt jaded by his long Wall Street run, Chip saw three dominant philosophical themes describing human existence: bad things happening to bad people, bad things happening to good people, and good things happening to bad people. Of the three, he observed that "good things happening to bad people" seemed to be the most prevalent theme of late on the trading floor.

It was time to go home, before the alcohol led him further down this depressing path.

"Good night, Chip," said Tracy who sensed it was time for her to leave.

"See you tomorrow, Tracy. Thanks for your help tonight," Chip said as he walked Tracy to a cab, only to return to the bar where Sasquatch ordered yet another nightcap.

"Alright, man, I gotta go home and get some sleep."

"All four hours of it; that is, unless you get lucky with Mrs. Smith."

"No risk of that happening, as you know all too well."

$ $ $

Chip managed to get the key in the lock on the second try. Mrs. Smith was already sleeping in the bedroom. He wondered if his wife was more tired of him than he was of her. He wasn't sure what he wanted anymore from his marriage. He was sure, however, that the feeling was mutual. His marriage had gone stale, much like the cold slice of pizza he was about to scavenge from his fridge. The immediate gratification of cold pizza, highlights of the Mets game earlier that night, and a brief glimpse of his sleeping kids were just what he needed before passing out on the sofa. Tomorrow would bring the same drill: wake up at five, shower, train, work, breakfast, work, lunch, work, beers with another client, back home...repeat.

In the longer run, he knew he had to somehow get his life back in balance. He, like so many on Wall Street, was paying a heavy price for the narrow pursuit of money and the heavy toll the banker lifestyle had taken on him and his family members.

$ $ $

Duncan Kerr, head of Debt Markets Worldwide, sat in his chair waiting for his protégé, Michael Feinberg, to arrive for their weekly meeting. He had a love-hate relationship with Feinberg; he loved the P&L Feinberg was generating for him but always felt uneasy toward his longer term motives for amassing power. This was Wall Street—the religion of money transcended this perceived threat, as long as they made money together. Making money was something they had managed to do well since Kerr hired Feinberg seven years ago. Kerr and Deborah Goodman, Feinberg's would-be-mother-in-law sat on a few charity boards together. At one function Kerr, seated between Goodman and her husband (a client of Smyth Johnston's), was convinced by Deborah to hire Feinberg. That historical connection, Kerr assured himself, would further serve to blunt the perceived threat he often felt from Feinberg's growing star-power.

Kerr's office had glass walls, allowing him to monitor the pulse of the trading floor—his financial empire—on the outside. Feinberg seated himself in one of the two wingback leather chairs facing the desk, such that Kerr could check his torrent of emails during the meeting.

Whether Feinberg reported directly to Kerr or not didn't matter. All of the bank's managing directors knew instinctively that Kerr in some way, shape, or form controlled their business fate. In fact, Kerr controlled everything insofar as Sales and Trading was concerned at Smyth Johnston. With the explosive growth in derivatives over the last 15 years, Kerr's Debt Markets Worldwide division contributed disproportionate amounts to Smyth Johnston's profits. This made Kerr, arguably, the most powerful person at the bank. If not the most powerful, there was no denying his status as the highest paid person at the bank, pocketing somewhere around $50 million every year, far outpacing Smyth Johnston's CEO.

Kerr opened the meeting in his autocratic and articulate style. His steely, serious eyes could seemingly pierce through those to whom he was speaking. There was no joking with Kerr. It was all business, all serious, all results, all the time. He knew no other way to conduct himself, perhaps the result of his rags-to-riches personal story of escaping his childhood as the son of factory workers in the industrial port city of Dundee, Scotland. He wanted a way out, and soon found that way out courtesy of his tireless work ethic and academic successes. After being awarded a full academic scholarship at London School of Economics, he went on to graduate number one in his class before landing his first job in banking in the city of London.

The only issue up for debate when dealing with Kerr was whether his intelligence or demeanor was more intimidating. Even his star performers, Michael Feinberg included, would become sweaty-palmed and feel inadequate in Kerr's presence. He was good at everything pertaining to the Wall Street game: doing deals, being ahead of the curve in identifying lucrative trends in the markets, schmoozing clients, and keeping his friends close and his enemies—threats to his throne—even closer.

Kerr trusted no one; the risk of misplaced trust was too great.

"Michael, good job this year so far. I see your year-to-date P&L at $350 million."

Feinberg became apprehensive, knowing that the compliments from Kerr were few and far between.

"Haven't looked at my P&L since this morning, but that's about right, give or take a few mill."

"We need every bit of that and some more to hit budget. Many of our core businesses in debt markets, let alone elsewhere in the bank are way down. Even some of the cash cow businesses like corporates and govies are way down. I guess they're in the mature part of their cycle with margins that are eroding as they get further commoditized. Both of those desks—on the Trading and Sales side—are going to shrink dramatically in the coming years."

"Those fixed income staples just won't drive the business like they once did. That's for my business to do. It's a new chapter in fixed income, a revolution in finance."

"Correct, Michael. We need you and the other high margin derivative desks to drive the results. What do you think your full-year P&L results will be, conservatively?"

"Conservatively… I'd say we can deliver somewhere in the range of $500 million."

"That's not going to work. I need you at $700."

"That's absurd. You want me to double my YTD in just four months."

"Okay. I'm holding you accountable to $600 million. End of discussion. I need that P&L to make up for the shortfalls in my other businesses," Kerr added, as he was mindfully calculating how close his division would get to the hefty three billion budget the board had given him. He was also calculating how his chances of landing the CEO's job would fade if he failed to deliver.

"Duncan, I have your back," Feinberg said, sensing the importance his desk's performance had on Kerr's ambitions of becoming the next CEO of Smyth Johnston. He knew his leverage at the bank had just increased.

"Same time next week, Michael. In the meantime, let me know if you need anything done. I need you to deliver."

"Got it."

Feinberg walked back to his desk. If Zeus got done at its expected billion dollar size, and the mortgage defaults kept creeping up as he thought they would, he would be able to book at least $100 million of profit from it by the end of the year. With a Zeus II and Zeus III he would be way over his new budget. Kerr would get promoted and so would he—right after pocketing another lottery-sized bonus.

Prologue – 2

Tuesday, October 14, 2008
12:42 A.M.

Presidential Suite, The Peninsula
New York City

Detective Victor Rodriguez stood at the doorway to the luxurious Presidential Suite at The Peninsula New York. The body was lying in the middle of the floor, drowning in a pool of fresh blood. A man had been shot in the head. As he canvassed the room from the doorway, noting the opulence of the room, his first instinct told him this had to be a murder.

Every minute that passed gave the assumed killer a head start.

Rodriguez opened up a camera bag and clicked a few photos from the door. He then carefully walked along the wall in hope that the killer's shoe prints could still be found. The location of the body indicated that someone had come in, shot the man, and walked out. Had it been a suicide, the man probably would've wanted to see the spectacular nighttime view of New York from the floor-to-ceiling window. It was all conjecture at this point, as he awaited the arrival of his Forensics team.

Rodriquez wanted to look for the victim's wallet but knew that would be a breach of police protocol to do so until Forensics had done their initial work. He thought better of it, choosing to shoot more photos as he waited. He felt instinctively that Jack Jones, the name the victim always used when making his reservation, sounded too common not to be an alias.

He had begun to agree with the hotel manager's conjecture that the deceased was a rich banker, shot at a luxury hotel, in the middle of a financial market meltdown. The expensive suit and lack of Hollywood flash made him that much more convinced he was looking at a Wall Street banker. So much for this being an open-and-shut case; a certain media feeding frenzy would follow.

Rodriguez decided to make two calls. The first call was to the homicide lieutenant on duty. The second was to his investigator, whom he would wake up to research the victim's background once he got his hands on the wallet, assuming there was a wallet.

He approached the body, as much as he didn't want to see the sad, grisly sight.

"I have my doubts as to this being a suicide," Rodriguez said to Detective Bush, his partner of five years, who had just arrived on the scene.

"Look around this place. Evidently he rented this room all the time for his escapades. There's a lot to like about being alive if you're this guy. Something doesn't smell right here."

"Got the feeling this is going to be intense. But I guess that's why we get paid the big bucks," Bush offered, tongue in cheek.

"Big bucks... The corpse here made the big bucks. Look where it got him—drowning in a pool of his own blood, with a mutilated head. Wait here for Forensics. I'm going downstairs to talk to the prostitute."

Chapter 4
So much pain, so little time

Tuesday, August 21, 2007
9:55 A.M.

Broadway Life headquarters
New York City

Mal had been hunkering down over the past week preparing the Zeus presentation to Broadway Life's Investment Committee. Hunkering down was a relative term, having to put in only 10- to 12-hour days in his new role as compared to the customary 12- to 16-hour days when he was on the sell side. He knew from the handful of prior deals he had recently presented just how rigorous the committee was prior to approving any deal. This rigor was particularly the case when dealing with a new asset class such as CDOs, in which the firm had limited experience and a healthy fear of the unknown.

The Investment Committee was no-nonsense in nature, with the senior-most people, including the CEO, CFO, and representatives from Risk Management, Underwriting, Legal, Accounting, and other key disciplines across the firm typically in attendance. The objective of the committee was to ensure that the firm engaged in quality transactions, often with many of its members playing devil's advocate by identifying reasons why not to do the deal. It was the business equivalent of defending one's dissertation. Some of the more aggressive members of the committee, skeptical about Mal's mandate in the first place, made every effort to embarrass him in front of everyone else in the corporate theatre of the boardroom.

Mal had been brought into Broadway Life as a strategic hire, in an initiative mandated by the CEO. Like so many major financial institutions—insurance companies, commercial and investment banks, hedge funds, asset managers, private foundations, and endowments alike—credit derivatives and CDOs were relatively new products whose market visibility had become difficult to ignore. In some respects, any and all financial institutions needed to be in the new product space to be taken seriously as a player in global finance. For Broadway Life, it was an opportunity to diversify its investment portfolio while targeting higher yields than were otherwise available in its ultra-conservative investment portfolio. As a former sell-side banker, Mal was given the mandate to build this new segment of the investment portfolio within its conservatively proscribed parameters.

Mal had done his time on the sell side in a number of capacities over the course of his 20-year banking career. With each passing year on the sell side feeling progressively less rewarding to him, the new position represented a fresh start as a blissful bank escapee to the buy side. Gone was much of the volatile sell-side banker lifestyle, in exchange for a more stable, albeit considerably lower compensation structure. The buy-side position represented the opportunity to achieve a more balanced lifestyle or, as he described it, the opportunity to reclaim his humanity. Don't do anything

A Wall Street Murder and Morality Tale

crazy, he reassured himself when accepting the new position; this could be the perfect retirement trade by which to conclude his career. It would also enable him to further solidify his financial future. It all made for a good three- to seven-year plan.

Zeus was the first deal on the Investment Committee's docket for the day. Mal entered the boardroom armed with volumes of quantitative and qualitative analyses prepared by his staff. He scanned his audience, mostly male except for the 50-year-old head of Legal, while seating himself at the opposite end of the boardroom table to the CEO. As with all presenters he sat in hopeful anticipation that he had cogent answers for any and all questions that might arise.

After receiving a nod from the CEO, Mal began.

"Good morning, Zeus is an ABS CDO deal brought to us by Smyth Johnston. As you can see from the previously distributed deal materials, my team has analyzed this transaction across countless scenarios— good and bad—and is asking for approval to proceed with $150 million participation on the most risk-remote tranche, rated triple-A by both Moody's and S&P."

He only wanted to do $100 million of the deal but thought he should ask for a larger approval if Chip needed to upsize him a little bit. He could use that to make a deposit into the favor bank—always good— while not needing to go back to the Investment Committee. The larger approval might also serve to thwart the outcome where he only received approval for a partial amount. Standard operating procedure.

Mal continued taking his audience methodically through the 80-page presentation materials. He had discussed the deal with each of the voting members of the committee in the prior two days. Pre-selling the deal was tactically the safest way to increase the odds that it would pass muster with the committee. Mal expected no surprises, though ultimately there was no way of knowing until the actual meeting.

"What do our proprietary models have to say in the worst-case loss scenario? What stresses did the agencies put on their analysis?" began the onslaught of detailed questions from Risk Management, who viewed themselves as the gatekeeper of the firm's self-preservation.

Mal was doing well in answering each of the questions, deferring on an as-needed basis to his quantitative team for the heavy-lifting.

"Could you please elaborate on Zeus' relative value," asked the CFO.

"Zeus offers 50 basis points over bank loan CDOs and 80 over triple-A rated corporates. We are definitely recommending the product based on its yield as well as its low correlation to other triple-A assets in our investment portfolio."

Some in the audience appeared pleased with what they were hearing, while others played it much closer to the vest as they awaited the CEO's reaction. There were always the skeptics, those who feared the unknown and all the sexy talk of cutting-edge new products that had been financially engineered by the Wall Street whiz kid crowd.

Mal continued.

"Our analysis shows that the default probability is .0001. So, to put that in perspective, if we did 10,000 of these deals, we'll lose money only once. Even if we've missed the analysis by a factor of 10 our odds are still 1 in 1,000."

"What about the rating agencies?"

"We've spent a lot of time with them as has the sponsoring bank, Smyth Johnston. Both of their analyses are broadly consistent with ours, with some slight methodological differences. I'm not sure how all three of us could get this wrong, not to mention the other investors who'll participate in the deal alongside us. Both S&P and Moody's have blessed it with the triple-As. We heard nothing alarming in our discussions with them."

After listening to the back-and-forth, the CEO finally weighed in.

"Apart from the numbers you've presented in support of the deal, how have you gotten comfortable with Smyth Johnston's motivation for doing the deal? As you know, we're never quite convinced that they always have our best interests in mind when they show up with an opportunity. We don't want to be naïve capital."

"Well, that's a fair question. As part of my mandate here, I have no intention of doing deals with everyone on the Street. Instead I plan to work only with a handful of banks that I know best and where I have the best relationships with my coverage. Having come from that side, I know how they work and Smyth Johnston fits that description well. That's the deal around the deal, if you will."

"Okay, but why are they doing the deal? Did you get any insight into that? In my book, that's the real deal around the deal, to use your words."

"Beyond the usual investment bank deal motivation of making money, they were selling the use of a third-party manager as a new deal type. Maybe they get some kudos in the market for that—you know, league table bragging rights. I did not get any specific red flags on the deal. It seems to stand out on its own merits."

The CEO looked around to judge the body language of his committee colleagues.

"We hired you for a reason. And we're not looking to do too many of these deals in the first place. ABS CDOs are not a core business of ours, as you can appreciate. By the way, how have the other deals you put us into performed thus far?"

"We've done three deals previously, all in manageable size and triple-A like Zeus. They're all new—it's too early to say how they're performing with any degree of certainty. I can tell you, however, based on the various performance reports from the bankers as well as the rating agency updates, so far so good from where we sit in the most risk-remote piece of the deal. Of course, there have been some mark-to-market issues, but those seem to be broader issues and not deal specific."

After an hour of defending his dissertation on Zeus, the deal was put to a vote, where it received unanimous support—a prerequisite at Broadway Life for approval on new types of deals—for $125 million. The committee was pleased with the expected return and the small probability of loss the analytics showed. In addition, it had the support of countless other capital market investors similar to themselves and the blessing from multiple rating agencies.

Mal was pleased with the favorable outcome as well as his team's hard work leading up to the presentation. He also had $25 million of additional approval if Chip needed to upsize his order. As with all deals, he reminded himself that he couldn't possibly know every risk associated with the deal. That said, the committee hadn't found anything bad that he might've missed in his presentation. He was sitting on the most risk-remote piece of the deal.

$ $ $

Chip pulled open the kelly green door of the Blarney Stone. Minutes earlier he had been sitting at his desk combing through his countless emails when his cell phone rang. He recognized the number: it was Jack Bonfiglio of the SEC. Chip, as a matter of precaution, or creeping paranoia, hadn't saved Bonfiglio's number into his contact list. There was no chance of his taking that call in the middle of the trading floor, reactively hitting the Answer button saying, "Call you right back."

Such precaution was commonplace on the floor, as extended cellphone calls were generally frowned upon and thought to be with a spouse or headhunter. The latter possibility always elicited some curiosity from those within earshot. To avoid that, Chip headed toward the elevator bank and the street. He recognized a number of other Smyth Johnston bankers milling around the lobby on their cell phones. He doubted any of them were talking to the SEC as he was.

Bonfiglio had wanted to meet with him again, preferably that evening. Chip agreed, despite suspecting he was in violation of company policy. He knew any communications with the media, much less a government agency, needed to be cleared internally as a matter of protocol. A stealth meeting such as this wasn't even in the gray area. He decided to have the meeting nonetheless, hoping to keep it quiet and to avoid the potential consequences, namely being fired.

The two had agreed to meet at the Blarney Stone again. It was as good a place as any to meet, with Bonfiglio tacitly recognizing it being off the radar with the banker types.

Chip ordered a Budweiser before spotting Bonfiglio in the back of the bar.

"Hello Chip, thanks for getting together again. I guess you're probably wondering what I'm up to, why I want to speak with you again," Bonfiglio said, immediately cutting to the chase. He had found that most prospective informants were suspicious and, for that reason, found it helpful to get to business right away.

"You could say I'm curious."

"I understand. Let me state the obvious: our discussions are confidential. I'm in the early stages of conducting an exploratory investigation of credit derivative markets. The SEC is aware of the enormous size of this business, the emergence of the shadow banking system, and the largely unregulated nature of over-the-counter products. We're trying to get our arms around any potential impact or risk to the broader financial system as a whole. All we're doing is gathering information at this point."

"Okay, but why me?"

"Neither you nor your firm are part of any investigation. In fact 'investigation' is a misnomer; the internal term at this point is what we call a 'matter under inquiry.' This is better viewed as us needing to better understand this hyper-growth marketplace. And I recognize you don't have to speak with me at all, so I appreciate your willingness to be here. You can be as vague as you wish and answer whatever questions you are comfortable with."

It all seemed awkward to Chip. But he controlled the flow of information and felt it was fairly innocuous despite this mild uneasiness. In the back of his mind, he thought, rightly or wrongly, that it might be an opportunity to call out some of the behavior he had begun to find objectionable. Doing so on the condition of relative anonymity made it that much more appealing to him. Or ultimately, who knew, he had fortuitously found a path to a job if and when he finally left banking.

"You didn't tell me why you got in touch with me."

"Complete coincidence. I had never even been in this place before. I was done with work and on the spur of the moment decided to have a beer and watch the end of the Mets game before heading home. Apologies for the eavesdropping, but when I heard you talking to some of your buddies, I thought, why not approach you."

"A fellow Mets fan? How bad can you be?"

"Mets and Jets. You might call me a glutton for pain."

"Mets, Jets, and trying to get up the curve on credit derivatives. You are a glutton for pain."

Bonfiglio, nursing the Budweiser Chip had brought him, jumped into the business at hand.

"What do you make of this so-called shadow banking system? There's a lot of discussion internally about it lately. What do you, as an insider, think is going on?"

"Here's my take. The shadow banking system is a bunch of unconventional financing transactions that obviate the traditional bank financing route. Basically it is investment banks orchestrating deals involving entities including hedge funds, insurance companies, and other highly-sophisticated capital market players. In the past, a commercial or local community bank makes a loan and then waits to get paid back. That's all fine, until those banks are no longer willing or able to make the loans desired by a given borrower. In these instances, your friendly investment bank structures a so-called bespoke transaction to provide the desired financing by tapping into the capital markets as the ultimate lender. It really doesn't matter what kind of a loan it is, as evidenced by the fact that it's happening in corporate loans, credit cards, car financing, mortgages, you name it. Even more basically stated, the investment banks are manufacturing financing in big size to keep the wheels of commerce turning."

"And all these transactions use derivatives?"

"Some do, some don't. It depends on the transaction form preferred by the players in a given deal. And in some cases, the bank may choose to get involved and take on some of the risk itself or hedge the risk in some portion by using credit derivatives. But the idea in general is for deals like this to create more efficient financing than in the past with greater dispersion of risk—a fundamental tenet of risk transfer—into a bigger and deeper pool of capital than the commercial banks."

"If that's the simple explanation, I'd hate to see the complicated one."

"These can get very complicated, cutting across different risk-takers, different accounting and tax regimes, and the like. As a baseline, just view the shadow banks as a means of marrying investors and borrowers in customized transaction that often use off-balance sheet mechanisms for better accounting and regulatory freedom. Being blunt, shadow banking is nothing short of ingenious."

"I can see that. How big has the shadow banking system become?"

"No one knows."

"No one knows?"

"No one knows because of their private, often off-balance sheet nature. But it's really fucking big. My guess would be in the trillions in the U.S. alone. Who knows how big it really is globally."

"Trillions and growing?"

"Yep. It's definitely growing. Why? Because it provides additional liquidity, credit, and risk transfer into the global financial system where the commercial banking system falls short. Just think about the size of the entire U.S. housing market: most of that is financed through the shadow banking system given its dominant role in securitization, repackaging, and distribution of mortgage-backed risk. And that's just one asset class."

"Is that good or bad? Does this add risk into the global markets or reduce it? Obviously that's what the SEC wants to better understand."

"Both probably."

"Very interesting information. I'm sure you want to get going soon. Are you willing to stay in touch? This has been very helpful."

"Let me think about it some more. I don't want to get too far down this road and run the risk of my bank finding out."

"We can set up ways to protect you—I can take you through that the next time we meet."

Bonfiglio stayed behind at the Blarney Stone after Chip departed. He was pleased with the discussion, having lobbed in a few easy, generic questions and gotten Chip to talk. He hadn't found out anything new, but that wasn't the purpose of the meeting. The idea had been to test the waters with a potential informant. It didn't matter what Chip said at this point in their dialogue, only that he was willing to talk. This was a great first step.

Soon he would find out more on Feinberg's activities from Chip. There was no way he was going anywhere near his compliance people. Chip could be very valuable to him.

$ $ $

Bure was holding court at the W Hotel bar on Lexington Avenue, a banker hotspot within easy walking distance of Smyth Johnston's office. The midtown Manhattan establishment, knowing full well its clientele was paying the bills courtesy of bull market expense accounts, had no qualms about charging $10 or more for a bottle of beer. The economic absurdity of it all fed on itself, with certain bankers tending, paradoxically, to prefer those places that sought to overcharge them the most.

It was as if the higher the price, the greater the statement a banker was making about his own career success. Restaurateurs, bar operators, and hoteliers throughout the city were more than happy to oblige. In the extreme, one bar operator thought nothing of charging $18 for a Budweiser. Never mind that a case of Budweiser could be purchased at your neighborhood Walmart for less than that one single bottle—different markets, one might conclude.

The session Bure was hosting was Michael Feinberg's monthly thank-you to those at the firm's support functions, who were in some way important to the smooth operation and success of his business. The attendees included junior traders and structurers from his fiefdom and crucial support staff from Risk Management, Legal, Accounting, Tax, and Treasury. All were essential parts of the firm whose cooperation Feinberg needed in order for his money-making machine to keep printing in copious amounts.

However obvious his intentions, it was a gesture those in attendance appreciated at some level. Feinberg was wisely keeping the troops happy. Ironically he would never attend the sessions himself, preferring instead to delegate the task to Bure while he spent his time either thinking about new trade ideas or self-promoting his successes to the powers that be. Whether it was a personality quirk or otherwise, Feinberg was somewhat socially awkward and thought it best to keep a healthy distance between those who would typically attend these sessions and himself. More downside than upside for him, so his trader instincts told him.

As Feinberg's right-hand man, Bure wore many hats. Drawing on his JD/MBA from the University of Chicago, he was in part attorney, strategist, negotiator, and business manager for the desk. One of the many talents appreciated most by Feinberg was Bure's near encyclopedic mastery of the International Swap Dealers Association (ISDA) documents that governed most over-the-counter derivative transactions. Such mastery allowed him to pursue an airtight standard on deal documents with clients. Airtight meant that the deal had safeguard upon safeguard—belt and suspenders—built into the deal documents to cover the firm against any adverse developments, however farfetched, in the underlying trade. Even the highest priced securities lawyers who were paid $500-1,000 per hour couldn't conceive of some of the farfetched scenarios Bure would contemplate.

Bure's documentation mastery often resulted in his ability to embed free options into the docs, most of the time without the clients either noticing or caring. Free options were windfalls that occurred when or if something unexpectedly adverse happened in a trade causing a trigger that would change the terms of trade, conveying economic value to Feinberg's desk.

His gain, the client's loss.

Bure never referred to clients as such, choosing instead to refer to them as the "other side" of the trade; they were nothing more than faceless counterparties to him. It was better for him that way—it allowed him to maintain an impersonal approach as he sought to extract maximum profit on any given trade. Let Sales do the warm and fuzzy relationship handling. They got paid a lot of money, too much in his opinion, to keep the clients happy.

He was a clear practitioner of Feinberg's zero-sum mentality, and those with whom he dealt had better do their homework if Bure was involved in the deal documents. There was a reason, as counterparty upon counterparty would attest, why he became known unaffectionately as Dr. Doom.

Feinberg viewed this well-deserved reputation in the highest regard, as it likely resulted in higher profits for his book. It was always more about maximizing the current trade's profit rather than worrying about a series of transactions that would otherwise define a long-term relationship with a client. He wanted to win, and win at almost any cost, on any given trade. That was the prevailing mentality for Feinberg's desk—it was how he kept score in his one-dimensional, money-centric framework.

Feinberg's event had grown to a dozen or so by 6:30. And why not attend? It was free as long as you did what Feinberg needed and "played nice in his sandbox." Both appetizers and cocktails were being provided in abundance, and, who knew, perhaps an opportunity for one of the back office staffers to be discovered and join the Feinberg Empire in the vastly higher compensated front office.

Ben Cook was a recent example of that opportunity, having left the legal department to join the desk as a junior attorney. His transition had been anything but smooth.

"The Sales guys are getting seriously pissed off at the number of credit events we're delivering to their clients," he said to Bure. "The economy is booming, corporate defaults are at historic lows and we're delivering credit events on the few high yield firms that have blown up. No wonder they're pissed off. We've managed to find the only firms that have defaulted."

A credit event, simply put, occurred when a company defaulted on its obligations, and the client, as risk taker, had to pay under the credit derivative contract. It's conceptually similar to an insurer paying a claim.

"Too bad. They get paid a lot to show these deals to their clients. And their clients are big boys who are capable of performing proper due diligence on the deals," replied Bure in his typical dispassionate fashion.

Money had no personality to him.

"When I walk back to the Sales desk, they know it's a problem and that some bad news is about to unfold. Sasquatch is still complaining about the ink not even being dry on the Hercules deal, when we triggered the first credit event notice."

"Ben, welcome to the front office. You need to be able to take the heat. If not, you don't belong here. Go back to Legal."

"Can I ask you about something else I'm not sure I understand yet?"

"What now?"

"What do you think about mark-to-market accounting? We hear FASB is considering changing some of the rules. What do you think we should do about valuing Eros, Hercules, and even Zeus? I see some of the P&L reports, and we are minting money. That's good, but should we be front-loading so much of the profit?"

Bure paused to consider his response to what was a complicated topic. There was no right or wrong answer. It was also a politically hot topic internally, with the bosses from Accounting always wanting to be more conservative than the trading desk in terms of P&L recognition. One of his many jobs was to deal with the accountants to make sure that Feinberg got to book whatever profits were available in as flexible a regime as was permissible within Generally Accepted Accounting Principles.

"Generally speaking, I believe we should be accounting for all of our assets and liabilities at fair value—the current market price. The progress over the past 15 years away from measuring everything at original cost has been a positive one. It produces more current, and thus more accurate information about companies and their true economic value. That's all good. As an example, think about buying a new house that you pay a hundred grand for. And then the price of it goes up to two hundred grand. Don't you think you own a house worth two hundred grand, not a hundred grand?"

A number of people from various groups had heard the question and had paused their conversations to listen in.

"Okay, fair enough for the stock market or other liquid markets where everyone can see the prices, but what if there's no observable market in your example? What do you do then?"

"We resort to the next best thing, which in this case are models and hypothetical data. I have eight PhDs in my group, including two guys who have actually worked at NASA, so I have a lot of confidence in our ability to calculate accurate values."

"But don't you have a lot of wiggle room in your assumptions? Doesn't it create a wide range of possible outcomes under this mark-to-model accounting?"

Addressing the attentive crowd, Bure responded, "It's not as wide a range as you may think. If our model assumptions vary too much from what others in the business are doing, internal and external accountants will see that as a red flag. We should all be thankful for mark-to-market accounting. Without it, where do you think the money would come from to pay your salaries or big year-end bonuses? You have to be able to show some current P&L in a trading book. In any case, this is not an Enron situation in terms of the accounting practices for us or anyone else using these products. I'm saying we may use our own assumptions with the numbers, but then again, so can everyone else. It's no different from commercial banks with their credit charges or insurance companies with their loss reserves. Be that as it may, the accounting folks are the ones who set the rules, we're just playing the game by their rules."

"So what happens if our models are wrong?"

"In practice, we use a model akin to the famous Black-Scholes model for stock options. What happens if the model is wrong? Slavish reliance on model output can lead to trouble as it can never predict all outcomes in market reality. A model can only capture foreseeable events; however, try as they may, it can never capture the unforeseeable or statistical outlier events. The inability to capture these Black Swan events is what wreaks havoc on markets. Long Term Capital Management (LTCM) serves as a healthy reminder of that slavish reliance and the trouble that can arise when reality fails to conform to the model."

LTCM was one of the largest and most successful hedge funds in the world. Relying heavily upon quantitative methods, it employed a number of Nobel Prize winners in economics and a host of hardcore quants who monitored the fund's every position. It blew up spectacularly in 1998 when reality failed to conform to the intellectual firepower of their models, requiring a Federal Reserve intermediated bailout. The bailout was born out of fear that the potential losses to the banks, all of whom had significant exposure to the fund, could collapse the economy. Systemic risk, too big to fail—a huge lesson was learned—and such a scenario was vowed to be avoided in the future or, at least, until the next time it happened.

"So basically, if the models get it seriously wrong, it's Armageddon Day. There are trillions of dollars of trades out there based on models. Our models are rigorously tested all the time against worst-case stress scenarios so we shouldn't have anything to worry about."

"Armageddon Day sounds ugly."

"Yes, theoretically it would be. The system has enough checks and balances to prevent it. What I mean is that on any given deal you have multiple parties that weigh in on its soundness. The buyer and seller of risk, numerous quants on both sides, risk management, internal and external counsel, rating agencies, bank regulators, the CFTC, the SEC in some cases, and the fed are all looking at this stuff. Let's hope that if they all manage to get it so horribly wrong, we'll at least pocket a few more big bonuses," Bure concluded with a laugh. "This is boring, so who needs a beer?"

Bure was deliberately redirecting the conversation. He knew the discussion was far from boring, and, in fact, it spoke to the essence of an inherent frailty in the otherwise wildly popular and positive story surrounding credit derivative products. What if, he often thought to himself, the models used for accounting as well as other purposes were challenged by a major market disruption event?

The fact pattern leading up to the Long Term Capital meltdown, Bure continued thinking to himself, had frightening similarities to what had been transpiring of late in credit derivatives. There were the aforementioned models built by legions of PhD quants. As good as the models were, he knew—as proved to be the case with Long Term Capital—that they could never capture all possible outcomes in reality. There could always be a statistical outlier, the so-called Black Swan or other unknown event. He also knew that the largest financial institutions globally were inextricably in bed together as incestuous trading partners. And what would happen, as it did with Long Term Capital, if market liquidity dried up? How would the market function in an orderly fashion if and when its participants sought to exit their positions at a time of intense stress?

Despite these parallels, Bure nonetheless felt that things were somehow different with the new world of credit derivatives. Long Term Capital happened nearly 10 years ago. A reassuring air of invincibility surrounding credit derivatives was strong among its global participants.

There was one notable difference, however, that alarmed Bure. If Long Term Capital defined the notion of *systemic risk*, credit derivatives had the potential of redefining that notion on a scale exponentially greater and more dangerous. It could spell Armageddon Day. Had it become a high-stakes, industrial form of game theory, with all market participants closely scrutinizing, in defensive fashion, one another's moves in the market? Who really knew—it was guesswork.

Bure, like most of his peers in the business, was left to merely hope that if his world were challenged by a market disruption event, it wouldn't be on his watch. Maybe he could actually collect those few more bonuses before it was over. Even if his world did blow up he had already made a fortune using OPM—other people's money. Taking some comfort in an otherwise scary thought, he realized that the Armageddon scenario might, perversely enough, lead to countless opportunities to reinvent himself at a hedge fund, another bank, workout firm, or otherwise. Heads he wins, tails he wins.

There was no sense in fearing Armageddon. He would be fine. Might as well, he concluded, keep the money machine printing at high speed.

$ $ $

Sasquatch and Chip returned to their three-by-three-foot offices from lunch. Tracy had just gotten off a call with Mal, who had confirmed his order on Zeus. The order was hugely valuable as it created momentum for the book and gave others in Sales leverage in their follow-up discussions with clients. It was the age-old scarcity demand tactic, in practice no different than a telemarketer using the "if you act now" ruse.

So important was the order that Feinberg visited Joey Karros, Chip, and Sasquatch to thank them for their effort, something that rarely happened, unless he was seriously concerned about the trade. No one—except for Feinberg, Bure, and a few select risk management people—was privy to the overall risk of Feinberg's book. In a world where actions speak louder than words, the order must have meant Feinberg had either reduced the risk in his book or just booked an enormous amount of P&L.

Chip wasn't sure which outcome had just happened. He was experiencing mixed emotions. Selfishly he was happy that securing an important order on Zeus would bode well for his bonus. He was equally concerned for his client if the trade went awry. He always had that uneasy feeling whenever he did a deal with Feinberg, as if a voice in his head was saying "Congratulations, you've just been fucked."

Seeing Feinberg approach, Karros hung up the phone almost mid-sentence and slithered over to him, never missing an effort to share in the glory.

"I told you Michael, my team gets it done. Who loves ya?"

"Joey, we're going to have a Sales and Trading celebration after Zeus gets inked. You get to pick the spot, but realize my guys suck at golf."

"Pebble Beach here we come," joked Karros.

"You're done on that," Feinberg responded, even cracking a smile.

Now warning bells were really going on in Chip's head. Feinberg was taking them to Pebble Beach. What had they just done?

"We have room for two more Sales guys besides me and Chip. We'll have four from Sales, four from Trading—two foursomes."

Karros, of course, included himself in the plan, quickly dropping Tracy who evidently was too junior to go on such a trip. It wasn't pretty being the bitch. The day couldn't come soon enough for her to have her own bitch to pull rank on.

An avid golfer, Sasquatch liked the sound of Pebble Beach. And why wouldn't he? It was an opportunity to see and play one of the world's greatest golf courses, for "free" in a manner of speaking.

"Okay, Sasquatch, I can see you want to play Pebble. I have a good feeling about getting another order. Work the phones this afternoon, show up with something, and you can go. Besides Pebble, we'll look like heroes by driving this deal across the goal line."

Karros dangled the carrot in front of Sasquatch.

$ $ $

After several hours of checking in with the clients to whom Zeus had been shown, another order came in.

Sasquatch, seizing the moment, yelled out across the desk "Order on Zeus."

Karros jumped up. "How much?"

"Twenty on the triple-As."

No sooner said than done, that Karros, Sasquatch, and Chip trotted over to Feinberg's Trading desk.

"Michael, we have good news and bad news for you. Which would you like first," asked Karros with a flair for the dramatic.

"Give me the good news first. Good news translates into money being made for the desk."

"We have another order on Zeus that ought to get you where you need to be. Basically, the boys have another order for $20 million of the triple-As. Two big orders in one day."

"That is good news."

Feinberg realized this would enable him to call Duncan Kerr with the good news. More specifically he could allay Kerr's fears that the market was going away. There still was a liquidity point for deals to clear. The sky was not falling. Arguably more significant than the deal getting done was Feinberg's ability to make the call to Kerr. He knew better than most that there was always the deal itself and then the deal around the deal—in this case pleasing his master, Duncan Kerr.

"So what was the bad news?"

"The bad news is that we are not going to let you off the hook on Pebble. No bait and switch this time. In fact we've already made our travel plans. All we need is your cost center," Karros smiled, sensing he had Feinberg in a cage.

"No problem. No bait and switch, though of course we'll have to go this weekend. There is no way I can be off the desk during the week. I assume you're aware of that."

Feinberg had once again gotten the better of the exchange with Sales.

$ $ $

Instead of staying in the city celebrating the deal news, Sasquatch decided to head home. He arrived in his typical state: tired, irritable, and hungry. After power-eating his dinner, he decided it was time to tell Kelly about his upcoming trip to Pebble Beach. He knew any and all pleasure to be derived from his trip to Pebble Beach was soon to be transformed to pain. It was not going to be a pleasant conversation.

"I have to go on a business trip, this weekend in all likelihood."

"Are you kidding me? We have dinner plans on Saturday night."

"Not anymore. I can't do anything about it. We have to go as part of getting a big deal done today. It's part of the game I have to play to get paid. No money equals no eat. Sorry."

"So I get to stay here once again solo with a one-year-old and a three-year-old all weekend."

"Yep. Still like this lifestyle? Let me know if you have any other ideas, like the trailer park. I just might hit the ground with a heart attack. Of course you'd probably like that... collect the life insurance and live happily ever after. The kids might miss me for a while, but I'm sure they'd get over it soon."

"Oh, c'mon Nigel. That's not fair. And where are you going? I can only imagine."

"Pebble Beach."

"You asshole! You call that work? Without spouses?"

"Yes, it is work, and yes, it is without spouses. Someone has to pay for this kind of stuff. You can't have spouses jump in on every trip."

"Great. So I will let the Reynolds know we won't be able to make their dinner party. Not that they'll be surprised—all the ladies in the neighborhood think we're antisocial anyway," she said, storming off upstairs to the bedroom where she slammed the door.

"Who the hell are the Reynolds? And feel free to tell them your husband is antisocial—that is, after being out until midnight for three of the previous five nights. Newsflash: I don't want to go out on Friday or Saturday nights. Seems to me like we've had this discussion before."

It would be hard to determine what gave him less pleasure—his work life or home life. If he could somehow compartmentalize the two aspects of his life, it would be much more tolerable. But he hadn't been able to do so yet, something that likely explained how he was on his third marriage. The third time was supposed to be the charm. There was very little charming about any of this.

So much pain, so little time.

Chapter 5
The scum rises to the top

Friday, August 24, 2007
1:55 P.M.

Smyth Johnston Trading Floor

Karros, Sasquatch, and Chip were standing around the trading floor, excited about their imminent trip this weekend, as in today, to Pebble Beach. Their plan was to pick up Mal at his office—he was the client chosen to attend, which would legitimize the business expense—and take a limo out to Teterboro Airport. They would meet Feinberg and crew there and board a private plane to fly directly into the Monterey airport.

Karros's phone rang. It was Feinberg.

"Joey, hey sorry about this, but I have some shit I have to deal with that's going to take me a few hours before I can leave. It might not be until very late."

"Okay, so should we just wait for you?"

"No, I don't want you guys to run the risk of not getting there tonight and missing your round tomorrow. Just have your secretary book some flights tonight. I'll have to meet you out there tomorrow."

"It is what it is, I suppose. Let me know what your plans turn out to be. I assume your trading brethren will wait for you, right?" Karros asked, masking his disappointment at the sudden reversal of fortune.

"Right. We can get some work done en route. I'll let you know once we're able to get out of here. See you out there."

Karros put the phone down and proceeded to tell Sasquatch and Chip about the change in plan, and then told his secretary to book the last-minute flights to San Francisco. Instead of flying directly into Monterey where they would land a mere 15 minutes from the Inn at Pebble Beach, they were now facing a two-and-a-half-hour drive south of San Francisco—a gorgeous drive, granted, but nowhere near the same as flying private into Monterey.

"I can see this is already getting off to a great start," Chip observed, ever suspicious of Feinberg.

People always had silent agendas they were harboring, something that had to be watched closely before taking action. Had Feinberg done this on purpose? Would he even show up at all? Chip had become conditioned to seeing the world through the lens of a game theorist.

"Going to be a long night by the time we get to the hotel. Well, just think of the destination. That will make it all worthwhile. I'm not going to complain about any of this," Karros replied.

$ $ $

Arriving safely in San Francisco, Sasquatch, Chip, Mal, and Karros claimed their luggage, golf clubs included, and met up with the prearranged car service that would take them south to Monterey. It was about an hour away from sunset, with temperatures in the low 70s with no humidity—yet another perfect day in California.

Rather than admiring the California coastline, they did what all bankers do, namely obsess on their Blackberries. Each of their inboxes had become littered since boarding the plane in New York. Rarely, if ever, would a day pass that a banker didn't feel overwhelmed with the sheer volume of emails to be managed, despite a vast majority of these emails always proving to be of little or no value whatsoever. Valuable or not, email had to be checked incessantly. Hence the notion of the Crackberry: useful technology that had the unrelenting propensity to run amok, much like teenagers and texting.

Mal was sitting in the front seat, next to the driver, on the phone. The three bankers were crammed into the back seat, with Sasquatch sitting in the middle.

Karros's phone rang, and Chip took the opportunity to whisper to Sasquatch, "I bet we come out of pocket for this trip. Brace yourself for about a five grand expense."

"Are you fucking kidding me, man? I can't wait to explain that to my wife. A business trip to play golf with work colleagues, on the weekend, paid by me. I guess she won't be getting her new window treatments. Oh well, tough shit."

"Even when you think you win in this business, you somehow lose. Bloody hell, he's got it," Chip replied in his mock British accent.

"It can't be that we get to pay for doing our jobs well. I've heard of bankers coming out of pocket for deal toys before, but this would be a first," Sasquatch said, clearly not amused at the prospect of coughing up an unexpected five thousand dollars. It was cash he really didn't have, given that his assets were mostly illiquid and his real estate business was now bleeding money. Bonus day, his next cash infusion, was still six months away.

Karros continued his conversation.

"Michael, okay, that's fine, I'll make sure the team makes the calls first thing on Monday. By the way, we just landed and are in the car heading to the hotel. What's up on your end?"

"Things are looking good here. We ought to get there tomorrow, maybe even in time to join you guys for golf as long as it's in the afternoon."

"Sounds good. Let me know if anything changes. I'll push back the tee time to 1 p.m., that way we'll be able to have plenty of time between golf and dinner."

"See you tomorrow."

Despite Feinberg now joining them and the fact this was a Sales-Trading deal celebration trip with a client, Chip had planted the seeds of doubt in Sasquatch's mind.

"So, am I correct in assuming this is a business trip—a deal toy—that Feinberg is covering out of his budget?" Sasquatch asked Karros, now fearing the worst.

"As far as I know, yes it is."

Chip chimed in, "I'll take the other side of that…bet you we somehow get screwed. It's Feinberg after all. He's the master of this type of bullshit. Always has a bait-and-switch up his sleeve, a hidden agenda; and worse yet, he doesn't find anything wrong with it. In his mind, it's okay to lie, cheat, and steal, not in the literal sense per se, but in the sense that the end always justifies the means. In a perverse sort of way, I almost respect the guy for his ability to get what he wants, ignoring, of course, the fact that he screws so many along the way, including us—again."

Chip and Sasquatch couldn't help but often engage in moralistic diatribe of this type, even when in the presence of a client like Mal, who, as a former sell-side banker himself, understood the sales-trading dynamic as well as they. They never ceased to be amazed at some of the behavior they witnessed and were no less amazed at how the same perpetrators of this behavior, who represented but a very small sample of the Wall Street populace, were the ones, like Feinberg, who had amassed the most money, power, and control as of late. It all seemed so counterintuitive to them, so toxic, that a business culture could be tainted by so few.

"You guys ever wonder how things could get so fucked up in this business? What is it that causes this to happen? How are they able to get away with it?"

Sasquatch knew Chip would take the bait.

"That's simple: the scum rises to the top," Chip responded with no hesitation, "then rewrites the rules to allow their agendas to thrive. We all have a choice to make about crossing that squiggly line that separates appropriate from inappropriate behavior. For those who don't cross the line, as you rightly point out a large majority, you do the best you can within the convoluted system and have faith that the scumbags' time on top will be met by a day of comeuppance in some way, shape, or form.

"But, it doesn't explain how they get away with acting like scumbags. Someone has to have oversight for them. I mean, if a complete asshole is in it only for himself, doesn't care about the firm, and does things that jeopardize the reputation of the firm, someone has to care. Joey, you're senior enough to shed some light on this, please tell me someone cares."

Karros took the high road, declining to join in on the rant, "We have compliance, risk management, and other checks and balances within the system to safeguard against this stuff...you have to rely on the system to do its job."

"I disagree. When the results keep coming in as positive as they do, those responsible for safeguarding against the questionable behavior get silenced. No one wants to hear that someone puked in the punch bowl. And management turns a blind eye to behavioral issues unless they're potentially damaging legally. Excepting the Enron-type behavior—that's not what I'm talking about here...it's more a case of management worshipping at the altar of profitability and wanting to believe in the sanctity of the results rather than really caring or wanting to know how they were achieved... 'don't ask, don't tell.' When you think about it, it becomes management by absenteeism, without adequate accountability."

"I guess the hope is that things have a way of policing themselves in the final result," Sasquatch added, hoping to bring closure to their backseat philosophy.

"Enough of this conversation. We're in California heading to one of the nicest places on Earth. We can resume this conversation once we're back in New York. Time for some happy pills. I'll buy the beers once we get there. In fact, let's pull over on the next exit and get this party started," Chip replied.

"Good idea'" chimed in Karros. "You guys spend too much time thinking about all the bullshit in this business. Just roll with it, be a chameleon, adapt. It's just a game you need to play. If nothing else, it'll keep you sane."

"It's the weekend and we're about to be in Pebble Beach. Things could be a lot worse," Mal said from the front, as they pulled into a convenience store about 60 miles from their destination.

Just enough time to consume the 12-pack of Budweiser Sasquatch was about to fetch.

$ $ $

"So when can we expect to see Feinberg and his boys? It looks like a nice day out there," Chip said over his first cup of coffee. He, Mal, and Sasquatch had stayed out later than planned and were nursing the all-too-familiar combination of hangover and sleep deprivation. This was something most on Wall Street learned to live with, an almost inevitable byproduct of the business.

"He'll land at 11 or so. I got a text from him as he was boarding the plane this morning," Karros assured his guys.

"So if he lands at 11, he won't be here until 2-2:30. I hope we can get our round in before it gets dark. Would hate to come all the way out here and not finish— imagine being out here and not playing number 18. It's one of the most famous holes in golf."

"No, he said he can get to the hotel by 11:30. He's flying directly into Monterey. Yes, the same plane we all could have been on had we left together yesterday."

"He screws up the plan and keeps the private jet for himself. Oh well, at least we're out here. It's hard to complain about that. Besides, you wouldn't really expect a credit derivative trader to be thinking about anyone other than himself, now would you?"

"Dude, you should know by now, it's just the nature of the beast. And, I hasten to add, it's his money footing the bill for NetJets. That's the way Feinberg rolls. Deal with it. He makes a lot more cash than you and can afford to do this. It's a rounding error for him. Maybe if you weren't on wife number three you could roll like this too," Chip said, inciting Sasquatch further. Not that he needed any help becoming irritated.

"Thanks for the reminder, Buddy. I know my life sucks. I don't need you to remind me of that."

"I'm from Wall Street and I'm here to help," Chip replied, laughing at his friend.

"We're all here at the service of the King. King Feinberg. All hail the King," Mal added, relishing that he had left much of this bullshit behind when he fled the sell-side of the business to join his new firm.

"Guys, listen to your client. All hail King Feinberg. Without him in the equation, you're not sitting here. Real money, not sales credits, has to pay the bills," Karros said.

"Let's hope it's not my real money paying this bill," Sasquatch said, convinced he was getting a big bill for the weekend.

$ $ $

Having flown directly into Monterey, Feinberg and entourage arrived on schedule, checked into the hotel, and were ready for golf.

He was actually going to deliver the round he had promised to the Sales team for their effort on Zeus.

As they teed off, with caddies, Sasquatch couldn't help but think how it felt to be standing on the first tee at Pebble Beach. His family back in the East End of London couldn't grasp what his life appeared to have become. Of course, they generally only heard about the moments of joy such as this one. As far as they knew, Sasquatch was getting paid a lot of money to play famous golf courses, dine at world-class restaurants, hang out in corporate skyboxes—all the trappings of the proverbial high life. It sounded so good, in the abstract, from the outside looking in. They didn't see the stress, the politics, the alcoholism, the blood pressure medicine, despite noticing the 40 to 50 pounds he had put on during his last 10 years on Wall Street.

The round was going well for all, were it not for the Crackberry addicts—mostly the traders—who strangely seemed to prefer being on their phones, on a Saturday afternoon, rather than playing golf or simply enjoying what was among the most spectacular natural beauty found anywhere in the world. Sasquatch couldn't help but laugh while plotting out his approach shot from atop the fabled cliff on number eight. The sun was out with the wind gently blowing from the ocean. He had 182 yards to the front left pin; maybe a four iron, the caddie advised loudly, as the A-Bauminator yelled into his phone to one of his minions running models back on the trading floor in New York.

How bittersweet it was to be experiencing this moment with a bunch of Wall Street traders, who had little concept of the hallowed golf ground they were walking on. Imagine what his mates back in England would think.

Sasquatch took a practice swing, looked at the caddie, and asked, "Are you sure it's a four?"

"Yes, nice slow swing, and you'll be right there."

Sasquatch swung, and watched the ball soar over the crashing waves in the bay, and land at the front edge of the green.

"What a clown this guy is," Sasquatch said to his caddie, referring to the A-Bauminator. "Good call on the four iron." He was doing his utmost to not let the others rain on his parade. Who knew, he might never get back to Pebble Beach.

Soto, who heard Sasquatch's comment, couldn't really get involved in badmouthing his boss, while Bure dismissed the comment as that of a dumb salesman who didn't have the intellectual capital to be on the trading side of things.

The caddie, evidently on the same page with Sasquatch, seemed utterly shocked by it all.

"So you guys are bankers from New York it sounds like. I hope it's not always like this for you. I mean you come all the way out to Pebble Beach and spend most of the time on the phone. You guys must be some serious high-rollers."

"Pretty sad, isn't it, but don't lump me in with those guys," agreed Sasquatch. "You'd think they could turn it off for something like this, especially on a Saturday. I did. I guess you can tell who the traders are in the group. Not everyone from New York acts like this."

"I sure hope not. If so, I'll be racing home tonight to tell my son, who has designs of going into banking, to avoid it like the plague. There are lots of people, in particular the college kids, who are convinced Wall Street is the be all and end all for them. The glamour, big money, big 'trades' to work on, and trips like the one you're on here today. It all looks pretty appealing through the eyes of a 22-year-old."

"I wouldn't necessarily tell him to avoid banking like the plague, only that the reality is a lot different than the perception," Sasquatch said, as he grabbed his putter for his next shot.

"It's hard for these kids to understand that there's a lot of good, bad, and at times ugly in all jobs. I don't know what that is in your business but I know what it was in mine. I retired a couple years ago from a corporate marketing job in San Francisco. I caddy for the exercise and the scenery out here on the bay—it makes me happy."

"Good for you. I have no idea what I'll do when I pull the plug on my gig… Or when the plug is pulled for me. Remind me to give you my card after the round. Your son can give me a call if he really is serious about banking. Believe me, I can give him everything he wants to know about it."

"Great. Thank you."

"Sure. Now let's get back to playing golf. I don't want to think about my job when walking Pebble Beach."

$ $ $

With dinner set for 7:30 at the Grill on Ocean Avenue in nearby Carmel-by-the-Sea, those in the pub looked at their watches only to realize it was 6:30 and time to go back to their rooms, get showered up, and be ready to meet in the lobby for the easy 15-minute taxi into town. As they were walking to their rooms, Sasquatch looked west toward the back of the lobby where the sun was beginning to sink, beautifully so, into the Pacific Ocean. What a place. One day he would bring his wife here for a nice stay. That would surely rekindle their relationship. Maybe he could convince her to play golf—God forbid that they have a common interest.

As they walked into the lobby at the Inn, Sasquatch, still thirsty, asked Chip and Mal if they wanted another quick drink before heading up to their rooms. As they sat down on the patio Mal noticed a couple on the far side of the patio enjoying a glass of wine together.

"Isn't that Feinberg over there? That's a pretty hot-looking email he's working on," he said in a hushed tone.

"Yep, that's him." Chip replied.

"So he brought his wife. Why not I suppose? Private jet, Pebble Beach, beautiful inn to relax at, all good. It seems so right."

Chip turned to see what his client was talking about, "It really does seem right, except for the fact that she isn't his wife. I've met his wife, Franny, at a business function or two."

"So who is she?"

"I have no idea. Maybe it's someone for hire from San Francisco or maybe, lucky her, someone for hire from New York who got a ride on the jet instead of us. You know, he has a reputation for hanging out with the hired help. And if I was a betting man, poor Mrs. Feinberg has no idea."

"See Sasquatch, you missed your opportunity to join the mile-high club with Feinberg. That could be you snuggling up next to him."

"Quite a shame."

"Thanks for the visual, gentlemen," Mal added. "See you in 20 minutes back here in the lobby."

$ $ $

Karros, who had been informed of the mystery woman, discreetly asked Feinberg who she was, as they walked into the restaurant together ahead of the others.

"Well, she's just an old friend of mine from New York. She had never been out here and I thought it would be fun for her—and I hope for me. No way was I going to bring that bitch that calls herself my wife. It's like a bad trade that's gotten worse—at some point you just have to write it off the books and move on."

"Good for you. Even better you managed to keep your marital woes out of the industry gossip. Not that I'm looking to do this myself, but how might I ask are you going to end it, if that's what you decide on doing?"

"Come on, Joey, you know the answer to that question. Sprinkle a little money at the problem. Basically, worse case, she's getting three million in exchange for keeping her mouth shut and going away. My lawyer will make sure of that when he finishes revising the pre-nup. I'm sure she'll bid for more, but it ain't going to happen."

"I would say that's a pretty good deal for you based on what I would ballpark your net worth at."

"Great trade, for sure. I really don't care if she thinks she's getting screwed too badly. She'll have three million to show for it. Pretty good walk-away money for three years of marriage. I'm sure she'll find someone else to sink her claws into. Make that she and her mother."

Feinberg was unemotional about it all. Marriage really was just another trade, a put option as he described it to his lawyer, Ira Rothman. No different than any counterparty to one of his trades, Franny was soon to feel like a lot of Smyth Johnston's clients that Feinberg had dealt with.

After being seated at a nicely situated table for eight, the dinner chatter began. Karros, ever the opportunist, sat right next to Feinberg. The others from Sales and Mal breathed a sigh of relief as they happily seated themselves at the opposite end of the table.

Karros took center stage and proposed a toast to all at the table for their work on Zeus. The toast was also a not-so-subtle reminder of why they were all in Pebble Beach together.

"Thanks to everyone at this table tonight for their hard work in getting Zeus done. Mal, that gratitude extends to you as our client. As I have often said, we are one team, one dream. This is what being a team is all about." It was vintage Karros. Chip and Sasquatch had heard his nothingness time and time again.

Feinberg chimed in by thanking Karros and his team, then proceeded to drop the bomb Chip had anticipated. "Joey, thank you for getting this done. And Mal, thanks for the trade. You'd think Kerr would be pleased by getting Zeus done although I'm not too sure. He's being painful on everything lately."

"Really, I'd think he'd be pleased as well," replied Karros. "What's up with him?"

"He's really on edge these days about everything. My guess is he's vying for the CEO position when Thomas retires and doesn't want any mishaps beforehand. In any case, Kerr called me before I got on the plane today and said he won't approve of this trip as a business expense. He's worried about the firm's expenses and even more worried about the potential for a market disruption event that may cause a meltdown. I think some changes are coming. Look, I've told him my book is well-hedged particularly after getting this deal done, but he didn't care. There's nothing I can do about it. Let's just hope he calms down soon. Obviously, Mal's paid for."

The table went quiet. Sasquatch was waiting for Feinberg to offer to pay for the trip out of his own pocket. The offer never came.

"Told you so," Chip mumbled under his breath.

"Screwed again," Sasquatch mumbled back.

"What did you just say?" Feinberg said, pressing the question.

"I said 'screwed again'."

"I heard 'jewed again'. Now just shut the fuck up and get your credit card out unless you want me to tell HR and Kerr about your anti-Semitic views."

"Michael, that's ridiculous. You know damn well that's not what I said."

"My word against yours... Let's see: a superstar trader who makes him a ton of money vs. a totally expendable journeyman salesman. Good luck with that."

Karros chimed in, "Hey Sasquatch, just get your Amex out at the end of dinner. We can sort this out later. Maybe we can get it covered within Sales. Besides, being fired *for cause* on Wall Street means no job, no stock vesting, and probably no chance of being rehired by a competitor. Your word against Michael's in the court of Kerr...not a good scenario for you at all."

Silence marked the rest of the dinner for Sasquatch and Chip as, much to their horror, Feinberg kept ordering expensive wine—1995 Opus Ones in three-liter magnums to be exact. Bure and the other traders were having a great time. So what if it cost a bit of money out of pocket. They were on Feinberg's team. They would be taken care of at bonus time. In effect they knew they were covered whereas Sales never knew that until the moment in time when they ripped open their bonus envelopes.

After begrudgingly getting their credit cards out to pay for the $400 per person dinner, Sasquatch and Chip, along with Mal, departed to the Inn. Too pissed off to go to sleep, the three of them convened at the lobby bar, hoping as they often did, that they could drown their pain with liquid solace.

"That fucking asshole. I wish I had called him a Jew. What a piece of shit."

"You think so, Sasquatch? And you wonder why I'm the way I am. Feinberg really is a piece of shit. The assholes have taken over this business. It's just another version of the same theme we discuss all the time. How much you want to bet he'll find a way to expense all the traders' costs for the trip, especially the dinner. I did notice that he picked up your tab, Mal, so he'll probably use that as the rationale to expense it all."

"Theme, huh? The theme being that the scum rises to the top. He'll get his one day."

"Exactly."

It was the same thought Chip had a mere handful of hours earlier on the golf course.

Wall Street's white glove culture had indeed been replaced by a toxic culture that favored the minority of those who figured out how to rig the system. A silent alliance of bad operators had waged and won the war on integrity, personal accountability, and responsibility. Somehow the bad operators had hijacked the business and were exploiting its vast upside disproportionately for themselves.

"It kind of feels like late stage Roman Empire to me," Mal summarily added. "Too much of a good thing is bound to unravel at some point. You have to believe that or you'll go berserk. Why do you think I finally went to the buy-side of the business?"

Chapter 6
It's just the market

Friday, December 7, 2007
12:05 P.M.

Fifth Avenue
New York City

Michael Feinberg looked at his watch, taking his eyes off the multiple Bloomberg screens for the first time in hours. It was time to leave for his lunch appointment with Ira Rothman. Anticipating the near-impossible task of hailing a taxi in midtown Manhattan during Christmas season, he decided he could benefit from the walk to his lawyer's office.

Fifth Avenue was abuzz with holiday commotion. At every corner were Salvation Army Santas ringing their bells and countless street vendors attracting hungry customers with the scents of roasted chestnuts and hotdogs. Piecing his way through the wall of humanity, he turned the corner where he was immediately struck by the sheer scale of the Rockefeller Center Christmas tree and the smiling onlookers. He couldn't help but think of the contrast between his life and those of the categorically happy crowd.

"Hi, Ira. Need to make this quick. My book is all over the place today—I can't be off the desk long. By the way, you're late. If I were on the clock like you attorneys, I'd be sending you a bill: my effective hourly rate is four to five thousand." Feinberg laughed, knowing Ira would appreciate the wry humor.

"Fine. I've reviewed the pre-nup. In brief, as per the original understanding with Franny, she gets half of your net worth subject to a cap of three million, That was a good number when the doc was signed, but of course that's a much smaller percentage than half nowadays. Does she know what you're actually worth now? I have the revised doc ready for your final review."

"I don't think so. I'm sure she knows it's a lot more than three million. At least judging by the amount she spends, you would think she knows."

"Well, keep it that way. You don't want her thinking you're worth more to her dead than alive. Remember how your estate plan works with the life insurance and how it all fits together."

"Sure."

"How do you propose we get her assent to the amendments you're proposing?"

"Ira, just leave that to me. I'll get her signature. After I bless the final document, get the execution copy to me and I'll do my part. Sooner or later she'll need to accept that this marriage is over and she's three bucks better off than otherwise would have been the case. A million dollars a year for not working while spending my money lavishly—that's pretty good work if you can get it. I gotta go… Thanks, Ira."

Feinberg chocked down the rest of his sandwich and raced back to the desk.

$ $ $

Chip and Sasquatch, who seldom shared Feinberg's habit, or obsession, of eating at the desk, headed off the trading floor to go to one of their mainstay delis for lunch. They seemed to have gotten into the rut of mindlessly choosing among three delis, a pizza place, and a greasy cheeseburger joint. Neither knew what any of them were actually called, relying on their instincts, much like dogs in a Pavlovian experiment racing to their food bowl. Today's choice was an easy, two crosstown-block walk from their office on Lexington and 47th.

As they walked, Chip stuffed a dollar bill into the can held by a beggar whose sign read, "Need help with my mortgage."

"What? How would that guy have a mortgage? Who would've lent him the money? Whoever it was has sold it a long time ago. Garbage in, garbage out. It probably sits on Fannie Mae's books festering like an open wound along with the rest of the subprime mortgages that never should've been made in the first place."

"Maybe it's sitting in Zeus. How's that for two worlds colliding?"

"If so, I'm sure the boy genius has already sent in the credit event notice."

"Good point. Speaking of default risk, I'm beginning to get a little worried about my real estate ventures. Bad scene if those head south on me."

"Looks like you need to have a good year with your day job. It's great seeing you in such despair," Chip laughed. It was his way of taunting his friend Sasquatch.

"Based on how things are going here, I think I need to crank up my personal market value and see if some other bank will up the ante for my fine services."

"There's not another bank dumb enough to hire your worthless ass—you're at the end of your nine lives in this game."

"You're making me feel great. Really, really great. I'll have you know I got a call from a headhunter yesterday about a position."

"Good for you. Who is it, Bank of Poughkeepsie or some other major player like that?"

"Nope. Must you know, it's Lehman."

"Even a blind squirrel can get a nut—Lehman's a top player. Might as well talk to them."

"Yep, that's what I figured. Basically, the head hunter tells me it's the same job I'm doing here, but with more money and a one-year guarantee."

"Dude, don't tell me you're a whore for the money and a guarantee. Surprise, surprise."

"You would be correct, sir. I work for money, especially guaranteed money."

"What about loyalty to the firm, to Karros, Feinberg, Kerr, and the rest of your colleagues here?"

Both laughed at the absurdity of it all. The new Wall Street engendered no loyalty whatsoever. Anyone who didn't understand that wound up getting squashed like a ripe melon.

After ordering their usual nine-dollar sandwich specials, the two decided they weren't ready to go back to the desk yet, instead grabbing a small table in the corner of the crowded deli. Ironically, the two felt more comfortable conversing in a crowded public place than the privacy of their office. At least in the deli they knew there were no taped lines or other ways to invite unwanted scrutiny. Anonymity was everyone's friend in New York.

"Let me guess, it's going to be the same downer conversation today."

"What else would you expect," replied Chip.

"Is this ever going to end?"

"Yep, but let's hope it ends on our terms. You have to hope that our business can sustain itself long enough to bank enough money and get on with our lives. The real downer will be if or actually when a massive market event happens and you don't have enough dough and whole businesses like ours get shut down. Happens all the time—how do you think the associates in dot-com banking felt around 2000? After spending hundreds of thousands on their education, going through a rigorous and painful interview process, training classes, et cetera, they think they're getting on the gravy train and then, kaboom, their business is dead. Imagine that scenario. You get to do this and then get blown out before you reach the finish line. Sure you might be an expert in CDOs and credit derivatives with a stable of clients, but what happens if there isn't a CDO market? What're you going to do then, hotshot?"

"The finish line sounds good to me, though it does seem like it just keeps getting further away. One step forward, two steps back, in a sense."

"I've been thinking about pulling the ripcord for a couple of years, but then again I've been saying that for a while. I don't need a Wall Street fortune, but I do need enough to live a decent life, which requires money, a fair amount of money. Be thankful we're on the Street. At least we can compress the money-making years into a shorter, hopefully much shorter, time span. It's my Constant Pain Theory."

"Huh?"

"Yep, CPT. The amount of pain for any career is constant. Whether you work 40 years as an accountant, insurance salesman, factory worker, or 15 years as a Wall Streeter, the amount of pain you go through is the same at the finish line. For us Wall Street guys, that amount of pain, as my theory has it, just gets compressed into a smaller time capsule."

"True, I can buy into that."

"On the topic of pain there seem to be some storm clouds on the horizon. But we should be okay for the next few years. The banking industry will always survive, especially with all the regulatory changes that have been emerging as of late, especially the new Basel regulations. You onto that?"

"Somewhat, but remind me."

"You know, currently banks are supposed to hold a particular percentage of their assets in capital. The rules, of course, are complicated. So, to simplify it: for regular loans the capital charge is 8 percent, but to lend to an OECD government it's zero because they never default. And banks domiciled in OECD countries have a 1.2 percent capital charge, because they're not as safe as governments, but safer than regular companies."

"Okay, sounds fair enough. But, if you have a triple-A-rated bank, flush with capital, in a non-OECD country, that still gets 8 percent?"

"Yep, exactly. So the bank regulators, to address that concern, have agreed that every bank can estimate how risky its own loans are and basically hold whatever amount of capital they deem necessary. All they have to do is get their regulator to validate the models."

"I'm sure the bank rocket-scientist quants aren't really going to get much opposition from the regulators. Not a very fair fight."

"Nope, if the regulators were that smart, why would they be sitting there making 75 grand a year rather than sitting here with the possibility of making millions."

"So basically, Feinberg and Kerr will be able to determine how much capital they'll need to hold against anything they do. How much you wanna bet that number is really low? It's strange that the regulators have put the wolves in charge of the henhouse."

"Yes it is, but I'm simplifying the situation a bit. There will be internal checks on the model, but what chance does an internal accountant have vs. Kerr if he wants to reduce the amount of capital? At least some of the external regulators will have some teeth. Return on equity is one of the metrics determining Kerr's bonus, so what do you think he'll do? So you think this gravy train's going to continue?"

"Hope so, at least the next couple years should be good. The bank should be able to leverage its capital much more effectively to make more money. Hence bigger bonuses for us."

"Unless…"

"Yep, unless the whole thing comes crashing down. Then it'll be ugly. Actually, make that 'fugly'…"

"Fugly it would be. But going back to the comp stuff," Sasquatch continued. He was prone to philosophical conversations and particularly enjoyed engaging Chip on the topic of compensation.

"Why do we make more, actually a lot more, than people in other businesses? We really don't add that much more value to society. My buddies back in England can't believe it when I've given them a peek in the box. I don't dare tell them exactly what I make— they'd have a fucking heart attack. They'd think Wall Street money is unfair to the rest of the people. Hell, some of these guys would turn hostile with envy despite being mates for most of my life."

"I wouldn't agree with the unfair notion at all. Let's face it, Wall Street has lots of seriously smart and ambitious people. Look around the trading floor. Virtually everyone is smart, with the possible exception of certain management empty-suit types. But the people who actually make the money are smart, sometimes scary smart. And they are competitive and hungry for success. No one has given them their seat on the desk; they've earned it. As you said before, they had to get hired in the first place, probably from a top university where they had to study their asses off to get the grades to earn an interview with the top firms. For the older guys with experience, they get promoted or hired away because of track records for making money. Performance. This ain't the charity business: you either have the desired background and are able to perform or you don't. Actually, it's completely fair, brutally fair."

"I guess so. It's really not that much different than a soccer pro for Manchester United, as an example."

"Or baseball player, musician, actor... People don't realize that for the most part it's all about performance to get in the game, and ongoing performance to stay in the game. If you can hit a 95-mile-an-hour fastball with 30,000 people watching, then I guess you deserve to make what the market bears. Most athletes, however, reap the benefit of multiyear deals, not to mention huge endorsements while we live bonus to bonus. From that standpoint, maybe it's more like golf than baseball. In other words, if you don't perform, you don't get paid. You know, it's just the market. Of course there are the few empty suits—for some reason Bonet immediately leaps to mind—who manage to make a mint without measurable performance. Maybe they're the real geniuses, like the guy sitting atop the pyramid scheme. I suppose that makes him a lot smarter than we give him credit for. I'd be happy to be a face man making ten million a year, or whatever it is guys like him pull in."

"I guess the general public just becomes so envious of all the bonus checks they hear about that they always want to put the *unfair* label on the object of their envy, rather than face the music that they aren't in the big leagues for whatever reason. Maybe it's because they don't have the talent to play in the big leagues or they've made the conscious choice not to make the necessary lifestyle sacrifices to build wealth."

"Yep. And to complete your train of thought, that envy becomes anger when someone in the big leagues appears undeserving of their exceptionally high compensation. A journeyman .200 hitter initially gets paid a lot for mediocre results, but will fade fast and will soon be out of the game. That said, the journeyman has put in the blood, sweat, and tears to earn the chance to play in the big leagues, starting from Little League, to high school to minors, etc. Same thing with some of the mediocre performers in our business—even they've had to earn the opportunity to get here, but they can only bluff their way through for so long."

Chip paused, before continuing.

"But going back to your value comment, there is enormous value, economically, socially, and financially, being generated on Wall Street. It's too easy to ascribe wrong-doing and be jealous of the evil bankers. The reality is that the world needs Wall Street to generate new products to enable businesses and individuals to grow and thrive. Think about the world where the original risk taker, say a bank making a mortgage, had no ability to hedge or transfer that risk into the broader capital markets. Your average Joe probably doesn't get into a house, can't buy a car, that flat screen TV, or new iPod. The money has to come from somewhere, and you can't expect a thriving economy to exist without credit being extended. Consider New York without Wall Street as part of its tax base? Lots of shit that people take for granted gets shut down without their taxes."

"But what about Wall Street compensation compared to Fortune 500 companies? I have a buddy who works at General Electric as a marketing exec or something like that. I think I make 3-4 times what he makes."

"It's just the market, as I said, and our market is fundamentally different than GE's and, again, if your buddy wanted to be in a different compensation culture then he should have come to the Street and work his way up the ranks like you did. And I would be willing to bet that a lot more of his compensation is in base salary than yours. Most of your compensation is in your bonus. Your base salary is pittance by comparison and certainly isn't enough to live the inordinately expensive lifestyle in this part of the country. You know, of course, that the bank pays most of your comp in bonus, which is nothing more than a free option for them to screw you every year, whether your performance merits your getting screwed or not. And they can always find a reason to screw you."

"I know that. My buddies don't really understand that the bonus is at risk compensation. There is no free lunch being handed out here. Produce or perish."

"They sure don't. They also have no clue about what the typical Wall Street guy has to put up with—the politics, backstabbing, volatile market conditions, general lifestyle trade-offs, hours…it's not the free lunch they think it is. It's a whole lotta pain to stay on your feet in this gig, a lot more than most people realize or would be able to handle. Here's a new concept for you— next time you have beers with your GE buddy, talk to him about pain-adjusted compensation, or my Total Pain Theory."

"Let me guess: TPT. You're a man of many theories, a modern-day Einstein. Maybe you'll find refuge in academia after you end this stage of your life."

"Einstein was smart enough to never do this for a living."

"By the way, I just refuted one of my theories. Who says there's no free lunch? I bought yours today. In terms of pain, I guess we'd better get back to the desk. Gotta get some stuff done to make the big money. Hopefully there's some meat left on the bonus bone at the end of the year after Kerr, Feinberg, Bonet, and Karros take their giant bites."

$ $ $

At a few minutes past three, Duncan Kerr strode into the conference room filled with the senior-most managing directors in Smyth Johnston's New York office. He had called the invitation only meeting earlier that day.

"There are some of us at the senior-most reaches of this bank who have become concerned about the pace and scale of risk within the bank. In particular, there's concern about the high correlation risk across product types, our inability to perfectly hedge our trading books, and what might happen when an unanticipated market shock occurs."

Kerr continued the lecture. No one dared to interrupt him.

"Effective immediately, no more risk will be underwritten until I have definitive proof that our exposure is manageable and we're not unduly vulnerable to a potential market shock. I want details on risk we currently own and the prospects for moving it off our books in the near term, the quality of our hedges, and our counterparty exposure. It doesn't seem like many of you understand that we're in the business of moving product rather than holding it in inventory. I expect each of you to provide me this detail by end of business tomorrow prior to my departure to London."

Kerr's dictum went over about as well as a loud fart in church. It signified that it was no longer going to be business as usual, that a change in business model was immediate and essential. No more origination of deals unless there was a taker for the risk. No more putting on deals, making money, and worrying about the exit of the unsold inventory later. For years, the game had been all about cranking out the deals in volume for purposes of climbing up the league table rankings and bagging other accolades such as Derivatives House of the Year. Such rankings and accolades had fomented a "build it and they will come" mentality, often resulting in lots of deals not being fully distributed and aggregating on the bank's books. The bull market had made everyone somewhat blind, blissfully so, to the risk that had been accumulating on the bank's books over the years. Those accumulated assets hadn't presented a problem since their value had increased during the bull market run, making all the traders look like geniuses with their unsold positions.

"Does anyone have any questions? This is an open forum; I want to hear what each of you is thinking. There are no stupid questions," Kerr assured his managing directors.

Failing to recognize the trap, one of the attendees from Sales fired away. "Duncan," he said, "my clients have begun to hit their limits on a lot of our deals. We're running out of bullets to get them to take more risk. We need trading to be more flexible about terms and price."

"Are you fucking kidding me? You're an MD at this firm. Maybe you shouldn't be if you can't get your clients to help us out. We've made your clients a fortune over the years. I discount you as a salesman at 50 cents on the dollar. No wonder we still own so much of this product on our books."

Everyone in the room knew that at that precise, unfortunate moment their colleague had plundered himself. Just like that, he had cratered any upward trajectory he might have had at Smyth Johnston. Being told he was discounted by Kerr at 50 cents was the equivalent of being worthless, below investment grade, a human junk bond of an employee. He knew he would either be fired or, worse, left to fester in a situation that had little if any upside.

Being left to fester, perhaps surprisingly so, was an age-old industry tactic—the equivalent of being sent to Wall Street purgatory, a leper colony of sorts—for those hapless souls who had to stick around, do the work, take the pain, while getting screwed on compensation year after year until they finally screamed *uncle* or found another job. As long as they remained, it meant they had no bid away, only increasing the firm's motivation to screw them come compensation time. It was a vicious circle of the worst kind. Wall Street firms often preferred this approach over outright firing as it provided them cheap labor and decreased the potential for wrongful termination lawsuits from bitter ex-employees.

A mere two weeks later, the ill-fated MD's seat on the desk was empty, a gaping symbol of the hara-kiri he had committed. No one knew if he was actually fired or fell on his sword in Wall Street samurai fashion. He had disappeared without fanfare, though most knew he would surface again at a competitor or buy-side firm sometime after the next bonus cycle.

Karros sought to diffuse the drama by redirecting the discussion back to the task at hand.

"Guys, I agree with Duncan. Each of us needs to make sure that every member of our team is focused on reducing risk. Smyth Johnston is best in class, and now we need to show it by leveraging our client relationships. We must make sure the clients look at our deals first."

It was Karros at his finest. If there was an ass to kiss—as long as it was someone senior to him—he was all over it. But somehow Kerr's ass got the most attention, whenever Karros had access to it.

"I'm sure I can speak for other salespeople in this room when I say that Zeus and some of our other deals aren't as popular as comparable deals from other banks. Unfortunately, there have been more losses on our deals and clients are unhappy, and, in some cases, skeptical of the trading desk. They feel our desk has sharper elbows than others doing similar deals," added another Sales MD.

Feinberg sought the need to defend his desk.

"There is nothing wrong with Zeus or any of our other deals. Yes, there is risk in these deals—that's why we're paying an appropriate premium. If your clients don't want risk, or the risk premium, sell them treasuries. And I can't prevent defaults from happening; I don't control corporate balance sheets. Your clients had the opportunity to do their own analytics, did so, and negotiated the price they needed as risk-takers. Ultimately they agreed to the deal terms. No one put a gun to their heads. Besides we own plenty of the risk ourselves, so we're in the same boat."

"That all sounds good, but the fact remains that our clients are saying our deals have performed poorly by comparison to peer banks. Hard to overcome that criticism, if that's the case. This shouldn't come as any surprise to the traders, but our clients are also clients of every other major bank. Guess what—that means they get to pick and choose what deals they do and with whom they do them. If they think our deals aren't as good as what they can see from others, then, 'Houston, we have a problem.'"

Kerr jumped in. He'd heard enough.

"You sales guys get paid a lot of money to move product. Let me remind you that I sign your paychecks, your clients don't. You're in my back pocket, not theirs. Is that simple enough for you to grasp? Trust me, I can interview 50 people for your seat by tomorrow morning."

Kerr held a pregnant pause. There were no more questions—nobody was dumb enough to say anything else. It was self-preservation time.

"That's it. Do your jobs and get the reports I requested done by close of business tomorrow."

Karros tried to follow Kerr to his office to continue his sycophantic advances, but was waved off, causing him to retreat to his own desk.

Taking mental stock of his team, Karros realized that many on his desk may not be good candidates to sell the inventory positions and help him curry favor with Kerr. Many were hired for strategic reasons, or so it had been portrayed to senior sales management, as part of his pitch to get himself hired in the first place. They were pieces of his derivitization plan. It was a catchy soundbite, a platitude that Karros, the personification of a derivative himself, had cleverly borrowed from the Street and deployed to inject an air of legitimacy to his team. As the pitch went, he held the keys to this new sales machine, a transformative, game-changing notion he had sold hook, line, and sinker to Smyth Johnston. His team would be the critical distribution arm, the missing link for harvesting the vast credit derivatives pipeline. A team with various skills ranging from legal, accounting, structuring, industry focus, and so on, that would bring these new asset types together with new clients. With margins being squeezed in traditional lines, businesses like corporate and government bonds, he was the future money machine. He was an essential cog in the Wall Street wheel of progress.

What Karros knew that management didn't, was that many of his strategic hires, while smart people with significant experience, were years and not months away from unlocking the profit potential of their client bases. In many cases, there were legal, tax, and/or accounting reasons precluding a given client base from investing in these new assets. They were works in progress. In other cases it just wasn't a product area that certain client types were ever going to meaningfully get involved with.

Karros, as he had done before with other banks, had sold Smyth Johnston's management a bill of goods under the impression that they needed to hire him and all his people in order to keep pace with the competition. Hoping that it would one day amount to something beyond competitive window dressing, he really had no idea when that would be. He did, however, have a few proven sales people who produced for him, making him look good at bonus time. In any case, Karros was hedged via his two-year guaranteed contract under which he would make at least $3 million a year. If things went well he'd get more than that, with the possibility of landing the coveted head-of-sales role, a title he was keen to hold. It was his dream. Hopefully the strategic hires would start producing by the end of his contract. If not, there were always other banks to whom he could sell the same deal. It was a great personal trade, if you will.

Some might consider this a fleecing, a sham, a charade of sorts. But it happened all the time on Wall Street: one bank wants what another one has—in this case a credit derivatives distribution arm that can unlock enormous, newfound profits—and pays up for the promise of greatness on the business horizon. Typically, the buyer, or the bank, was handicapped in the amount of due diligence it was able to carry out when dealing with high-priced hires such as Karros. Too many market rumors of a bank about to make a big hire might start a bidding war, increasing the cost of winning the war for talent.

But now Karros was in trouble, with his proven producers having almost all but tapped out their clients on credit derivatives. The strategic hires were nowhere near making sales. How would he be able to look good in front of Kerr?

It was a rhetorical question for Karros. He knew exactly what to do: ingratiate himself with his bosses by any means—dinners, drinks, meetings off the desk, whatever it took to get on the good side by managing up. After the rebuke from Kerr, Karros decided to set up a meeting with Jean-Pierre Bonet, global head of Credit Sales, who had just arrived at the office. Bonet commuted from Bermuda most Monday mornings. Judging by the picture on his office wall, Bonet's Bermuda getaway, one of several scattered around the globe, was spectacular. It made one wonder why Bonet even bothered with Wall Street anymore.

The answer, of course, was that the elixir of money, power, and control was what defined him as it did many others on Wall Street.

A Frenchman and graduate of the Sorbonne, Bonet had the stereotypical polished European persona that: bespoke suits, race cars, immaculately coiffed hair, wine snobbery—the self-styled international playboy. He was the kind of guy, as a colleague once described him, who one could easily picture getting manicures, pedicures, and facials on a regular basis. Bonet was the proverbial sales manager with limited knowledge, let alone interest, in the details of the business lines for which he was responsible. He thought of himself as an asset allocator whose task it was to get the right people in the seats, pay them a lot of money, then let them worry about the details. Many of his underlings, having soon grown weary of his ivory tower detachment, thought his compensation of $10 million per year was all but a waste of shareholder wealth.

Karros managed to stake out Bonet's office, and snuck in after seeing him put the phone down.

"Joey, I'm sorry, but I'm already late. Traffic from Teterboro was terrible," Bonet started in his haughty-sounding Euro accent.

"I just need a few minutes, Jean-Pierre."

"Fine, Joey, first tell me more about your business. I would like to know how I can help you grow your business." It was the typical Bonet hollow banter that could be used interchangeably with any one of his many subordinates.

"Let me tell you about some issues my guys are having with Feinberg. Some of the deals in the past have blown up and now we need to move more product."

"Feinberg, he is a great trader."

Before Karros could continue, he was interrupted by the ring of Bonet's Blackberry.

"Joey, sorry, I need to take this call. Let's catch up later. Maybe we can have a glass of wine tonight over dinner tonight. French wine, of course. Life is too short for any other type."

Karros wasn't holding his breath. This wasn't the first time a meeting with Bonet had been cut suddenly short. As soon as Bonet realized he actually might need to do something, like discuss a controversial topic with Feinberg or someone else within the power structure at

Smyth Johnston, the meeting came to an abrupt end. Bonet's strategy was to avoid confrontation and political crosshairs at all costs. Avoid controversy and let his flamboyant European personality carry the day.

Alternatively, when finding himself in the middle of a political hot potato, he would always promise action to his subordinates, then simply never do what he promised. Subordinates and their clients were a lot easier to deal with than taking on Feinberg or, worse, finding out that he was on the wrong side of Kerr's position on an internal battle. It was far better to play the do-nothing, managerial rope-a-dope than enter the fray. Like it or not, at $10 million the strategy seemed to have worked brilliantly for him. Sure, he would never be Kerr and make $50 million, but 10 years of $10 million would work fine, thank you very much.

Karros had learned that wastes of shareholder wealth were more commonplace on Wall Street than he had imagined. Sure, he earned his $3 million a year by being an internal networker and having the right guys in the right seats, but Bonet? The guy was next to worthless. He could do so much better in that seat. But he had to be patient; his time would come.

Although Wall Street was a produce or perish environment, with theoretically flat organizational structures that make it tough to hide (especially on a trading floor), there were those who, either by their own cunning or as the result of politically-expedient circumstances, were able to create very cushy, seemingly bulletproof, positions for themselves. Bonet had figured it out, and Karros was trying to follow suit.

$ $ $

SEC Detective Jack Bonfiglio sat in his windowless office at the World Financial Center, across the street from the poignant ruins of the World Trade Center. He was reflecting on the credit derivatives matter of inquiry he had been investigating for the previous six months. In contrast to his former law enforcement counterparts at NYPD, he never worked on such a thing as a garden variety case. Each case was defined by a unique set of facts and circumstances—and for that reason, his life as an SEC investigator was more interesting and challenging than it had been when he started at NYPD many years ago.

He had gathered vast amounts of information about the arcane world of credit derivatives. Despite his fact-finding efforts, he struggled mightily to advance the matter under inquiry. What he had learned thus far about the brave new world of Wall Street was dizzying. Was there even a violation to be investigated? If so, what, specifically, was the nature of the violation? Fraud? He knew something about that, given his involvement in the Enron case. Market manipulation? Bid-rigging? Disclosure violations? It would be far easier to move forward with a case if he were operating in a mature, better understood market. But no such luck; this was different.

There were few market conventions or precedents that could provide him a roadmap on how to proceed. Such conventions and operating guidelines were being invented day by day, in real time. Bonfiglio felt the pace of innovation in this business moving one step ahead of the regulatory bodies—the SEC included—that had jurisdiction over the market. At times what he was learning failed to fit neatly into any particular regulatory box. How much should he be working with the FBI on this? What about the CFTC? What about the state regulators? The New York Department of Banking, or was it the Department of Insurance? Were credit derivatives a form of insurance? Tough to chase a moving target.

Chip Smith was among many with whom he had been fact-finding over the last six months. It had been two or three months, he frankly couldn't remember, since he last spoke with Chip. What he could remember, however, was the disdain Chip felt toward Michael Feinberg. Feinberg had emerged as one of many credit derivative traders whose name continued to surface as a person of interest in his inquiry. Perhaps that fact, he thought, could be useful in getting Chip to cooperate more broadly. There was only one way to find out.

"Chip, it's Jack Bonfiglio calling. How have you been?"

"Fine. And you?"

"I'd like to speak with you again about the credit derivatives case we talked about before. Can you talk now, or do you prefer meeting in person?"

"I'd like to meet in person, but can't tonight. Are you on your cell phone or office phone."

"Office phone."

"Ok, call me back on your cell phone, and we can talk." Chip was wary of speaking on any land line, a healthy concern for any denizen of a trading floor where every call was recorded and thus retrievable. It was no different than email in this respect.

The two reconnected minutes later, with Chip having secured a private location off the trading floor where he could have the conversation.

"So, I've learned a hell of a lot since we last spoke. The matter under inquiry has evolved into a potential violation of the Securities Acts. And, your buddy Mr. Feinberg is on the short list of persons of interest."

"Okay," Chip replied, intentionally being more guarded than usual given that Feinberg's name had been mentioned. "So what's the case?"

"That's where it gets a bit nebulous. There's really no precedent for any of this since it's a relatively new market. Let me cut to the chase."

Chip sensed the stakes were about to be raised.

"Okay."

"I'd like you to be an informant for the SEC."

"An informant—how exactly does that work?"

"It's pretty simple: you cooperate with the investigation on a confidential basis. No one knows, not your colleagues, not your clients, your employer, family members...not anyone. If a case gets brought against your firm, you are protected under the statutory whistleblower laws."

"Whistleblower? What the fuck? This is serious."

"Yes, it is serious. SEC violations are nothing but serious. People lose their jobs, pay fines, lose their careers, and maybe go to jail if there are criminal charges, too. You have the benefit of being protected, kept anonymous should this case move forward and Feinberg is implicated. After all, judging by the last time we met, you didn't seem to be in love with your job. What do you think, Chip? We need your help."

"How would this go down if I said I agreed to help."

"We prepare a whistleblower agreement, you'd sign it, and then we go from there."

"Well, I can't do anything now. We're in compensation season. I can't do anything to jeopardize my bonus. Of course, I may get totally screwed anyway."

"I understand. I can tell you that signing an affidavit will not be an issue insofar as your bonus is concerned. We can talk about a make-whole clause in our arrangement as well, if that's what it takes for you to help us. Think about it and call me back in the next day or two. Maybe this is your way out of banking."

"I get it. I'll get back to you soon."

$ $ $

The trading floor at Smyth Johnston was filled with bankers in town from many of the bank's global offices—London, Paris, Hong Kong, Sydney, Singapore, Toronto, to name a few. That could only mean one thing: it must be compensation season. It was time to come to the headquarters in New York and kiss the ring—make that ass—of senior management. Anyone running a business of any size was in town to strut their stuff, no different than a pack of wildebeests preparing to rut as mating season begins.

Meetings, coffees, lunches, dinners, and other soirees were the order of the day. With two weeks until Christmas, the performance clock had stopped, as had by no small coincidence, deals getting done. It was the Wall Street equivalent of the lame-duck session. Year-end numbers, as of November, had been gathered from all businesses and sent up the chain to senior management and the other key members of the compensation committee. For those businesses with deals in the pipeline soon to close, soft credit was allowed so that profit from them could be included to buoy their numbers. There was always the attempt to have the deal count in that year and the next, the double dip. The next three to six weeks would determine the aggregate bonus pool and, most importantly, the allocations from the bonus pool to the various desks.

With all the seasonal commotion, it was difficult to lay low. Try as they may, Sasquatch and Tracy circled floor upon floor for any open meeting rooms, only to find them filled with serious-looking faces in the midst of bonus expectation management conversations. Chip, as head of one of Karros's coverage teams, had the misfortune of having to partake in the generally unpleasant year-end pageantry and other mundane management responsibilities including performance and peer reviews.

"Okay, let's call up our lawyer about closing on the Hoboken building," Sasquatch said to Tracy after finally securing a meeting room on the 14th floor. "Although, prospective tenants aren't exactly lining up to rent the units."

Tracy had gotten involved with Sasquatch on a number of his real estate ventures. She was a minority interest investor and a provider of sweat equity on various tasks such as finding tenants for the three buildings Sasquatch owned in Hoboken. Tracy had lots of recent college graduate peers living in or interested in living in Hoboken.

"Not sure what the problem is. Hoboken is hot. College grads, Yuppies and Dinks (Double Income No Kids) are everywhere in Hoboken. You don't think we're going to have issues hitting our break-even occupancy rate if we go through with the purchase, do you?"

"Nope, it's just strange that the tenant demand hasn't been as high as expected."

"I guess we can renege on the deal and forego the earnest money. Glad we negotiated that amount down."

"It's a good building, in a good location, with better than Manhattan rents."

"Even if the building value falls, the cash flows make up for it. And we do have decent funding despite having to put up more equity. My sense is we go through with it. The teaser rate may not be around forever."

"And I spoke with a friend of mine on the mortgage desk. He said our terms are good and we should lock them in. If the rate spikes when it goes from fixed to float, we can always refi. Getting money, cheap money and lots of it, is not the problem in this game."

"Keep in mind, this is New York. People from all over the world want to live here. No chance will real estate values or rents go down and stay down. It's free money, or as close to it as you can get."

"Okay, let's get the attorney on the line."

A declining real estate market was the last thing Sasquatch needed. His real estate ventures had been intended to help dig himself out of the two-divorce-induced financial hole he had dug for himself. It also was designed to hedge himself against losing his job, something he knew could happen each and every day in the precarious world of Wall Street.

A declining real estate market would turn his hedge into a double-barreled shotgun pointed at his own head. One barrel contained a bad bonus or, worse, losing his job. The other barrel contained a real estate market with growing illiquidity risk combined with high amounts of borrowed money. If the value of the buildings dropped and he didn't have enough tenants to cover the mortgage payments, he would take a suicidal financial hit. His plan for a more comfortable lifestyle, post-banking, would be retarded even further if either barrel fired.

Had he paved his own road to hell, albeit with good intentions? Though he kept telling himself he had not, in fact he was no different than most who had become real estate investors with the objective of diversifying away from the broader stock and bond markets. As an investment, real estate offered a lot to like in addition to the diversification rationale. Cheap money—other people's money—was flowing, with inordinately high loan-to-value ratios that produced attractive, leveraged returns. Even better was the long-standing, steep price appreciation on almost all types of real estate in the New York tristate area. As to the rental market, it was hard to go wrong in places like Hoboken, which had no shortage of excess demand.in the rental market.

It had been easy for Sasquatch to rationalize his real estate ventures based on the circumstances at hand. Besides, if he got it all wrong, he'd be in much better shape than the countless others who were playing the same investment game with lesser means than he. It was as if everyone, seemingly without regard for financial wherewithal, was riding the real estate wave. He often wondered how some of the investors had managed to qualify for their mortgages or how they could possibly service the debt in the slightest of downturns. Was this an extension of the Community Reinvestment Act, where funds flowed liberally, courtesy of the political ideal that all Americans had the right and were entitled to own real estate? Regardless he knew that he had begun to feel less confident in the "can't lose proposition" he once held for his real estate ventures.

Anxiety was on the rise for Sasquatch.

$ $ $

It was 4 p.m. and time for the mandatory meeting scheduled by Jean-Pierre Bonet, head of Credit Sales. Everyone from Sales was there, except those who had been fired earlier in the week as part of the thinly-veiled annual cost-cutting initiative. The culling of the herd always started before Christmas so that those getting the axe wouldn't qualify for a bonus.

Merry Christmas, you're fired.

The staff awaited the opening salvo from sales management about what to expect in terms of bonuses for that year. That expectation would be set by Bonet's discussion of the year-to-date performance of his sales force, as well as Smyth Johnston's prospects in the year ahead.

For those who had been through the annual rite of passage before, it would be a perfunctory mix of carrot-and-stick platitudes intended to motivate the sales force to even greater collective heights in the coming year. As the veterans of the process knew all too well, it was management's way of purposefully managing expectations downward to the extent their bonus pool allocations turned out to be unsatisfactory in the final result. It all seemed so predictable to those who had been through the drill before: under-promise, over-deliver. For those new to the game it was an adrenaline surge at the prospect of netting that first big bonus check, an outcome that both financially, if not psychologically, would serve to justify the chosen career path that had led them to Wall Street.

"Ladies and gentlemen, thank you for your efforts this year," Bonet began as he stepped up to the podium. "And thank you for your attendance at today's Year in Review/Year Ahead meeting. Looks like we have a full house," he chuckled.

The ass-kissers in the room laughed with him, but Chip texted to Sasquatch: "Fuck I hate the Euro Boy. This is going to be a crock of shit. How do I know that? His lips are moving."

Sasquatch could only nod his head in agreement, hoping, however, that in a fleeting moment of blind optimism, he would hear some positives spew forth from Bonet's lips. After going ahead with the purchase of another addition to his real estate venture, he was in the market for good news.

Bonet continued with his antiseptic spiel, turning to the PowerPoint presentation one of his minions had put together for him. It was highly unlikely he had even read the presentation beforehand. He was the kind of guy, glib and bristling with his own self-styled greatness, who performed better unrehearsed. In another life had he not been in banking, he would have made an excellent game show host.

"As you will see, the numbers are up year over year across the board. The quality of the numbers has also improved year over year, which dovetails well with the strategic vision we have for top-scoring the sales force."

Now it was Sasquatch's turn.

"Top-scoring? Who the fuck comes up with this type of nonsense?"

"Probably people like Karros—who makes a lot more than you. You see, the key to success is to use buzzwords like top-scoring, empowerment, paradigm shift, reengineering…"

"Shoot me."

"Please, me first," Chip texted back as they both returned, agitated, to Bonet's spiel.

Page after page of performance numbers later, Bonet lapsed into the more grandiose, visionary part of the presentation.

"The platform at Smyth Johnston has made tremendous strides this year and in recent years. We engaged in an aggressive hiring plan earlier this year for a handful of new businesses that are strategically important to us. All of us in management are confident this investment will be accretive to everyone in this room as we stay the course. Patience and focus will win the war."

"Get ready to bend over!" Chip texted right on cue.

"For all of the positives that are undeniable, there are a growing number of us in management, Duncan Kerr included, who have become cautious of the market and our existing risk positions. We are actively looking to reduce our value-at-risk, as many of you know. Sales performance in this is critical, and will weigh heavily in our year-end conversations. There is also some concern over the lower margins in our traditional businesses. For these reasons, Duncan has imposed a hiring freeze, effective immediately. Any exceptions need to go through him."

"Told you so." Chip could only smirk at the grimace observed on Sasquatch's and many other faces in the room. He knew from previous experience that a hiring freeze did not bode well for bonuses. Bonet had done his usual masterful job of under promising, exactly as predicted.

"Senior management has recognized that the P&L numbers have decreased in the last quarter, but what I can tell everyone in this room is that I'm personally vested in your success at this firm. I'm also vested—as is your manager—in the best possible year-end outcome for each of you. If it were up to me, all of you would be very happy on February 11. I'll be fighting for you. I view our client franchise as the most important facet of the firm, and you deliver that franchise to us. However, we need to be cognizant of the market realities as well as the P&L contributions across the firm. This year, especially, we need to recognize the true top performers and reward their contributions over just the average ones. Stay tuned."

"That's code for we're all screwed," Chip texted.

After finishing the 30-minute-long PowerPoint slide show and fielding a few questions from the sales force,

Bonet concluded the meeting.

"Smyth Johnston has a footprint second to none. Each of you should be proud to be a member of this firm. Some of you will have an opportunity to jump to another firm. There's a war for talent out there. The stars will always get competing bids and that's why we need to take care of them. For all you top performers, I encourage each of you to think long term. This has been a great place to be. It will continue to be a great place to be in the years ahead."

Tepid applause followed.

Just like that, the compensation game had officially begun. The game was no different than any other management vs. labor conversation, at least not in concept. It did differ, however, in one important respect: dollars at stake. An average bonus was in the hundreds of thousands, with low-level employees getting tens of thousands and the mega-performers reeling in multiple millions.

Most bankers hated this time of year. Their preoccupation with compensation robbed them of any, if not all, ability to enjoy the holiday season with friends and family. Everything was riding on a payout they wouldn't know with certainty until the official envelope was handed to them in early February.

No one knew why so many banks willfully lapsed into this annual lame-duck session. In some cases, the productivity hiatus could last as long as two full months—from the beginning of December, when management started looking at P&L reports, to February, when bonuses were divvied up. Theories abounded as to why such a prolonged lame-duck was permitted, though never with any definitive proof other than its dismissal as an arcane market practice. The only thing definitive was that one-sixth of the year was spent by virtually all of a firm's high-priced talent doing the compensation dance rather than deals.

Joey Karros was the exception to the rule—he actually loved this time of year. As a manager, this was his time to demonstrate his value, both to his subordinates as well as his superiors. He was in his element: endless politics, ass-kissing, reaffirmation of the numerous internal alliances he had built—such as the one with Michael Feinberg—general posturing, and anything else he could come up with to elevate his footprint internally. Karros loved every minute of the human chessboard, with him and others jockeying for position. Deals, clients, or technical knowledge didn't matter now. What mattered most at this time of year was who could play the game the best. He was masterful at it.

"Hey Chip," Karros said, catching up to him walking out of the meeting. "You have a minute to talk?"

Karros wanted to make the rounds with each of his business leaders over the next few days.

"Sure. Where do you want to go, maybe grab a coffee first?"

"Why not? I could use the jolt. I have dinner with Jean-Pierre tonight. Gotta be on my game."

After loading up a quick coffee from one of several kitchens on the trading floor, they walked back to Karros's office that he shared with another manager; luckily, the guy was not there. They could speak in private—never an easy task when working on a trading floor.

Karros launched into his own expectations management game with Chip, "Your team is one of the top producers on the desk, again. You guys hit budget in the first half, I want to say early June or something."

"I guess I sandbagged you on my budget," Chip passed off as a joke, smiling.

"I'm not suggesting that. Our business can be lumpy at times in terms of deal flows, you never know when the elephants, like Zeus, will hit. We all hope we can smooth that out as the derivitization platform matures. You're not the only team on the desk who has that issue."

"Yep. Believe me, I wish we could make it more predictable."

"We just need to figure out a story for Bonet and others. They will ask why your production fell off in the second half. You have Zeus and some smaller stuff on the books."

"I know they will. For what it's worth, the sentiment coming out of our clients is that the deal flow slowdown in the U.S. is temporary. It's a chance for the market to catch its breath, to reassess what deals it wants to see going forward, and a lot of clients are reloading their product allocations for next year. Maybe that's a healthy thing, as is deals getting printed over in Europe and elsewhere. The pie is definitely getting bigger, and we are going to be a big part of it."

"I hear you. Pretty good spin on things."

"It wasn't intended to be spin. It's current market feedback, directly from my clients."

"So tell me, buddy, are any of your guys a flight risk?"

"I worry about Sasquatch at times. He's the type of guy who could get lifted by a competitor at a similar level but with a guarantee. At his stage it might be just what the doctor ordered for him."

"Do you know he's looking? Does he have an offer from anyone?"

"I'm pretty sure he doesn't have an offer, but I suspect he has gotten calls. By the way, so have I. No surprise there. The headhunters are getting positioned for the annual frenzy that follows comp season."

"Okay, keep me posted on Sasquatch. What number does it take to keep him?"

"He's going to be more axed to fly the coop if his year-over-year bonus isn't something similar to last year's. That's always the starting point. Maybe a little kiss on top of that as a feel-good gesture."

"Maybe a $100K kiss on top of last year's level?"

"Something like that would seem to be fair to me, and I think I could sell him on it as a good outcome, whether he thinks so or not. Now Tracy is a different story. I'd like to see her double year over year."

"Double? C'mon, this year with what's going on in the market?"

"Yep. Taking her from $200K to $400K is nothing, a rounding error based on her role and our hitting budget like we did. She's the real deal."

"I like what I see with her. I could use her in 10 different roles. Great optionality. But it's a different story for you and Sasquatch. I keep telling you that you need to branch out more than you have, either into new products or expand your client base. If credit derivatives to life insurers crumble, I will be forced to put a bullet in your head."

"A fact not lost on either of us. I know."

"One more topic I want to cover with you. There a number of traders who think you and your team are difficult to work with."

"You can say it, Feinberg thinks I'm an asshole. Well, the feeling is mutual. And isn't that a natural part of the sales-trading dynamic anyway?"

"No doubt. I'm just telling you that he can create trouble for you. Kerr tells Bonet what to do, and Kerr definitely takes feedback from Feinberg as who's been playing nice in the trading sandbox."

"I know that."

"Just be careful with the smart-ass comments and play the game intelligently. You don't want to be known as a troublemaker. Those guys are the lead candidates for getting crushed come bonus day. That's it. Have Newberry stop by. I want to get his comp feedback before my dinner with Bonet tonight. The game has started."

Chip knew the game had started and was being played on many different levels. Karros wanted to have time to prepare for his dinner. Having a good sense of his team's individual bonus expectations gave him a better ability to play the compensation game with Bonet. It would also, importantly, enable him to better position his own bonus expectation. How he did that would be a function of the firm-wide bonus pool, the allocation to Sales vs. Trading, the specific allocation to his team and how he decided to meet, or not meet, each member of his team's expectations within those constraints.

Tonight's dinner would begin to fill in some pieces to the puzzle, at a minimum providing Karros with a far better idea of how much he had to work with and how much internal selling he had to do over the coming weeks.

$ $ $

"It's only 7 a.m., Franny. Why are you calling so early?" asked Deborah Goodman, after seeing it was her daughter calling. She had the maternal sense something was wrong.

Franny wasted no time. "I think he's going to file for divorce, if not now, soon. We had a terrible fight last night. He told me he was tired of me, and that I'm living on borrowed time with our marriage. Then he left to go somewhere else for the night. I can tell he just doesn't care about me. He's married to the money, not me."

"Calm yourself, get a shower, and come on up to my place for coffee and something to eat."

"Okay, I'll be up there as soon as I can."

Within the hour Franny had gotten herself ready and in a taxi for the journey to her mother's apartment on Park Avenue. She was shaken up by last night's events. As she stared out the taxi window, questions raced into her mind as quickly as the street numbers increased. What was wrong with her marriage? Was it really any different than her many friends who were married to Wall Streeters? Had she blindly headed down a destructive path or was it the path she had become conditioned to head down?

Lots of questions, with very few answers. Hence, the cottage industry of marriage counseling that had become a booming business in New York.

Deborah Goodman greeted her daughter as the doorbell rang. "Come in, Franny. Tell me what he's done to you."

"I told you, he said he was tired of me."

"Why did he say that? You've done everything a wife can do...gutted the SoHo place, rebuilt it from scratch, redecorated the beach house; you attend his boring business functions, are well known in the right social circles...what more does he want from you?"

"He said he's tired of me doing nothing but spending money, and he included you in that. He told me that 'leech' of a mother-in-law needs to get out of his life as well."

"He did, did he?"

"He called both of us money-whores, and said we're only concerned with spending his money."

Mother and daughter both decided another coffee was in order.

"And what other venom came out last night? How dare he call me a money-whore!"

"It just kept going round and round, always concluding with how tired of it he was. He said it was a destructive marriage, with him getting nothing out of it."

"What does the marriage counselor say about it all?"

"She's offered a number of suggestions, but Michael won't listen to any of it. That assumes he shows up for the session, which hasn't happened in a few months, at least."

"Maybe you need to speak with a lawyer, just in case he does something."

Franny shuddered at the thought, as the conversation continued for the better part of an hour before she headed back to SoHo. She couldn't get out of her head the fact that she had recently signed their revised pre-nup. Wishing not to think of her marriage in negative legal terms, she had signed the revised pre-nup after only a cursory read, at best. Feinberg had told her not to bother, that it's the type of document that needs periodic updating.

For her part Deborah Goodman withdrew into her own thoughts, dominated mostly by her maternal instinct to protect her scorned daughter. How dare that ingrate treat my daughter this way? Had he forgotten that it was her husband, now deceased, whose asset management firm had been a client of Smyth Johnston's when Feinberg was hired? It was she who, at a dinner function almost seven years ago, had spoken about Feinberg to Duncan Kerr, who was seated next to her. Franny had been dating Feinberg, when Deborah had sold Kerr on this math whiz kid with an astrophysics degree from MIT. At the very least, she helped Feinberg fast-track his entry onto Wall Street.

Prologue – 3

Tuesday, October 14, 2008
1:12 A.M.

The Peninsula
New York City

Rodriguez introduced himself to the Chinese woman who had been detained in the hotel manager's office for questioning. Li Juan was the name of the leggy girl in a miniskirt. She presented a New Jersey driver's license that indicated a Jersey City residence.

The forensic team arrived. Rodriguez asked Officer O'Roarke to brief them on the preliminary findings and guide them to the suite.

The detective turned his attention back to the girl.

She said she was a professional escort. That sounded much better than prostitute or whore, a euphemism of sorts.

Li Juan was high end for this business, Rodriguez thought, definitely not the type to be marketing her wares in the shadows of the Lincoln Tunnel. She was shaking noticeably as Rodriguez continued his questioning.

"Who called?" he asked.

"Well, he introduced himself as Jack Jones and asked me to come here at midnight."

"Why so late?"

"It's not unusual. Some people want to go drinking first, and then get a woman. For others, it's the other way around. In my profession you get used to everything. It's part of the business. If a client says show up at midnight, for $5,000, that's what you do."

Rodriguez nodded, "When did you get here, precisely?"

"About five minutes before midnight. I talked to the guy at Reception for a few minutes. He checked the guest list, which was marked with a suite companion, gave me a key, and I took the elevator up. I opened the door, saw the body, and returned downstairs. The hotel manager called 911. Since then I've been here."

"Do you have another gig tonight?"

"No, thank God."

"Did you know this Mr. Jones? Had you seen him before?"

The woman shrugged her slender shoulders. "Hard to say, because I didn't see his face. The man was lying sideways when I saw him from the doorway."

Plausible explanation, the detective thought.

"Why did he call you?"

"I don't know. He called, I answered it, and I promised to come. Someone had recommended me or else he had seen my ad online. You should ask him."

"He's dead."

"I didn't have anything to do with it. My business is hard enough without getting involved in homicides. Think about it."

"You okay with immigration?" Rodriguez asked.

The immigration ploy was an old police maneuver. If she got nervous, he would press more. Despite being *unnerved at what she had just witnessed, she maintained enough poise to convince Rodriguez of her honesty.*

She smiled. "Call INS if you want. But I can tell you something, my countrymen will soon own this place."

Chapter 7
Yo, Cabana Girl

Friday, February 1, 2008
1:15 P.M.

Pool deck, The Breakers
Palm Beach, Florida

South Florida in February was attractive to any banker, particularly Chip, Sasquatch, and Tracy who were less than two weeks away from bonus day. With their deal drought, now six months in length and still underway, the annual credit derivatives conference in Boca Raton was more welcome than ever. In the past, the conference was a must-attend for Sales and for traders who agreed to be off their money-making desks to meet with clients—not a large population. It was the place to "see and be seen," with each firm doing its utmost to put on a show more impressive than its competitors. Cocktail receptions, dinners, deep-sea fishing, golf outings with celebrities, yachts, and anything else the firms would indulge, in hopes of one-upping their competition and generating goodwill with their clients. In keeping with this spirit, one firm anchored its own yacht at the conference hotel dock, where it could flash its customized on-board trading floor. As if that weren't enough, the *pièce de résistance* was the corporate helicopter parked on the upper deck, also fully-equipped with an on-board trading floor.

"Great call on staying away from the conference hotel. The Breakers is pretty sweet, not to mention all the assholes we get to avoid."

The three bankers basked in the glorious low-80s sun on the pool deck. It was a lot nicer than what they left behind in New York.

"Tell me about it, Sasquatch. Beautiful day out, we're hanging by the pool, mahi-mahi tacos and stiff margaritas in hand. There's a lot to like…time for another dip in the pool. Looks like the Cabana Girl should get her head out of her Blackberry and do some real work right about now," as Chip motioned to his empty margarita glass before casually falling into the oceanside pool.

"Yo, Cabana Girl," Sasquatch hollered at Tracy. "Earn your keep. Why do you think we got you out of the office?"

"I know, I know. At your service gentlemen," she replied, taking the whole derogatory role play in good stride. Being the Cabana Girl by the pool at the Breakers in Palm Beach wasn't exactly bad work, even though it wasn't quite what she envisioned as a recent graduate from the University of Virginia. But then again, few things on Wall Street were. At least she got away from the office, where anxiety about the upcoming bonus day was starting to reach a fever pitch.

Chip stepped out of the pool and dried himself off as he sat back down in his chaise. The Cabana Girl had done her job well. A fresh margarita awaited him.

"Tracy, you're the best Cabana Girl in the business. When you get sick and tired of this gig, you have a great future in the hospitality business."

"No thanks. I signed up for this career to make some money, then maybe try something else when the wolf is away from the doorstep. That's the Wall Street dream, right? Is the dream alive, or am I a victim of bad timing. You guys keep talking about the end…"

"Good point. Chip, you should stop talking about the end. It can't be all that bad out there. Besides, you don't want your Cabana Girl to lose all hope."

"You're right. Tracy, don't forget this all will be yours one day. Give it another year, maybe two and this can be all yours after Sasquatch and I bail…or get nuked."

Trying to hold back the laughter, Sasquatch continued with his attempt at putting an optimistic tone on the business prospects.

"Seriously, it can't be all that bad. The Dow has roared back to 12,800 up a good 5 percent in the past week. The sky can't be falling if the equity markets are so bullish. Maybe our business is just taking a break, taking inventory of the last few years. That can be healthy in the long run."

"Dude, I hope you're right. I guess that's what we're down here to find out. Speaking of which, what time are we heading over to the conference tonight?"

"Let's try to get over there around 6:30. That ought to give us enough time to round up the clients for the fishing trip tomorrow. And we have the Mal and Feinberg meeting on Zeus. That means we have a couple more hours hanging here, with the best Cabana Girl in the business at our disposal."

"I heard that," said Tracy. "Just let me know when you're ready for another."

"Don't worry—we will."

$ $ $

It was an easy drive from Palm Beach to the conference hotel in Boca Raton, straight down I-95 about 30 miles. With Chip and Sasquatch feeling the bliss from their multiple margaritas, they handed over the keys to their rental Chevy Malibu to Cabana Girl, also doubling as the designated driver. The Malibu was in keeping with their intended low profile at the conference. Let the other bankers hire drivers and put on the show. Not to mention the last thing they wanted was for Karros to accuse them of profligate spending, with bonus day so close.

Provide no reason to get screwed on the most important day of the year.

Walking into the hotel they immediately noticed the swarm of industry players. Bankers, buy-side investors of all types and regions, asset managers, rating agency personnel, lawyers, accountants, and actuaries were everywhere, most wearing their blue blazers with khaki pants as if a requisitioned military uniform.

Settling in at one of the many bars scattered around the hotel, it was time to begin the search for their clients, particularly those who had agreed to go deep-sea fishing with them tomorrow.

"We need to find Mal first. Tracy, shoot him a quick text to let him know we're at whatever bar this is."

"Good idea: always better to drink before talking to Feinberg," Sasquatch declared.

Minutes later, Mal arrived and pushed his way through the horde to join the three.

"Yes, vodka and tonic please. Need some attitude adjustment, as I might go apeshit on Feinberg in the suite."

"Wow. That didn't take long. C'mon, at least have the meeting with the guy before you start to throttle him. What's up?"

"My senior management has become very nervous about Zeus and the other deals we've done since I was brought into the firm."

"Seems like everyone has an edge these days, including us. You know we haven't closed a deal of any consequence since Zeus. Everyone, except for the Euros, Middle East, and Asians are taking a break. Why do you think that is? What has everyone spooked?"

"I wish I knew. It's not like we're getting hit with losses on Zeus or the other deals yet, but the fall in market prices, from a liquidity perspective, is pretty scary. I guess they're reading a lot of the industry rags that seem to be spreading the fear factor about defaults and foreclosures being on the rise."

"Fear of the unknown. Maybe that's a healthy thing and good for the market longer term. I mean, the deal calendar has been a runaway train for a few years now. We all have to keep in mind that these deals are not risk free. "Free money" is just a hollow notion. Let's face it, these deals have risk. But that risk has been rated by multiple rating agencies, it's mitigated by a lot of protections built into the deal structures, it has managers whose reputations are staked on deal performance, and it has numerous marquee-name global investors who have participated far more than we have in the space. That's a lot of collective diligence in the process."

"That's my spiel to my management team. These guys are very conservative and are glass half-empty, defensive in nature. I suppose that's probably a good thing for the franchise."

"Alright, let's chug the drinks down. Time to go see your buddy Feinberg."

"He's everyone's buddy. Don't let me monopolize him—there's plenty of him to go around."

$ $ $

Chip and company escorted their client up to the suite where they were to meet with Feinberg. The suite was one of many rented by the banks in attendance, typically used both for client entertainment by night and private meetings away from the hotel lobby chaos by day. Feinberg had seen fit to reserve the finest suite available, complete with bar, food, a lavish master bedroom, and balcony which seemed to protrude into the ocean. Chip and Sasquatch had often speculated on whether that was the real reason Feinberg, otherwise highly inaccessible to clients, liked to go to these conferences.

"Michael, you remember Mal McMahon from Broadway Life. He's an investor in Zeus," Chip said, as if to remind Feinberg the specific purpose of this meeting. In fairness, Feinberg had had countless meetings throughout the day with various clients.

"Hi Mal. Good to see you."

"Thanks, Michael," replied Mal, the pleasantries abruptly coming to an end. "So, what has everyone so nervous about the Zeus-type deals? My management team has their antennas up and is wondering if I've delivered them a bill of goods."

"Sorry to sound cavalier about it all, but these are trades. Some are winners, some are not. Zeus has been fine except for a few defaults that impact the lower tranches. No one likes to see that. You should call 14th Street to speak about the specifics of those defaults. As to the broader market, do I see any type of default contagion, correlation across asset classes from subprime about to take off? No, I do not."

"Would you be willing to speak with my guys about your view?"

"No, I would not. I'm just a credit trader, not a clairvoyant—besides, the manager is the one they need to hear from, not me."

Mal could only wonder if Feinberg was being evasive or outright misleading. He struggled to separate his prior knowledge of Feinberg as a sharp-elbowed win-at-all-cost trader from the facts at hand on Zeus.

"I see. Blame it on the manager if this thing goes pear-shaped."

"You can look at it however you want. The fact of the matter is that the manager, as the portfolio selector, is the one you need to talk to if you are really worried about this deal. That's the right path for you; and as you know from the offering documents, they are the party legally responsible for the deal's performance."

"Now you're going to hide behind the legal crap…what about the relationship I have with your firm? You think I did the deal because of the manager, which, by the way, I noticed is not exactly a major force in the business."

"Same old nonsense from you credit derivative rookies. You live in fear that the big bad traders are going to rip you off, then when we insert a third-party manager into the mix to protect your interests, you still think you're being ripped off."

"A rookie I'm not. I know the game pretty damn well after sitting on your side of the business for so long. Thanks for the lack of transparency and double-speak. Hey Chip, this meeting is over. I need to go take a shower to wash off the slime."

As the meeting that had been scheduled for thirty minutes came to a less than cordial, premature close, Feinberg pulled Chip aside as Mal and the others waited in the hallway.

"Chip, sorry, but I'm triple-booked tomorrow. I can't go out on the boat with you and your clients."

"You are fucking kidding me. I set this up as an opportunity to spend time with you, the head credit trader, to talk about upcoming deals, the market, issues you see on the horizon, the whole bit. Some of my guys came down just for this. What do you want me to tell them?"

"Tell them I'm triple-booked and had to bail. I can talk to them another time back in New York. Make it go away—that's the way it has to work."

"You are totally screwing me in front of my clients. These are the same clients who are beginning to think you're screwing them. And you expect these guys to keep doing deals with you... I'm doing all I can to keep these guys in the game, and you walk away from the trip tomorrow. Suit yourself but don't blame me when your U.S. investors tell you to fuck off after you show them the next deal."

"And I guess you're out of a job at that point in time. Maybe I should call Bonet and Kerr right now... That will be too bad for you, not that I will care, as I can find more clients elsewhere through the global sales force," Feinberg said as he shooed Chip out of the suite. He had other business to attend to.

Chip went to find Mal and the others. Bailing on the trip was tantamount to telling the clients he doesn't give a damn about them, or far more importantly, their outcome on Zeus or the other deals they had done with his desk in prior years. In essence the fishing trip had backfired even before it got started—hardly the reassurance he was hoping to provide his key clients.

"Fuck I hate that guy. He just told me he isn't going on the fishing trip tomorrow."

"Typical from Feinberg. Didn't he just screw us a few months back in Pebble Beach as well...hmmm, seems like a pattern is developing."

"Very disappointing. That means I don't get to hold him over the side of the boat, chumming the water with him tomorrow. I was really looking forward to having that guy out in the ocean with nowhere to hide," Mal added.

"Let's go do some emotional eating. I made a reservation at Don Shula's nearby," Tracy said. A couple of other clients were supposed to be joining them.

$ $ $

After a heavy steak and red wine dinner—a Wall Street culinary staple—it was time to head back to the conference hotel for some additional market reconnaissance. Chip had learned that some of the best market insight could be gleaned late in the evening at these conferences. Rumor, fact, innuendo could readily be picked up from clients, competition, or other market participants—some of them completely in the bag. There was always something interesting to unearth, simply by milling around the lobby talking with others in the business.

"Guys, thanks for dinner. I'm going to catch up with some other folks. I have plenty more time with you clowns tomorrow on the boat."

"No worries, Mal. I'm sure we'll bump into you some more tonight anyway," Chip added. "Alright boys and girls," speaking to Sasquatch and Tracy, "let's go round up the guys for tomorrow and make sure everyone has all the details on the trip."

"If they don't, then they're asleep at the switch. I've sent them emails, called them, the whole nine yards.

Everyone is confirmed and says they know where to go in the morning," Tracy reassured her bosses.

"Dude, she's not just the best Cabana Girl in the business; she's the best events planner in the business as well. She has many talents, remember. That's why we hired her." Sasquatch often relished the fact that Tracy was on the team now. He used to have her role when he started with Chip. Now, there was someone in title and responsibility lower than him on the totem pole. Never mind the fact he had been playing the role of team bitch until recently while she was doing so at age 22.

"She sure is. You've trained her well. Hey, let's go smoke a cigar on one of the yachts out back."

"A cigar would be good right about now—take the edge off the booze a bit. Tracy, you're in," as if to tell her she needed to set aside any gender tendencies and join the alpha male cigar club.

"Tracy is in—this is an equal opportunity team," Chip commanded, in typical flippant fashion.

Chip pulled three Montecristo #2s from his blazer pocket as they walked outside and boarded one of the many yachts parked at the hotel dock. Along with the others on board who had the same idea, the world didn't seem so bad if only that precise moment could be frozen in time. Maybe the world wasn't coming to an end after all, despite the widespread trepidation they and their clients had begun to feel recently. The cigars took them to a happier place.

After making the rounds aboard the yacht, the three agreed it was time to extinguish the Cubans, get some sleep, and make the drive back to their self-imposed retreat in Palm Beach. As they headed back through the main lobby, Chip told Sasquatch and Tracy to give him 30 seconds. With that, he pulled out his phone and inconspicuously snapped a photo of someone across the lobby.

"What are you up to now?"

"I thought it might be a good idea to snap a photo of Feinberg with his date."

"Seriously?"

"Yes, seriously. He's a bigger asshole to his wife than he is to his clients and salesmen. Imagine that."

"Apparently. I guess the only question is whether he screws us or his hookers more."

"And to think people like this are the supposed captains of industry these days. How and when did it go so wrong in this business? Makes me sick. Let's get out of here."

As they waited for their designated driver, Tracy, to retrieve the car, Chip glanced at the photo. A bit grainy, Feinberg was easily recognizable as was his companion whose attire left no doubt as to her profession.

$ $ $

The next morning came entirely too quickly. At 7:45 a.m. Tracy arrived at the harbor. It was earlier than the others, as she, in her servile Cabana Girl capacity, was to ensure the boat and arrangements were as had been discussed. Erring on the safe side, everything seemed more than adequate, with enough food and drinks for twice the number of attendees. Not counting the captain and two deckhands, she felt certain the 120 beers would suffice for the 10 people in total making the scheduled five-hour voyage. Anything leftover would augment the tip they'd be giving the captain and crew

Shortly after 8:15 the shuttle transporting their clients arrived, most of whom appeared tired and hung over from the prior day's 16 hours of nonstop conference activities. Smoking, drinking, and fine dining, decadent as it may seem, takes its toll.

"I don't know, Chip, this is either going to be a great time or a frickin' nightmare for me. I feel like shit and we haven't even gotten on the boat yet. By the way, where's Feinberg?" Mal said, still upset at last night's all but useless meeting in the Smyth Johnston suite.

"Well, sorry to say he bailed on this. The guy decided to triple-book himself today. Fear ye not, I got him to agree to sit down with you and anyone else who wants to meet with him when we get back in New York. I'm not happy about it either, given that it makes me look like an asshole in front of some of my best clients."

"I'm sure Feinberg cares about your feelings, really," quipped Sasquatch, walking a few feet behind them.

"I'm sure he wouldn't care if I fall overboard and get savaged by a shark today."

"Actually, there might be some social appeal in that outcome for all of us—one less Wall Street sales guy to worry about," Mal smiled as each attendee took turns climbing aboard. Shortly after, they cracked open a breakfast beer while loading up on food and Demerol.

Blue skies were on the horizon. It looked like a nice day for some fishing, despite it being on the cool side at 52 degrees. About 45 minutes into the one-hour voyage to their destination, the wind had picked up and the sun had receded into the clouds. Plowing their way through the choppy seas, no one wanted to sound the alarm that this had, at least for the time being, ceased being enjoyable. The boat pounded up and down across the waves, as the collection of bankers and clients began to sit down and hold on for stability.

"This voyage seems to be going about as well as the credit derivatives market right about now. You know, life imitating art, or business. Something like that," Mal said.

Chip swallowed hard, taking deep breaths of the sea air. "This will settle down, just like the business will settle down. It's a bump in the road, man. We've made a killing in this business the last 10 years. I call this a correction. All markets have to go through this stage. It's a form of market legitimization. Seriously, you think a multitrillion-dollar-sized market is just going to stop after it encounters some issues?"

"Can you talk to my management team?" Mal added. "These guys are convinced we're getting screwed with our paltry alternative asset strategy."

"Dude, you work for a life insurance company. There's no one more risk-averse than your guys. Tell them to grow some balls—I mean, they're so far removed from the real risk they ought not to be getting paid anything."

It was interesting to hear the divergent perspectives on the market: gloom and doom on the one hand, with business-as-usual optimism on the other hand. Of course, everyone hoped for the latter, with the current rise in credit losses and turmoil being in fact just a bump in the road, an otherwise healthy sign in a high-growth market.

"I'll quote you on that as soon as I get back to my office. Hey, anyone up for a social?"

"A social, already?" asked Chip incredulously.

Not that he was objecting. A social was a spontaneous call to have everyone at a given function shotgun a beer. It was typically done as a rallying cry to get everyone in good spirits when at an outing such as this one. They could occur in the morning, on the golf course, late at night...anytime, anywhere, even in the middle of the ocean.

Despite the churning sea seeming to only gain force, most, out of false bravado, participated in the social as they approached their deep-water destination. The captain and crew, feeling no ill effects from the sea, readied the equipment for use. No sooner was the first pole placed in the water than the first client went below deck, proclaiming he wasn't feeling well. Sure enough, he began vomiting as the others laughed hysterically, finding perverse humor in his plight.

"What a pussy," said the client manning the chair. "Tell him to get some balls. By the way, someone get me another beer."

As the fallen comrade lapsed into full-stage seasickness below deck, others followed suit. One after another, as if in a chain reaction, either went below deck or, more expediently, clung to the side rails of the boat as profuse quantities of vomit cascaded into the ocean.

"I want to jump out of my skin. Why did I sign up for this?" Mal yelled, in between projectiles.

"Someone shoot me, please," commented another client.

"Great call on doing that social. It seems to really have helped everyone."

As time wore on, with little abatement of the seasickness, Chip thought it might be time for some discretion. He should at least ask the question if for no other reason than as a matter of client service.

"Should we turn back and get the hell off the boat?" Chip offered up.

"Fuck no, get me another beer to wash down the vomit," screamed the same client manning the chair, seemingly the only one actually enjoying himself. Except of course for the captain and crew who must have found considerable humor in seeing a bunch of high-flying banker types brought to their knees by Mother Nature.

Battling through the pain for another two hours, snagging one good size yellowfin tuna, unanimity was mercifully reached about aborting the mission and heading back to shore.

For Chip, Sasquatch, and Tracy, the outing could not have gone any more awry. Though it would be memorable, being trapped on the open sea with everyone on board violently seasick was not exactly as drawn up in the client entertainment playbook.

"Thanks a lot for the great time. Can't wait to puke again with the industry watching," said one client disembarking the boat.

"I have to hand it to you—that was a nightmare not soon to be forgotten," said another.

"Note to file: Stick to golf or other less adventurous outings. We've done race cars, hunting, skiing, golf, tennis, you name it. Nothing will compare to this outing. At least let's hope not," Chip said as they got the clients back on the shuttle and back to the hotel.

Tracy took care of the captain and crew with a tip that combined money and about 100 of the 120 beers they started out with. It was time to retreat to The Breakers and recuperate for tomorrow, the last day of the conference. Thankfully, they had nothing formal planned for that night.

Chip and the others were left to ponder whether the fiasco of a fishing outing was a metaphorical glimpse into their futures, or, more benignly, simply a rough patch or pregnant pause in the credit derivatives market.

Chapter 8
My ass is on fire

Monday, February 11, 2008
7:45 A.M.

Smyth Johnston Trading Floor

Most bankers viewed Bonus Day as their Christmas, Diwali, Hanukkah, or other relevant multicultural holiday, with the role of Santa Claus played by whomever was handing out the all-important envelope. The fact that Bonus Day did not coincide with the actual calendar year created a different conception of time. Much like January 1 in the rest of the world, Bonus Day became that mark in time that separated the new from the old, rendering the calendar year all but meaningless, apart from being a measure of time by which profit was calculated as a determinant for Bonus Day outcomes.

Anxiety had reached an expected crescendo. No one was doing any productive work; adrenaline was pulsing through the veins—aided in many cases by obscene quantities of caffeine—and the bathrooms were noticeably overcrowded. Entering a bathroom was done at one's own peril, invariably being immediately greeted by a cacophony of bowel movements and, at times, vomiting, both unmistakable proof of the power stress can exert over the human body.

Beyond serving as the unofficial New Year on Wall Street, Bonus Day also provided an even more important "signaling effect" to bankers. The size of the bonus check answered many questions: What is my perceived value? Does the firm value me as an employee and want to keep me around? Does it value the prospects of my future contribution? Does it like my business and believe it to be part of the core, forward-looking strategy?

A good result, defined either in absolute terms or relative to one's peer group, meant it was time to head into the "new year" feeling positive and ready to do the 364-day dance all over again. A bad result, using the same metrics, meant heading into the new year feeling negative, underappreciated, or just plain unwanted by the firm. For those in the latter camp, it meant that it might be time to search for a new job, a better offer from a competitor.

Playing the *bid-away* game was the only means by which an employee could exert leverage against their firm. It was a tried and tested tactic: show up with a bid-away, point the shotgun at the firm's head, and turn on the truth machine. It was a strange if not unsavory convention, widely accepted as a legitimate way to demonstrate one's personal market value in times of career distress, typically executed right after receiving a bad Bonus Day result. It was the Wall Street version of free agency in sports, but with shorter contracts. Guaranteed bonuses were only for a year or two at the most, and in scant supply.

As with free agency in sports, it was a practice that engendered a two-way street of disloyalty between employee and employer. It was, quoting many an inarticulate professional athlete, "just the business."

Translated into even more prosaic language, it said, "If I can get a better deal elsewhere, then I will. And why wouldn't I get paid what the market bears? I don't really care what logo is on my jersey or business card. Besides, I can only do this for so long anyway. Go for it, it's all about ME."

The bid-away game could be played a discreet number of times over the course of a Wall Street career. No one wanted to gain the mercenary reputation by shopping firms too often and thereby broadcasting their lack of company loyalty. In addition to the financial rationale, there was, not to be diminished, the ego-assuaging rationale for playing the game. Not surprisingly, with high compensation came large egos. What better way to even the score of a bruised ego than by showing up weeks or even days later with the loaded shotgun. In a flash, that ego is transformed to its previous gargantuan state.

Following what undoubtedly was a restless night, the Smyth Johnston professional staff marched into work with the anticipation of a child running down the stairs on Christmas morning. The numbers were in; actually the numbers had been in for at least a week. There was no longer anything that could stop someone from getting their envelope.

No time was left on the compensation season clock.

No time for further backroom politicking, ass-kissing, pandering, or anything else of the sort. In the span of a few hours, everyone's questions would be answered with the anticlimactic opening of the envelopes, followed shortly thereafter by the predictable banter and mixed emotions for the rest of the day. The next day, as if a giant "reset" button had been pressed, it would be back to the business of making money with the annual lame-duck session having officially ended. Alternatively, it would be time to start calling headhunters.

This particular bonus season had been one of the most challenging. The overall numbers for the year were good, but in the second half, business had dropped off. Apart from Kerr and his senior managers, nobody knew what that would mean for bonuses. There had been rumors of anywhere from near zero bonuses for some to 50 percent less than last year. The rumors engendered a certain element of neurosis, with some on edge and more anxious than others.

Exemplifying the anxiety, Chip ran into one of the mortgage sales guys in the cafeteria.

"Hey Chip, you ever notice how the muffins are mispriced here? Definite arbitrage opportunity. They are three bucks here, but only two on the street. What you can do is buy them down there and then set up a little stand outside of here and sell them for two-and-half, and shazam... You got yourself a trade... What do you think there, buddy," he rambled on deliriously. "Maybe that's what I'll do if I get screwed today."

Chip laughed politely, sensing Jim's abject level of anxiety. People reacted to Bonus Day in different ways.

"We'll see, Jim, we'll see." He turned around and rolled his eyes to Sasquatch, as if to suggest their colleague needed a long vacation. Get a grip on yourself.

After Chip and Sasquatch had grabbed their coffees, they settled into a conference room off the trading floor.

"So, how bad did Karros screw you?"

"No worse than I'm about to screw you," replied Chip, laughing. "It really wasn't too bad. These guys are really good. Somehow every year they're able to hit that number that doesn't blow you away, but doesn't have you walking out the door either. I kind of wish I'd gotten screwed much worse, and would easily be able to walk out the door. I feel like a crack addict—as long as I get a decent fix, it's hard for me to break the habit."

"Okay, without further ado give me the fucking envelope, please. I'm about to shit in my pants. I have the constitution of a jellyfish right about now, and I've been to the bathroom five times today already. My ass is on fire."

"Well, Sasquatch," Chip started into his spiel, "you had a pretty good year, your production numbers are good, but as you know there were some issues in other parts of the firm."

He could only laugh as he trotted out the same stilted, antiseptic managerial language he had just been on the receiving end of.

"I really went to bat for you, to the mats, balls to the wall to get the best result for you."

Sasquatch couldn't take it anymore. "C'mon, man, the envelope."

"Look, you ought to like the number, and if you continue to kick ass there'll be more next year. Tomorrow, tomorrow, it's always a year away." Chip was now taunting him as he humanely handed him the envelope.

As Sasquatch tore open the envelope, Chip reminded him that the balance of cash vs. stock was better for the director level than for the managing directors. Sasquatch's all-in amount was 20 percent less than the previous year, but still an impressive $850,000. It broke down to $150,000 salary and a $700,000 bonus, further consisting of $500,000 in cash and $200,000 in stock.

The amount of cash vs. stock was another potential Bonus Day surprise. Instead of cash, anyone making more than a hundred grand received some percentage of their compensation in Smyth Johnston stock. The stock was typically packaged as a grant, phantom stock, or options. The stock award, however structured, gave the recipient the opportunity for outsized returns if the firm performed well in following years. Stock grants were the firm's way of aligning its success with the employees. The downside for the employees was that the stock was always restricted for several years and geared such that the upside would pay off only in extraordinarily positive circumstances. As part of the compensation mix they could expire worthless if the firm performed poorly in the ensuing years, in effect retroactively shrinking the bonus. Not exactly *money good*, cash in the bank.

Thankfully, the stock award this year was actual shares, which would vest in three years. It wasn't cash but it was better than options or some other form of compensation with performance conditions, more specifically, conditions outside of one's control.

Chip gave Sasquatch some time to digest the news as he studied his facial expression intently.

"Not bad. Thanks a lot for your work here. It's a bit more than I expected to tell you the truth. The stock I'll get in three years, and the half-mill bonus will be something like $275,000 after taxes, et cetera. That'll keep the wolves at bay for a while," Sasquatch said. His honesty was unusual in these discussions, reflecting their long relationship. Most bankers acted disappointed to their boss, always conveying that they wanted more.

"I feel pretty good about the results. There was a lot of back and forth about the second-half business slowdown. Frankly that could have absolutely killed us, so I guess we may have dodged a bullet."

"I know. They could have screwed us outright or stuffed us full of illiquid company stock."

"I'm sure some people are looking at that reality right now."

"For the record, believe me, I like cash. Hard to pay bills with restricted company stock."

"So what are you doing with the money? What color Porsche are you buying?"

"I've already bought my Porsche, actually two of them. One was blonde, the other brunette. Both were very expensive and, ultimately, not nearly as much fun as they should've been," Sasquatch answered, lamenting his first two marriages.

"That sucks, but at least this can help pay for part of the next settlement," Chip laughed.

"Dude, don't say that. Way too painful of an idea. Like you and a lot of people around here, I don't want to do this forever, and another divorce would mean I'd have to work until I'm 80 or something."

"What are you gonna do? Put your check in the bank? Are you reloading for another year? Any news on Lehman?" Chip asked.

"Yeah, I have to keep doing this at least until my real estate empire gets back on track. I guess I'll talk to Lehman some more to see what they have to say, but I think it would need to be something pretty compelling for me to make a move. So what are you going to do with your bonus?"

"I'm sure my wife already has taken care of that. Can't wait to get home tonight to find out what she has in store for me. Quite a division of labor: I make the money, she spends it."

"So you guys are looking at a summer place or what?"

"Nope… I think I'm happy with what we have, don't want to expand the empire yet. I think muni bonds or my mattress sound good right around now."

"Chip, I know you've been thinking about leaving the business, but let's roll for one more year. By the way, there's no way I'll stay to deal with Feinberg and his henchmen without you."

Sasquatch wanted Chip to stick around for another year. Selfishly he knew Chip's departure would put him in a precarious position. The team would have less bandwidth, both in terms of productivity and internal credibility. With this would come less leverage and seniority to work the system, particularly compensation. He needed that leverage to keep the money coming in. He wasn't out of the woods yet, financially speaking.

"I'll think about it, but we need to figure out how to get the deals cooking. We were spared this year. Next year there'll be no stay of execution if we don't do a consistent flow of deals. Okay, I'm done here. You get to have the chat with Tracy."

As Chip left the meeting room, Tracy, who had been waiting outside, walked in. Soon enough she had opened her envelope.

"So, what do you think?"

"Well, it's okay. I was expecting a little bit more," Tracy responded, in a tone that Sasquatch couldn't tell was sincere or feigned.

"Hey, I can tell you $250,000 is a good outcome for an associate. You have a different comp curve, much steeper than mine, as mine is to Chip's, and his to Karros's. You're an associate; keep that in mind. It takes a while to prove yourself internally, build your own client relationships, et cetera. For now, you're part of a productive team learning the ropes and getting seasoned for the future. Don't forget, you're in a much better position than most of your associate-level peers."

"I know. I guess I can pay off some of my student loans."

"You can pay off all your student loans and most of your future kid's student loans. This is good."

"It's a lot of money, for sure. My friend in a similar seat at Goldman brought in $350,000. What's the difference?"

"Tracy, do yourself a favor. In this business be thankful for everything you get, and even more thankful every time you get it. Each year you survive represents a quantum leap closer to financial independence. You can always point to someone else at Goldman, here at Smyth Johnston, or anywhere else on the Street whose bonus outcome appears better. You'll drive yourself crazy if you spend your time this way. The system works, if not year by year, in the final result. That is, if you can survive long enough."

Similar conversations to these were playing out in virtually every office or conference room in the bank. Absent getting totally screwed, most who were in productive roles at the bank received payouts that were on balance "fair" in relative terms. There really were few instances where someone opened up their envelope in complete horror. Expectations were always well-managed, typically within a range of 20 percent. If someone was going to get screwed, they knew it beforehand or had been fired well in advance of Bonus Day.

In absolute terms, the payouts, regardless of stock vs. cash components, were a lot of money by any measure, which meant an instantaneous opportunity for lifestyle improvements. There were those who paid off student loans, mortgages, divorce settlements, and other financial obligations—cleaning up their personal balance sheets so to speak. Then there were those who did the exact opposite by acquiring more material possessions having little if any utilitarian purpose. Second or third homes, race cars, exotic travel, wardrobe upgrades; you name it, the acquisition race to the top was in full stride, with caution being thrown to the wind.

Today was a good day to be a banker.

$ $ $

Duncan Kerr, as was his custom, made a practice circling back with Smyth Johnston's star performers, the biggest money makers, to ensure they were content with their compensation outcomes. Michael Feinberg was atop that short list.

"Before we talk about yesterday, how is everything going at home with Franny? This is a tough business on marriages, and I know how hard you go at it here."

"My marriage sucks, to be frank. Very little if any joy coming out of it, but I'm not interested in thinking about it, here or anywhere. It is what it is at this point."

"So when I see your mother-in-law at the next business or charity function, I'll have to listen to what an asshole you are?"

"Of course. It's all my fault. Franny has nothing to do with it whatsoever."

"Just be fair about things if it heads to the divorce court. So how do you feel about yesterday?"

"You know, $12 million isn't that much. I think it should've been higher. It's less than four percent of my desk's total P&L contribution."

"Michael, you know you're in the upper echelon of payouts across the firm, not just in my division. You also know the comp curve flattens out the higher the contribution."

"What about outside of the firm? Look, you and I both know I can find another bank willing to guarantee me more than four percent of my book. Or, there are the hedge funds, where the house doesn't pocket 90 percent of my team's work product. Not to mention the favorable personal tax structure I could have if I wasn't working at a monolithic bank. You're getting a steal."

"Michael, I know that. But what they can't do is give you what you have here. I'm talking about the platform at your disposal here, the internal credibility you've built, and the commitment from senior management to support your business. You never know what you might be walking into at a competitor, or the dangers you may face at a here-today, gone-tomorrow hedge fund. I've seen that trade not work many times."

"Yeah, except for a 3 by 15 guarantee," Feinberg said referring to a guaranteed bonus of $15 million per year for 3 years.

"Multiyear guarantees are hard to come by, even for you, Michael. Even if you find one, it will be hard to replicate what you have here. To be clear, you have a money-printing machine here and a high delta of it continuing. So far, the firm has paid you more than $50 million in your 7 years here, including your first 2 years as an associate making peanuts."

"Maybe there is another way of showing me some love, beyond the dollars," Feinberg added, sensing Kerr was willing to listen to his spontaneous demand.

"Michael, let's not play games with each other. Tell me what you have in mind."

"I clearly outperformed the guys in London. Don't you think I ought to assume responsibility for them as well? I know you like the London crowd a lot, but frankly my team is much better than they are. The proof is in the pudding. The same applies to Asia."

"A lot of those guys are new to the firm over there. I think it's too early to start changing the game on them in terms of reporting lines. I don't want to have an exodus and have to rebuild the desk. Let's give them a chance to acclimate to the Smyth Johnston system."

"Think about it. If my comp curve is flattening, then I want my power base to be upward sloping. Sort of like how I notice yours has been in recent years."

"Fair enough. Let me think about it…just don't do anything stupid. Before we wrap this up, I ran into the CEO of Broadway Life the other night at an industry function—by the way, the type of function you'd need to go to constantly when in senior management. He told me he wasn't happy about the Zeus deal. He said he received a mark on their tranche that has them deep underwater. He said they're thinking about suing; they think you stuffed them."

"This would be a great business if the clients weren't such whiners. Spreads have widened on the portfolio, and we had a couple of credit events causing losses on the lower tranches. It's always the same shit with these guys. They're miles away from actual losses. Spreads widen, spreads tighten, and their mark-to-market changes accordingly. That's the way this works. If the clients don't comprehend that, then Karros and the other sales guys suck at what they do."

"Yeah, that trade seemed to have added a few million to your bonus, didn't it? The trade was good, we needed it, but we don't need any undue adversity or publicity with clients these days. I have enough issues to deal with in the rest of my division as well as the others. Talk to Karros. And keep up the stellar results this year, I need more Zeus deals, a lot more. Keep going short, but just make sure the sales guys know what you're doing."

"Okay, I know my official budget is $500 million, but what's the unofficial?"

"I need you to deliver $700 million this year."

"$700 million? Only a 40 percent increase, in this environment?"

"You deliver me a 40 percent increase, and I'll deliver you a 40 percent increase. Besides, Bear is about to go belly up, so that will mean less competition for you. Our platform will get you more business."

"Can you put that in writing, or is that the full faith and credit of Duncan Kerr, just like my last bonus?"

"Stop fucking with me, Michael."

"Give some serious thought to my global role. At $700 million that makes me 25 percent of your entire division, based on last year's numbers. And don't think I haven't noticed the declining state of some of your other businesses."

Kerr detected the not-so passive-aggressive power play, a grab for the throne, when he saw one. Feinberg had designs on the empire he had built. Tens of millions of dollars were no longer enough for him. It was an act of aggression, both disrespectful and disloyal to all Kerr had done for him, including hiring him.

He had no intention of handing over the keys, at least not as of yet. He would need to be careful with Feinberg, even after he ascended to the CEO's office.

As the meeting concluded, Joey Karros, who had been chatting with Kerr's secretary during some of Feinberg's time in the office, quickly departed. He had seen Feinberg enter Kerr's office and thought it might be useful to get a closer look at what was transpiring. Charming as he was, his idle chat with Kerr's secretary was nothing more than a ruse.

Ever the political tactician, he wanted to stay abreast of any developments within the Smyth Johnston power structure.

$ $ $

It was a new day, a new year, a time to turn the page and move forward to begin the next 364-day survival campaign. That had to be the mindset, a necessary psychological defense mechanism that enabled most to justify the prospect of tossing another year into the Wall Street abyss.

Chip walked onto the trading floor, following yet another life-sapping, two-hour commute from Long Island. Today's journey included the all-too-common 20-minute delay just outside of Penn Station. The reason, most likely contrived, was not having an available platform to come into. At least it wasn't the hackneyed excuse of "mechanical problems" or "accident on the tracks."

Inexplicable delays of this type somehow occurred over and over again. It was part of the daily rigor of commuting into Manhattan, something any seasoned commuter such as Chip would strive to avoid letting become a source of aggravation—with varying degrees of success. At least today's mishap wasn't in August, with the accompanying air conditioning malfunction to ratchet up the quotient of pain. There were times when Chip felt he was on the brink of snapping, akin to a killer pleading temporary insanity. He often wondered why more people didn't snap.

The trading floor was quiet as he settled into his tight operating quarters, certainly quieter than the prior two months during compensation season. The parade of visitors had retreated to their home offices, meeting rooms were suddenly available again, and the multitude of desks were filled with bankers "locked and loaded" for the year ahead. The natural buzz of the trading floor, replete with its animal spirits, had returned. Chip had become inoculated to the buzz, so much so that he no longer heard it. By contrast, anyone else visiting the trading floor for the first time would've thought it pure pandemonium.

It was a relief to have the drama of Bonus Day behind them, despite the unsettling thoughts of what they would need to do in the ensuing year to garner another satisfactory bonus payout. The slate had been wiped clean—none of their production from the previous year mattered—it was time to start putting points on the board again.

What have you done for me lately?

That unsettling feeling for Chip, Sasquatch, and Tracy resumed where it had left off before compensation season. Would their drought of deals persist, or would there be renewed interest in credit derivatives from life insurers and elsewhere in the U.S. investor base? There was only one way to find out. If the former proved to be the case, they'd better reinvent themselves by figuring out other deals to do with their client base.

"Hey, Chip, you feel like a coffee?" asked Ben Cook, who had snuck up to their desk without fanfare.

"Actually, I could use a reload—my commute sucked today."

"Let's head to that deli on the corner. I may grab a bacon, egg, and cheese sandwich. Besides, I have something to tell you."

The two, having received their breakfast supplies in inimitable New York efficiency, sat down in the nondescript corner deli across the street from their office.

"Okay Ben, what do you have for me?"

"Don't kill the messenger... I'm telling you this as a friend, and to note I'd get fired on the spot if Feinberg found out about our chat. You can't tell anyone, not even Sasquatch."

"Talk to me."

"Look, I work for the guy, but telling you this is the right thing to do. I need someone around here to drink beer with from time to time. Anyway, I hear that Feinberg has Compliance pulling tapes and emails on the Zeus deal. Not sure why, but it started happening right after a meeting he had with Kerr yesterday."

All phone conversations on the trading floor were recorded. Most trades were done verbally over the phone, and banks taped the conversations in case a client tried to renege on a deal. Tapes could be used for other purposes, too.

"Pulling tapes? What the fuck is that guy up to? We bail his ass out on the deal and now he pulls this type of shit."

"It's not the first time I've seen him do it. My guess is that Broadway Life has either sued or is threatening to do so. That's the drift I caught after he came out of Kerr's office yesterday. Trouble on the horizon, and he is not going to be the one taking the heat. He is going to hang someone out to dry, and usually that means a sales guy."

"I guess I don't need to finish the coffee," Chip responded as his mind frenetically raced to recollect what transpired over the course of his team's involvement in getting Zeus done.

"Sorry man, but I wanted you to know what your buddy Feinberg is up to."

"I appreciate it. It's nice to know there's some decency left in this game."

"It probably means I'll hit the glass ceiling in this business sooner than later."

As Chip returned to the desk, Sasquatch immediately sensed the panic in his eyes.

"Dude, you look like you saw a ghost. What did Ben tell you?"

"Let's get off the desk ASAP. Grab Tracy. She needs to hear this. Baptism by fire time for the young lady."

The three quickly secured one of the many available conference rooms off the trading floor. Chip needed his team involved, despite Ben's caveat of keeping the information quiet.

"Ben just told me that Feinberg is having Compliance pull tapes and check our emails on Zeus."

"Are you kidding me? Makes perfect sense—we bail the guy out and he looks to screw us. Why am I surprised?" added Sasquatch, as his blood pressure started cooking.

"Of course. The three of us need to go through every email and phone conversation we had on Zeus and find out if there's anything he can manipulate against us," Chip said.

"Welcome to Wall Street, Tracy."

"Thanks a lot. This is really fun."

Chip realized that his bonus check had not yet cleared, and might not for as long as another couple weeks. What had been panic, minutes ago, became paranoia. Had Feinberg somehow caught wind of his conversation with Jack Bonfiglio from the SEC? Could the bank actually not make the wire, cancel his bonus? Whatever the case, moments like this explained why investment banking can be terrible for one's mental health.

"Hey Sasquatch, Tracy—when do bonus checks clear? Have yours cleared yet?"

"I thought they were supposed to hit our accounts anytime now. Mine hasn't as of this morning. And believe me, I'm checking multiple times a day."

"Mine hasn't cleared yet either," Tracy added in an attempt to ease Chip's mind.

"See what this game will do to you? I'm not paranoid, just that everyone is out to get me. Let's do our homework on Zeus. Triage mode for the rest of the day."

Back on the desk, the three spent the rest of the day scouring any and all emails, recounting, as best they could, their Zeus phone calls, and even retracing their drinks session with Mal at the Whiskey Bar several months ago. It was all such a waste of their time, a purely defensive waste of time at that. Chip had had to do something similar to combat traders before, but never had Compliance pulled tapes on him. He wondered if there would be some note in his HR file, or would it even matter? In any case, it was not a good start to the new year.

By the end of the useless day, Chip, Sasquatch, and Tracy went to their favorite refuge off the trading floor: the Blarney Stone. Chip was convinced Feinberg had nothing even remotely incriminating on him or his teammates. The facts, however, as Chip well knew, need not necessarily apply. Feinberg wielded a far bigger stick and would not be bashful about using it.

"Fuck this guy. Maybe we can even the score with Feinberg. Maybe we can do more than that."

After saying that, Chip hesitated, taking note of the curious looks from Sasquatch and Tracy, then continued, "Maybe it's time for another meeting with my new friend, Jack."

"So, you're wondering who this guy Jack may be."

The two had no clue about what was about to come out of Chip's mouth, but Tracy managed, "Yes, I am."

"This has to go deep into the cone of silence with both of you."

Both nodded.

"Sasquatch knows a little bit about this already. Basically, I met a guy from the SEC Enforcement Unit recently. I guess he overheard me talking about our business when Sasquatch and I were out late last year. In any case, he introduced himself to me, and we talked for a while after Sasquatch had left. The SEC is working on what they refer to as a 'matter under inquiry.' It's not actually an official investigation, more of a fact-finding mission, into the world of credit derivatives. Nothing specific, he said the SEC was just trying to get a handle on who's who, what the products are, how they work, and so on and so forth. He's looking into Feinberg and a number of other star traders at the major houses. I didn't tell him too much but we've been in touch over the past few months."

"What, you're an SEC informant?" Sasquatch curiously asked, somewhat indiscreetly.

"I'm not sure I would put it in those terms, but I guess I could be if Feinberg tries to fuck with us. 'Hey Feinberg, you want the SEC knocking on your door, Mr. Big?'"

"That does sound like a pretty nice pocket-nuke. He shows up to fight with a toothpick and we're carrying a bazooka."

"Before you turn into an SEC informant, can you please wait for our checks to clear?" Sasquatch joked.

"Maybe this is the perfect end to it all."

"Not funny anymore," Tracy said sensing a seriousness in Chip's tone. "Don't leave your friends behind, gasping, bleeding to death on the battlefield."

"You guys are young, resilient. At least you are, Tracy. Sasquatch, you're dead meat."

"Tracy get this guy another beer. We gotta get him back on the reservation before there really are no more bonuses coming our way. Man, you can't hate Feinberg any more than the rest of us."

"Yes, I can. I'm so tired of punks like him. Look what's happened in this business over the last 10 years. You tell me, how does a 32-year-old wind up amassing so much money, power, and control in so little time? He doesn't care about the bank, his colleagues, or anything other than how much money he makes for himself. Let's face it, we're all into making a lot of money, otherwise we would never have gotten into this shit in the first place. But I'd like to think we have some governors around our behavior—this type of guy is getting rewarded for being a scumbag.

"Just call me Chip Smith, SEC special investigator or informant or whatever. It has a nice ring to it. Not a bad way to retire either."

$ $ $

"Good evening, ladies. May I get you a drink?" asked the handsome bartender with slicked-back black hair. He was the stereotypical New York bartender working in a trendy restaurant, most likely an actor or artist looking to supplement his income while waiting for his big break. There would be a day when he, too, would be sitting on the other side of the bar, ordering outrageously priced cocktails without batting an eye.

Franny looked at her mother, as the two were seated at the beautifully restored antique bar at Ward III on Reade Street in Tribeca.

"Yes, we'll have two cosmopolitans," her early evening drink of choice.

"So, Franny, where do things stand with Michael?" Deborah asked, sounding a bit more concerned than the last time she broached the topic with her daughter.

"I haven't had a chance to talk with Michael at all in the last week. He's been at work from 7 in the morning and doesn't get home until 10 at night, best case. I know that the last couple of weeks have been bonus time. He's been unapproachable for any conversation."

Deborah Goodman's eyes lit up at the thought of her son-in-law's bonus. It was as if she somehow felt entitled to share in his success, that somehow she was responsible for his success by having introduced him to Smyth Johnston.

She wasted no time going in for the kill. "Franny, how much was his bonus? You need to know these things about your husband. I don't care how poor you think your marriage is these days."

"He hasn't told me."

"He hasn't told you?"

"I told you, he's barely been around. I do know his bonus last year was $7 million, and his team had a much better year this year. I'd be surprised if it wasn't more than $10 million this year."

Deborah liked what she was hearing, at least on the financial side of things. She needed Franny to somehow stay married to this jackpot of a husband. Having all but blown through what her deceased husband had left her, she needed someone to finance her *nouveau riche* lifestyle. New York was much more enjoyable for those with money.

"Another cosmopolitan? Michael can afford it."

Deborah Goodman had trained Franny well. Their behavior had become culturally endemic in New York circles, particularly for the brash new breed of traders who had indelibly inherited the Wall Street earth in years past. Bigger was better, more was better than less, new better than old, trendy better than traditional. It was behavior that fomented contempt and envy, not only on the part of Main Street but also by the vast majority of bankers. Many went so far as to attribute this unbecoming behavior as a provocation for Al Qaeda's symbolic strike at the heart of Western culture at the World Trade Center on 9/11.

Not that Manhattan was the only place where this behavior had been developing. It was seemingly everywhere; a slow but certain value system malaise had woven its way insidiously into broader society well beyond the boundaries of Wall Street. Hollywood, sports, music, academia, politics had shown a parallel deterioration of values. Even Main Street had fallen prey to the behavioral malaise.

People across the country as well as socioeconomic strata were living lifestyles of abundance, fueled in too many cases by inordinate amounts of debt. Ironically, these lifestyles developed in no small part due to the innovation on Wall Street that eased the flow of credit. Deborah and Franny Goodman, like so many others, felt inexplicably entitled to live however they wanted. Boats, expensive vacations, new cars, label-conscious clothing, pools, and flat-screen TVs littering nearly every room in over-sized houses had become the cultural norm. America was living a financial lie.

Whether the Wall Street/Hollywood bon vivant set or the Main Street living-beyond-one's-means set was more contemptible remains a matter of opinion. At least in the case of the former, there was a far greater ability to afford the lifestyle of abundance. Regardless, both groups presaged an economic bubble that eventually would have to burst.

As Franny sipped her second cosmopolitan, she debated whether or not to let her mother know about the revised pre-nup she had signed. Though she had not yet heard back from her lawyer, she had the disquieting feeling that Michael might have committed a marital sleight of hand when he told her she didn't need to review the revisions. His behavior as of late gave her reason to believe so.

"I just hope I can talk with him and get things back on track. He can't ignore me forever."

"Yes, Franny, you need to find out what's going on with him... $10 million is a lot of money."

Deborah Goodman had her eyes on the prize. Gold diggers always do.

Prologue – 4

Tuesday, October 14, 2008
1:30 A.M.

The Peninsula

The manager confirmed the hooker's story.

He wasn't able to tell Rodriguez any other details about who else had been in the lobby. Guests had their own keys. If the elevator accepted the key, then upstairs they went. The Presidential Suite required a special key, provided only to those on a pre-specified list.

"What about the stairs?" the detective asked.

He said that for fire code reasons the stairs remained unlocked from the hallway side, but from the stairs side they were locked.

"Anyone check them yet?"

"Housekeeping and hotel security are responsible for that; but in reality it's difficult to say. The stairwells don't have any alarms."

"Isn't that a security risk?"

"The VIPs—rock stars, athletes, actors—always bring their own bodyguards to check them."

"So it's possible that someone could've gone to the suite using the stairs?"

"Yes, but they would still have had to go through the lobby," the manager said.

The case seemed more interesting by the minute. It wasn't a robbery, and would've needed at least some planning. If the elevator had not been used, the killer would've had to have used the stairwell to reach the top floor.

"Does your computer track elevator usage? Can you tell who's gone up there?"

The manager shook his head.

"Our technology is from the '90s. This is a hotel, not a bank. People come and go on a daily basis. The lobby has a receptionist 24/7."

"Can your computer system tell when this Jack Jones reserved the room?"

"Yes, the receptionist can generally track that."

"Good. When did Jack Jones reserve the room, and when did he check in?"

"The room was booked over the phone earlier today at 7 p.m. Can't tell you anything more."

"And checked in?"

"I was here then. It was around 10:30, but I can't remember the exact minute. Nobody reported any gunshots. This suite is totally soundproof, so you can play that grand piano or play the stereo as loud as you want without disturbing anyone."

Okay, Rodriguez thought, the time of the murder was between 10:30 and midnight.

How did the killer know that the victim was coming to this hotel? Was he followed? If so they could look at surveillance cameras; there was no shortage of those in New York following 9/11. Access to the suite, if not on the pre-specified list, required planning and preparation.

"When did you last check the stairway locks on the top floor?"

The manager laughed. "No idea."

"Who's the head of security?"

"He's not working at this time."

Rodriguez said he wanted to review the surveillance camera tapes.

"Also, I need a list of the hotel guests for the past week. Of particular interest are those who paid in cash."

Chapter 9
I love this business

Tuesday, May 6, 2008
5:40 P.M.

Wheeltapper Pub
East 44th Street

"Dude, Zeus is a really bad situation," Mal said, wasting no time getting to the heart of the matter as he greeted his longtime friend who was coming down the entrance steps. He and Chip had known one another for the better part of 15 years, enjoyed one another's company and, most importantly, trusted one another. Theirs was an old-school Wall Street relationship.

The two were sitting at the front bar of the Wheeltapper Pub, a nautical-themed Irish bar on 44th Street on the east side of Grand Central Station, where Mal caught his train home to Westchester County. Mal had taken the liberty of ordering a pair of Smithwicks, knowing that Chip would show up with a healthy thirst for beer.

The two had decided they needed to get together to discuss Zeus and the imminent prospect of a suit being filed against Smyth Johnston by Broadway Life. Both knew the gravity a lawsuit would bring to bear not only on their firms but also, by extension, on themselves.

"We received a mark from Feinberg at 75 yesterday. It was 85 a week ago. I'm fast running out of ammunition internally."

"Ouch. The mark-to-market loss hurts, yes, but it shouldn't be the end of the world. It's not like you're paying cash losses. And the portfolio has a long time to recover."

"I know that and you know that. But these life insurance guys aren't used to any loss that arrives unexpectedly, even on a mark-to-market basis. To them, it's all about smooth, predictable results on both the underwriting and investment sides of the house. And let's face it, the spread widening doesn't appear to be abating anytime soon…the stats are the stats…defaults and delinquencies have been on the rise for a while. These guys are feeling like they've been fleeced by the Wall Street sharpies."

"You don't really believe you've been fleeced? You've been on this side of the street before."

"At this point, it doesn't matter what I say or try to tell them. Perception has taken hold of reality. There's no way I'm going to convince these guys that they haven't been fleeced as long as the mark keeps deteriorating. All I keep hearing in my head is the CEO asking me during the Investment Committee meeting whether or not we can trust 'the strangers from Wall Street bearing gifts' when referring to Zeus and this new product type, in other words my mandate. My internal credibility is shot, as is any chance of a decent bonus. Hell, if this thing goes severely pear-shaped, they're going to shut down my business and fire me."

"C'mon Mal. These guys can't be that put off by one deal."

"You'd think not, but we've done a host of deals in the space, and these guys assume, right or wrong, that they're all highly-correlated. The fear got elevated yesterday after my visit to 14th Street, the so-called portfolio selector/asset manager of Zeus."

"You went to talk with them without the banker being present?"

"Yep, I'm afraid so. It was a direct order from the head of Risk Management. Nothing I could do, including letting you know."

"I'm going to have to pretend I didn't hear that, or now I'm the one getting a bullet in his head. Feinberg, Bure, and their guys would have a fucking aneurism if they found out. It looks like you and I are on the same page, the path to mutually-assured destruction. So what was the gist of the meeting?"

"14th Street told us that Feinberg was the de facto portfolio selector, that he had given them a list of names he 'encouraged them to add to the portfolio.' He said the names were optimal for liquidity purposes or something to that effect. They, at 14th Street, were not happy with Feinberg either. This is one of their first deals, and they're wondering if they're dead on arrival. The docs are the docs. On paper, 14th Street is responsible for selecting the assets, but in actuality Feinberg ran the show. It's just another trick from Feinberg and Bure to legally hide behind a wall of paper and documents. It smells like a mix of dubious ethics coupled with a lack of transparency and duty to disclose. That's what our outside counsel is saying, anyhow."

"I'm not sure how much more of this I want to hear," commented Chip, as he reflected on his earlier suspicion as to what purpose the asset manager was actually serving in the deal. Could it be that the A-Bauminator had engaged in trader double-speak or, for that matter, was there any truth in how he had sold the deal internally?

"You have the gist of it. You also need to know that we're probably going to file suit against the bank, unless we can restructure the deal. I'm trying to stop it. The lawsuit may be the only way I keep my job. How's that for a bizarre turn of events? Suing my buddy."

"I love this business."

As the conversation wound down, both agreed, in the spirit of their friendship, to keep one another posted as the fur began to fly once the lawsuit was filed. Mal left to catch his train, to a house and lifestyle he could only hope to continue to support. Chip meandered across town to Penn Station, hoping to soon secure additional liquid solace from Don Pepe, the beer vendor extraordinaire.

Walking west on 42nd Street, Chip wondered whether his days on Wall Street were setting, much like the sun he was watching fade. How quickly things had changed. It wasn't that long ago that he was in Pebble Beach celebrating the completion of Zeus with Mal. Now his best client was filing lawsuit against his firm. Worse, the suit was born out of the same suspicion he had harbored about Zeus.

Feinberg and the other zero-sum, win-at-all-cost traders had taken over the business as management sat idly by, watching the enormous P&L get manufactured to their benefit. Chip envisioned a picture of the three "hear no evil, see no evil, speak no evil" monkeys with the faces of Kerr, Bonet, and Karros superimposed on it. In their defense he wondered if anyone sitting in their seats, as direct beneficiaries of the credit derivative money-machine, would have rightfully intervened. Imagine Kerr having a conversation with the board, who is asking why everyone else on the street is printing trades in credit derivatives except for Smyth Johnston. Taking the higher road by questioning the ethics and transparency of Feinberg would have been self-inflicted career suicide.

Chip had learned that Wall Street behavior is shaped by current market circumstances. In hyper-growth markets, credit derivatives being a prime example, certain behavior went unnoticed as the afterglow of the profits blinded its onlookers. As with all markets there would be a correction, with eventual firings for those responsible for losing a lot of money or damaging the client franchise. A new cast of characters would enter and the cycle would invariably repeat itself. It was just the way it worked—no amount of regulation would be able to stop it. Armed with a Foster's oil can, courtesy of Don Pepe, he stepped onto his train, left only to his musings of the devolution he was witnessing in his business. Had he been complicit in the devolution, was he part of the cultural problem himself?

He knew it would be very painful when Mal's firm went through with the lawsuit. He'd weathered many periods of stress since becoming a banker. For the first time in his 20-year career he was feeling tired, a feeling of numbness from the neck up. He didn't care anymore how any of this worked out.

Like so many bankers, he had hit that disconsolate point of no return.

$ $ $

Jack Bonfiglio sat at his desk, his office decidedly unadorned in its governmental, bureaucratic minimalism. Not a Starbucks man, he was sipping the near-flavorless black coffee he had grown immune to over the years. To him caffeine was caffeine and existed to serve its functional purpose. He was trying to digest the enormity of an anonymous call he had received the prior evening.

The caller had provided him an inordinate amount of specificity, including the deal name, names of individuals, transaction details, the various parties involved in the transaction, and current deal performance. It was as though he had been given the full anatomy of the stealth world of the shadow banking system—all gift-wrapped in one phone call.

His boss, assistant director Phelps, popped his head into the office.

"What's going on Jack, you said something about an anonymous call last night."

"No idea who this guy was. All I know is that he gave me chapter and verse on a deal named 'Zeus,' which bank was involved, Broadway Life as a pissed-off investor threatening lawsuit, and lots of transaction details. I was doing my best to jot it all down but I didn't really understand all of it. It's almost a foreign language. I'm trying to piece it together to make sense of it."

"Interesting. Sounds like the guy did you a big favor."

"I think so. I mean this may be enough to launch a proper investigation, you know, after we verify some of the facts."

"Is it insider trading-type information?"

"No, it didn't sound like insider trading to me. More like some type of misrepresentation. Or maybe it's a failure in terms of duty to disclose…hard to say, really."

"Anything of a criminal intent? Do we need to get the feds involved?"

"Way too early to conclude that. I need to get a copy of the deal docs to start with. Sounds like some questionable ethics. Where that crosses into criminal intent... I'll leave that to our legal guys once I gather more facts."

"I assume you have an insider at Smyth Johnston."

"As a matter of fact, yes I do. I met this guy by chance one day when I was grabbing a beer after work to catch the end of the Mets game before heading home to Queens. I overheard him talking about Wall Street, how much he hated some of the people in the business, so on and so forth. I approached him out of the blue, we talked and I gave him my card. We've actually met a few times since then. I get the sense this guy wants out of banking, like yesterday."

"He sounds like the perfect guy. You might want to think about having him get on our side."

"The thought has crossed my mind, even though I'm not sure I need him after this call. The problem is that no one in their right mind is going to leave their banking job for lowly government work."

"Probably true—unless, of course, he thinks he may not be getting a bonus this year."

"Bingo."

$ $ $

Sasquatch found himself sitting at his eight-year-old son's baseball game at Manhasset Ball Fields. It was a rare occasion for him to be participating in one of his children's activities. Not being able to participate in most family stuff was one of the many lifestyle sacrifices an investment banker had to make. It was an inherent trade-off that had to be accepted. It was part of the deal.

The evening was beautiful, 74 degrees with a calm breeze—perfect weather for baseball. His mood, however, was anything but perfect. Fear and loathing had reigned supreme for the three months following bonus season. Deal flow remained slow, if not nonexistent, for many of their clients who were seeking to hedge or exit their credit derivatives positions altogether.

The recent Bear Stearns saga—once viewed as a an isolated sideshow—had been casting a wider and more indelible pall over the credit markets. The bank had been bailed out by the Federal Reserve and then merged with J.P. Morgan. As the rise in mortgage delinquencies manifested itself further, the smell of a meltdown became unmistakable to those in the know, namely the banks, investors, and other market participants who constituted the mortgage-backed securities market and the broader debt markets. Everyone was on high alert. In contrast, the equity markets provided an underpinning of financial market confidence with the Dow Jones continuing to hover around the 13,000 level. Sasquatch wondered what was driving the difference in market sentiment between the equity and debt markets.

His son wasn't up to bat yet, and the pitcher couldn't throw strikes. Rather than watching the endless walks, Sasquatch's mind kept taking him back to work, the spectacular implosion of the two hedge funds culminating in Bear Stearns bankruptcy earlier in the year, and its continued impact on the markets. The two funds had levered themselves to the fullest extent possible, as had many hedge funds, investment banks, and other shadow banking system participants. Even Smyth Johnston's leverage ratio of 25, while less than the market average for its peer group, was astounding by historical standards. Leverage had become an accepted, common practice, and the road to generating attractive returns and maximizing investor and shareholder wealth.

The Bear Stearns funds were prototypes of how leverage was typically deployed. In simplistic terms, the funds borrowed money in order to obtain higher returns for their investors. With the borrowed money they would purchase triple-A-rated CDOs of subprime mortgage-backed securities. The funds borrowed to buy more and more CDOs, with their cost of borrowing obviously being less than the return on the investments. To hedge themselves, the funds then purchased credit default swaps as a form of insurance against adverse performance on the underlying triple-A CDOs.

All that was left to do after netting out the cost of leverage and cost of hedging was to watch the money train—*positive carry*—come to town. And that train roared into town without incident time and time again for the Bear Stearns funds as well as countless other investment vehicles using roughly the same structure. To be sure, the Bear Stearns funds were anything but outliers.

Such a leveraged investment strategy works perfectly well in the assumption of normal markets, statistically speaking. Everybody is a winner: The investors make high returns, the hedge fund managers get handsome fees, the CDO market gets heightened liquidity, rating agencies make their fees, the bankers earn deal origination fees and asset sales, homeowners get access to easy credit, and, last but not least, the vote-seeking politicians claim enhanced availability to housing.

Unfortunately, however, the problems with subprime delinquencies began to snowball well outside normal boundaries while beginning to inflict losses far greater than the amount of portfolio insurance purchased. As the losses began to roll in, the banks' lending to the funds sought greater collateral to offset the decreased valuations on the subprime bonds. Margin calls forced the funds to sell bonds, further depressing the price of the bonds and leading to a self-fulfilling prophecy: a death spiral of debt.

The more the margin calls came in, the more the market realized that Bear Stearns was in trouble. Blood was in the water. The more it tried to sell each fund's bonds, the more the prices declined, and the more the losses mounted. Before long, the feeding frenzy ceased, as the carcass had been picked clean. The funds were bankrupt, with Bear Stearns, the sponsoring investment bank, having run out of cash as well. Seeking to avert the systemic risk posed by a "chaotic unwinding" of investments across global markets, the Federal Reserve had engineered a March 14th-midnight $30 billion loan to J.P. Morgan to buy Bear Stearns for $2 per share. That purchase price was less than 7 percent of Bear Stearns' market value two days prior. Fear of a Bear Stearns contagion overwhelmed any market confidence engineered by the Fed's "too big to fail" bailout. Diminished confidence began to trickle down from the institutional to individual level. Sasquatch was no exception. He, along with millions of others, was orbiting alongside Bear Stearns in a parallel universe of leverage.

His son's baseball game continued, one laborious walk after another. Try as he may, Sasquatch's mind dragged him back to work and his precarious financial life.

As he gazed out at the field, occasionally making eye contact from afar with his son, he sat there on the cheap, aluminum bleacher seats worrying about whether he had become his own liquidity trap, his own Bear Stearns leveraged investment vehicle, albeit one with far fewer zeros to count. He also knew there was no bailout coming his way, apart from filing for Chapter 7, an act that would officially expunge everything he had worked toward and derail any hope of riding away from Wall Street into the sunset of a nicer lifestyle. He would jump at any opportunity to sell a piece of his real estate holdings.

That opportunity arose when he least suspected it.

Another dad came over to sit next to him. He knew Sasquatch was involved in the banking business; he was on the equity side of things himself.

"Nice bases-loaded walk from Robert. He seems to be catching onto America's pastime pretty quickly."

"Sort of hard to tell with all the walks out there."

"Good point. Hey, can I ask you a business-related question?"

"Sure—fire away."

"I heard you play around with some real estate ventures on the side. I'm looking to diversify my portfolio, and it seems like the real estate game has been a great run. I'd love to pick your brain sometime."

Sasquatch thought to himself, "Are you kidding me: this guy must be clueless about what's been happening on the fixed-income side of things. He's got the eternal optimist, institutional-equity-sales hat on."

"Well it has been a pretty good run for a while. Of course there's some noise in the market as of late," Sasquatch responded in understated fashion.

"I've read something about all of that, the Bear Stearns meltdown and all. It seems pretty complicated, though I admit I don't really understand the subprime mortgage-backed market too well. Even so, looks to me that the situation there was isolated and a function of mismanagement, taking on too much risk or some catastrophic mistake being made. I'm looking more at smaller scale, residential real estate anyway. And with this noise, I think it's a great opportunity. You know, buy on bad news…"

"I have several properties, all residential, I could talk to you about. I'm potentially looking to sell some of them. Things have been pretty hectic at work, and I haven't been able to spend as much time on the real estate stuff as I had hoped. Anyway, the building's in Hoboken. Nice townhouse, has five apartments in it and has rented well for a long time, mostly with young professionals. I've had it for five years. For the right price, I'd like to get out."

"Okay, sounds interesting. Maybe we can talk about it some more one of these days. Why are you selling it?"

"I've held it long enough and was able to buy it at a distressed price in 2003. And, I'm trying to move all my ventures closer to home here in Long Island."

"Send me the details… You can get my email address from the coach, right?"

Sasquatch went back to focusing on his son's game. He felt the ethical dilemma confronting him if this guy truly was serious about the Hoboken building. How much does he tell him about what was going on in the housing market? Was this guy that naïve or did he have a fundamentally different view of the risk? Caveat emptor, he thought. It was something he could easily rationalize as he contemplated the grim prospect of getting caught in his own personal Bear Stearns leverage and liquidity trap. If he could sell the building, make a little money, life would be looking better. Maybe the extra cash would help with things at home, certainly when considering the way the year was going. With virtually nonexistent deal flow, he and his team were irretrievably behind in production compared to last year. At this rate he wasn't going to get a big bonus, let alone any bonus at all.

He wondered if he'd actually find himself on the receiving end of "Hey, you got a minute?" from Chip, followed by a long, awkward walk to HR to get his pink slip.

The situation with Mal didn't help his case either. He wondered if he'd have to testify in some courthouse building downtown, with expert witnesses, a jury, aggressive lawyers, and press hanging around looking to fell another evil banker type. That sounded like it would suck, and certainly wouldn't help his prospects for getting paid.

And then there was Feinberg pulling the tapes on Zeus. He must not have found anything on the tapes since it had gone quiet. Or was Feinberg just waiting for the right time to strike, preserving his optionality to extract something out of Sales as part of a greasy backroom deal. Internal greenmail. That would be typical Feinberg, whose Machiavellian ways were never to be underestimated. Did he have Compliance and HR primed, ready to waltz over to the desk and haul each of them to conference rooms to deliver their walking papers for cause? Being terminated for cause was tantamount to a career death sentence—say good-bye to any severance, unvested stock, and, realistically, the chance to ever work on Wall Street again.

No wonder things hadn't been going well on the home front lately. The constant stress, both at work and on his real estate ventures, was like a voracious disease eating at him. Was he headed to divorce court again, the third time being no charm? He knew the act had grown old, as he stared lost in thought at the trees on the other end of the field, completely oblivious to what was going on in the game. At least he was there.

Chapter 10
Fired for cause is not a good thing

Thursday, May 15, 2008
9:34 A.M.

Smyth Johnston Trading Floor

Joey Karros returned to the trading floor from a meeting with senior sales management. This meeting had been different than the typical weekly managing director meeting. There were no opportunities to manage up or engage in any other self-aggrandizing tactics. The gamesmanship was conspicuously absent. Instead, everyone in the room was rapt with attention as they listened to Duncan Kerr brief them on the deteriorating state of the debt markets.

Kerr was of the strong opinion that Bear Stearns would not be an isolated event. He saw the excessive leverage built into the markets, knew the perils of model-risk, the inextricable web of interbank relationships, and the underlying liquidity risk inherent in the shadow banking system. The game-changing implications this market could have on the thousands of bankers on their acre-sized trading floors across Wall Street had become progressively evident to him. There was no more delusion—this was going to get ugly, really ugly. He had heard the rumors that Lehman was in trouble, probably the next to implode. The bigger question was, who would be next? Would the dominoes ever stop?

Sasquatch yelled at Karros, "Joey, can you pick up on two with Chip and I... I got one massively pissed off client on the line who wants to talk with you."

"Who is it?" Karros responded.

"Mal McMahon...you know, the guy we were celebrating with in Pebble Beach a year or so ago."

"I don't want to do this now. I thought Feinberg had restructured the deal for him," Karros said, thinking the potential issue with Broadway Life had been addressed.

"Not quite. You can assume Feinberg's proposal was not to their liking. Mal called me earlier and asked if Feinberg was kidding; basically the proposal amounted to their taking a large realized loss in exchange for Feinberg breaking the trade."

Karros jumped on the phone as Chip released the mute button.

"You fucking assholes. You've completely screwed me," screamed Mal into the phone as soon as Karros picked up.

In barely less than a year of the deal's expected seven-year life, his triple-A-rated investment was being valued—courtesy of the most recent mark-to-market calculation provided to them by Feinberg's desk—at 68 cents on the dollar. Historically for a triple-A deal, 98 cents was viewed as catastrophic. Seventy-five was unheard of.

Worse yet, having left his sell-side position at an investment bank, Mal had sold these deals to Broadway Life as a smart, relative value investment—one that offered superior risk-adjusted characteristics than similarly rated alternatives—to his otherwise highly-

conservative life insurance employer. He had staked his
claim on his credit expertise on the Street and, more
importantly, on his long-term relationships in the market.
That was his value proposition, one he was helplessly
left to watch evaporate before his very eyes. He was
watching his own career train wreck.

"I don't know what to tell you, Mal, this is something
no one could have foreseen. You saw all the modeling
runs, did your own diligence, made the same
assumptions we all did on default rates," Karros replied,
evasively.

"Get that piece of shit Feinberg on the phone. I'm
going to kick that guy's ass. That is, right after I get a
pink slip any minute now. His attempts to restructure the
deal were nothing more than attempts to screw me
further. This is a catastrophe. You think a life insurance
company is going to like the headline about how they
got fleeced by Wall Street into playing the credit
derivatives game? You guys better figure this out. Our
PR machine is ready to talk to the press. Better figure it
out. Glad I just upsized my house in Rye; thanks for
ruining my career. You have four hours to send in
another proposal or the lawyers get involved."

Karros, Chip, and Sasquatch could only listen to the
dial tone after Mal slammed the phone down.

"Ouch. That wasn't pretty. What are we going
to do?"

"Boys, you guys get to handle this one… I have too
much other shit to deal with," Karros said as he ran off
the trading floor to an apparent meeting. Controversy
was beneath his pay grade. Lead not by example, but
instead by delegation. It was the stuff Teflon geniuses
are made of.

"Well, dude, looks like you're a true scumbag.
Congratulations. You have a great career ahead of you.

Go out tonight and celebrate, having just ruined someone's life. I can't believe I even associate myself with you," Chip added facetiously, for the obvious purpose of inciting Sasquatch.

Sasquatch was livid and marched across the floor to find Feinberg. He had reached the saturation point. Hope for salvaging something for Mal on Zeus was lost, as was, consequently, a long-term client of theirs. Deals were hard enough to get done in this environment, losing clients like Mal made it near impossible.

Feinberg saw him coming as he approached his desk.

"Hello Sasquatch, let me guess: you're here about Broadway Life and Zeus. Look, I can't hold your hand on this one. He's your client. He bought the deal, agreed on the pricing for the perceived risk, and lost. He's a big boy, a qualified institutional buyer. Move on. It's called trading. I have plenty of positions I'm getting torched on in my book. What do you want me to do? There's nothing I can do. The mark is the mark; we tried once to work with them, and they were being completely unreasonable. Now fuck off and get out of my face."

"Really? He told us he had another bank mark the portfolio—at 90 cents instead of 68. I'd suggest you revisit the mark your desk provided him or figure out a way to restructure the deal in good faith. He said that your last attempt was a joke, of no value to him."

"Stop shouting and get out of my face. My proposal was in good faith. What do you want me to do, let him off the hook entirely? I wish it worked that way, but it doesn't."

"So, you want me out of your face, how's this?" as Sasquatch got right into Feinberg's face. "How is it your deals always perform worse than similar deals from other banks, and it never fails? You have a long list of people you've pissed off, including lots of us in Sales."

"Get away from me, unless you don't want to work here anymore. Make that work anywhere on Wall Street."

As Sasquatch slowly retreated, Feinberg picked up the phone and called Karros on his cell.

"Your guy Woodley just physically assaulted me. I have witnesses. I'd suggest you have him removed from the building, unless you want me to go to Kerr with the full account of how you can't keep your staff in check. You can't have your guys storm over here like that. And it won't reflect very well on you."

"I had no idea he was over there. Hey buddy, just keep this under wraps. I'll take care of it," Karros whispered.

"Good idea. I have enough stress without this freak threatening me. Don't make me tell Kerr what the real problem is here."

"What are you talking about?"

"What am I talking about? I'm talking about what a joke your sales team has turned out to be. Everyone in trading knows it. It's your job to explain these deals to your clients; not to mention, assess their suitability for entering a trade like Zeus. It can't be that all your clients clamor to get in the game, then scream bloody murder anytime a deal has an issue. This guy is screaming bloody murder over a mark that changes daily or weekly. He's not even paying losses, yet. Someone in your clown show over there needs to understand that's the way derivatives sometimes work."

"Yeah, I know. It's not like these deals were sold as risk-free."

"I'm beginning to wonder how they were sold, and for that matter how good your so-called strategic hires really are, fucking empty suits."

"Michael, that's not fair."

"Life's not fair. You have to manage your clients better than this. I can't have them crying wolf every time a deal doesn't go their way."

Karros panicked, fearing Feinberg would call out his team with Kerr and others. He was one call away from being tainted as damaged goods. Some unflattering commentary from Feinberg to Kerr could derail him off the track to becoming the next head of sales. His career plan might be hanging in the balance. Feinberg, with one comment, had gone from friend—or better, an ally of convenience—to potential foe. Karros would not allow Feinberg to ruin him; this was self-preservation time. Karros started to think about his options.

$ $ $

Karros wasted little time deciding which option was most expedient.

His decision was to fire Sasquatch, report the assault to the police, and have him hauled downtown. It would be the best way for him to acquiesce to Feinberg in hope of preserving his all-important alliance of convenience. True to form he delegated the firing responsibility to Chip, who had opposed Karros's pandering to Feinberg and making his friend collateral damage.

Shameless politics that made for unnecessary drama. As if there hadn't been ample drama on the Street over the course of the prior six months without Sasquatch getting fired. The week had passed, mercifully so, without any headline incident capable of roiling the debt markets any more than was already the case. It was simply more of the same; everyone was on edge, as if they tacitly knew there was more pain heading their way. The hope engendered by the Bear Stearns bailout, such as it was, had collapsed under the weight of fear, with all deal flow being directionally one way: sell.

The party was over.

Major market participants within the shadow banking system, as if a panicked and thundering herd, stampeded through the credit derivatives exit doorway. Their exit efforts proved mostly to no avail as the specter of market gridlock—illiquidity—had arrived, irreversibly.

In many ways Chip perversely felt envious of Sasquatch for having just been culled from the herd. At least he didn't have to come into the office to observe the train wreck every day. There was nothing for him to do while in office, apart from watching himself, Tracy, and countless others search for the end of the internet. Manufactured 3 p.m. client meetings at the nearest pub became standing operating procedure. At these meetings, he would hatch the next golf outing with a client or two, always wondering whether the firm would reimburse him on his expense account. All bets were off. It was a risk worth taking, he calculated, when compared to being in the office. At a minimum, being out of the office would spare him more of the same office nothingness and depression. Spending time with his clients was something he had always enjoyed, despite the current acrimony over the pain they were experiencing on Zeus and other deals they had completed recently. He could also use the time out of office as a faux career counselor for Tracy, who faced the prospect of getting blown out before pocketing an ample number of handsome bonus checks.

His situation had devolved into a no-upside, all-downside proposition. Even in the unlikely scenario where he was granted a stay of execution in the coming months, he knew survival was a hollow victory given the nonexistent, or best-case vastly reduced, bonus he might receive in the next bonus cycle. Either way he knew it was a bad trade—an unacceptable pain-adjusted return on his time.

$ $ $

Chip received a call later in the day from Sasquatch's attorney.

"Mr. Smith, can you come downtown to bail out your friend Nigel."

"Of course. Now?"

"He's free to go once the $10,000 bail is posted; he'll need a cashier's check."

"Okay."

"Nigel told me he was also fired for cause. After all, that likely spells the end of his time on Wall Street. Nice guy. In any case, go to the Manhattan Detention Complex on White Street; they will help you there."

"Okay, got it."

Within the hour, Chip had been to his bank where he obtained a cashier's check, arrived downtown, bailed out Sasquatch, ran into a nearby deli for a six-pack of Budweiser, and found himself and Sasquatch being whisked over the Triboro Bridge into Queens, seated together in the back seat of a town car en route to their homes on Long Island. Hastily having arranged the town car, two thoughts dawned on Chip—first, he would have to pay for the car himself, since bailing out a colleague did not qualify as a reimbursable expense, and, second, this was his friend Sasquatch's final ride in a company town car, a symbolic funeral.

"Dude, you physically assaulted Feinberg?"

"I didn't assault him. Sure, I got in his face a little bit, like I have in the past with other people, but never did I make contact with him. I'm not that stupid."

"That's the story I'm getting from Karros, who of course is stroking Feinberg to save his own pathetic ass. Fired for cause is not a good thing. We all may be toast soon anyway."

"It's all good. Game over. I don't really care. I hate this business and lifestyle. There are too many assholes to deal with, anyway. If it isn't Feinberg, it's too many others. Spiritual death by a thousand cuts. The business never used to be this way, at least so it seemed. And with the meltdown going on, it's not as if my unvested shares of Smyth Johnston will be worth anything to me."

"Consider yourself lucky. Though I think any hope of an offer from Lehman just went bye-bye."

"Actually, I do feel lucky. I managed to sell that apartment building in Hoboken. My bank account is flush with cash. And I don't have to deal with those pricks anymore. I don't care about the Lehman possibility. How's my buddy Feinberg? Tell him I really miss him, and I'm sorry I didn't get the chance to snap his scrawny little neck before HR perp-walked me out of the building. I'm surprised he didn't have me paraded through the trading floor on my way out. Nice gesture on his part."

"You get fired and you're the happy one. What a business. By the way, what moron did you get to buy an apartment building from you in this market? Let me guess, someone with money who doesn't know how to read; I mean, seriously, who's stepping into that game at this time?"

"He's the dad of one of the kids on my son's baseball team. He's actually an institutional equity sales guy. He told me he wants to diversify his portfolio away from financial assets into real estate while picking up some current cash flow. And he likes the Hoboken market, given its proximity to the city."

"Don't call me when he realizes you just fleeced him."

"Hey, he said he knows what he's doing, blah, blah, blah. All I know is, I have a nice cash infusion into my bank account, net of paying down my note on the place. And I'm not hanging out at fucking Smyth Johnston anymore."

"You fleece this poor bastard, then leave me for dead at the bank. You're screwing more people than a porn star these days."

"Speaking of screwed, how's our boy Mal doing? He sounded pretty pissed off earlier. Still have a job or did the kinder, gentler buy-side firm of his put a bullet in his head? Before you go there, you're the one who sold him Zeus, not me, let the record show. Now who's the scumbag," Sasquatch laughed as he swilled his beer.

"Man, oh man, I spoke with the guy after the call with Karros. He is seriously bumming. I invited him to a Yankees game later this week, to the Skybox no less, and he said he couldn't go."

"Why not? He loves that whole scene."

"He does, but he's convinced the bullet is coming any day now. He's paranoid about not being in the office."

"The music is going to stop and he has no seat. I feel his pain. Very few are going to escape this meltdown without a lot of pain: financial, family, or some type of lifestyle pain."

"I got the feeling his pain may be more than yours and mine. It sounded bad."

"Sounds like the lifestyle trap to me. You know the 2.2 kids in the wealthy suburb in a house bigger than you need. Make that the house you can't afford when the shit hits the fan, like now."

"Think about it. He's got the house in Rye that he just added onto, at what now appears to be the height of the market, with huge property taxes, four kids in private school, a weekend place in Vermont, the whole works. He's trying to sell the Vermont place; but, guess what, his market is largely other Wall Streeters who are also shitting in their pants to get rid of second homes or first homes of their own. He even said he hasn't gotten laid in three months. All this on top of the beating he's taking now in his personal account."

Sasquatch took a moment to absorb Mal's plight.

"Thanks for that. I feel a lot better. But what's his real problem? Never mind that he potentially has no income, massive expense creep, no liquidity, and an investment portfolio about to tank further. My gig seems pretty good compared to that. By the way, you were right about your theme of bad things happening to good people. You know what is really scary about all of this?"

"Tell me, please. I feel like getting more depressed."

"When and if the blood continues to flow—and I think it will—Mal's story will be one of thousands. I mean, no one goes into this game thinking it will end so abruptly and in such spectacular fashion. Most crushing will be the limited ability to do much about it. It really is a lifestyle trap, a perfect storm that will leave people reeling with few options to escape."

"Everyone will be victims to varying degrees if the Street melts down. No two ways about that."

"So what's he going to do if he gets nuked?"

"Who knows? Work at Burger King perhaps. I just hope he doesn't fly off the deep end and do something drastic."

Minutes away from their respective homes, Sasquatch requested that the driver pull over. He was hungry and needed more beer before arriving home and having to tell Kelly that the game was over...and, that he might need to defend himself in court against an assault charge.

She wouldn't be impressed. A burger and beer at one of his Long Island mainstays was a must, given the predicament he found himself in.

"Good idea—no, great idea. We need to strategize on how you're going to roll the news out on the home front."

"How about something like this: hey Kelly, I got fired today and my time on Wall Street is over. Let's sell the house and all the bullshit we don't need. It's time to do something else with our lives. Maybe less of the race to the top and more trying to find happiness of some sort. We don't have to live this way."

"Not bad, might as well get right to the point. This is the way the story ends for a lot of people on Wall Street. Not necessarily the fired for cause part, but the part about the game just coming to an end, whether it be for a market disruption event or a change in strategy that results in an unexpected decision to shut down whole businesses or products. Circumstances change, often well outside of anyone's ability to control them. Call it a simple twist of fate in a perpetually volatile business."

"Blah blah blah…more beer," slurred Sasquatch who was feeling the ill effects of the day's inordinate stress.

"No need to tell her about the fired for cause part of the story. After all, there are going to be lots more people getting served their walking papers soon enough. Tell her you're part of the first wave."

As Sasquatch made his way to the bathroom he slipped and fell to the sloppy, beer drenched floor where he lay in his suit, as if a human mop. Chip and another struggled with his mass of dead weight, eventually helping him to his feet.

The fall was a harbinger for the human toll that had begun to unfold across Wall Street.

Chapter 11
Something had to give

Wednesday, September 17, 2008
5:00 P.M.

Smyth Johnston Trading Floor

Something had to give, Michael Feinberg decided, as he took his seat on the trading floor toward the end of the day. In the three preceding days Merrill Lynch had entered into a Letter of Intent to be purchased by Bank of America, Lehman had gone bankrupt, and AIG had cratered and was on life-support courtesy of a taxpayer-funded bailout. As if that history-making market volatility weren't enough, Kerr was on his case to show more profit while tension with Sales had escalated to a fever pitch. Not that Feinberg was bothered by any of this; in fact, the volatile markets had propelled his book to enormous profitability. The volatility that bothered him was that of his deteriorating marriage to Franny. He decided it was time to end it, much like he would terminate a trade that had gone bad. The trader in him saw marriage like a put option: he owned the right but not the obligation to continue the relationship. To him, it was about optionality, opportunity cost, and cutting losses—all hallmarks of a successful trader. The lines of distinction between his work life and personal life had become all but meaningless.

Earlier in the day he had let Franny know he wanted to speak with her that night at their home in SoHo. Though they had been spending little time there together in recent months—evidence of a souring relationship—it was best, Michael felt, to be in private when he sprang the news. Who knew how she would react. Would she be surprised? Would she care? Was she so blinded by the materiality of her lifestyle that the news would be met with self-denial? He didn't care what her reaction might be. A good trader keeps his emotions in check. Get it done and move on. The moment of truth arrived.

$ $ $

"So Franny, it's clear this marriage doesn't seem to be heading anywhere. I want a divorce."

Though she had sensed it coming, she nonetheless reacted surprised that he would do this to her. It was no longer something left to ponder in the abstract. Michael stayed the course, refusing to get drawn into the emotion. "Do you want to know why? You seem more concerned with your lavish lifestyle than anything else. It's as if I'm just the faceless guy paying for everything, as if that's my obligation. And it's as though you think you have no obligation to me, other than to spend money on whatever you want. And your mother makes it 10 times worse. She's a gold digger of the most blatant kind. I've expressed this to you many times, but nothing ever changes. It's like I have two wives I don't want."

"Maybe we should just separate for a while."

"No thanks. And no, no more marriage counseling. That hasn't helped at all. Look, we have a pre-nup in place. Let's just get on with this, get it over with. I'll have Ira, my lawyer, get you the paperwork."

Franny was speechless, deciding to leave their soon-to-be-former marital nest, returning uptown to her mother's place on Park Avenue. Before leaving she went into their bedroom to retrieve a document she had stored in a safe alongside her jewelry. It was the pre-nup agreement she had recently signed, to reflect "some amendments that needed to be made periodically," so Michael had told her.

Thoughts bombarded her as she sat in the back of the taxi. How could Michael do this to her? Was she the cause of their failed marriage, as Michael had just suggested? Panicked, she pulled out the current pre-nup to see what she had recently signed on blind faith. As best she could tell she would receive up to 50 percent of their combined net worth, except that the 50 percent would be subject to a capped amount that was prorated as to how long they had been married. She would receive $3 million based on the carefully crafted language.

Three million dollars, to most, was a lot of money. One million dollars for each year of marriage does not exactly constitute a hardship. However, Franny knew her husband was worth many multiples of that amount, which she would be receiving but for the divorce.

Franny stepped out of the taxi after arriving in front of her mother's doorman building, where she rode the elevator up to her mother's apartment.

"What happened, Franny? You look shaken up."

A mother can always sense problems with her daughter.

"Michael is filing for divorce."

"Just like that?"

"Just like that. He said it was my fault, that all I was concerned with was spending money on a lavish lifestyle."

"How did you leave it before you left? Did you ask to go through more marriage counseling with him? Separation time?"

"He said he was done with the counseling, that it didn't do anything to help, and that he wants this over as soon as possible. I grabbed a copy of the pre-nup before leaving."

"Let me see the pre-nup. What does it say? I'll get my lawyer on it first thing tomorrow morning."

"It's actually been amended recently. Michael told me it needed to be amended every few years to better reflect our financial circumstance."

Deborah immediately went to the amendment.

"Why did you sign this? Do you realize what it says?"

"Yes. I do now, at least I think I do."

"It says you're entitled to receive a maximum of five million that gets adjusted down to three million based on how long the marriage lasted. And what do you think he's worth? Let me answer: a lot more than that. Didn't he just get a $10 million bonus, or something like that? He's probably worth $100 million at this point. Half of that is a lot better than what this now says."

Franny just sat there listening to her mother berate her. Maybe Michael had a valid point—she was acting like a gold digger.

No aspect of her financial life with Michael had been left unexamined—amounts to be received with or without the divorce, enforceability of the pre-nup, life insurance, and anything else that may have a bearing on what Franny would receive. It was as if her mother was more concerned with the financial outcome than her daughter's emotional well-being.

Deborah was acutely aware of the impact the revised pre-nup would have on Franny if the divorce went through.

"Well Franny, it may be that you just paid a gigantic stupidity tax by signing this thing. Not even the photo of him with the Florida prostitute can save you. He's not going to do this to you."

$ $ $

Chip's cell phone rang. It was Sasquatch's ringtone. "Dude, I have him by the nuts. Feinberg is going down." His excitement was pouring through the line.

"Talk to me. By the way, I thought you were happy to be out of this bullshit."

"I'm happy, and thanks again for firing me. I'm going to be a lot happier after Feinberg is screwed. Consider it vigilante justice."

"Okay, what do you have for me?" Chip was now very curious.

"So here goes...I decided to call up Bob Lancer of 14th Street Asset Management to see how he was doing on Zeus, and to dig a bit into his relationship with Feinberg. By the way, he seems like a decent guy. Let me sum it up by saying that he feels about the same way about Feinberg as we do."

"You went rogue, commando-style in other words."

"If you insist. He told me exactly what went down on Zeus, the forced portfolio that was crammed down his throat, the whole background on the deal. Lancer feels thoroughly deceived and thinks his business may be in jeopardy because of Feinberg. By the way, he has been doing some market reconnaissance of his own: Feinberg never covered his positions. Zeus was a pure short."

"As we suspected, Feinberg was up to no good when he went out to hire a manager for the deal. It was a ruse, an attempt to bring in third-party asset management expertise as a shell game for the investors. You mean our good friends in Trading lied to us? If Feinberg was positioned a billion short on Zeus, and asset prices have dropped 40 percent, that means he's sitting on a $400 million gain."

"Imagine that. Lesson number one on Wall Street: some people lie. That lesson holds true everywhere else as well. Hidden agendas are nasty by nature. A $400 million gain is what you would call a good trade," Sasquatch laughed sarcastically. "There has to be something wrong about what's gone on here, be it illegal or not. At a minimum, to me it smacks of deception or some form of securities violation. Knowing Bure, they did just enough to cover their asses legally in the docs. And, our new best friend Lancer phoned in an anonymous call to the SEC to tip them off. He said he might eventually file a formal complaint."

"I wonder if my guy Bonfiglio is involved."

"He is. Lancer told me that Bonfiglio was the guy he spoke to. You might want to contact him to see what's going on with the investigation."

"Yep, thanks for the heads up, Rambo."

$ $ $

Holy shit, Chip thought to himself, as he digested the call from Sasquatch. Feinberg may really be in trouble. And for good reason—selling a deal as a regular CDO with an asset manager and then shorting the deal. Very damaging to Smyth Johnston's reputation, at a minimum.

It was time to get off the desk and take a walk.

Chip grabbed his Blackberry and told Tracy he was going to lunch. He headed to Bryant Park, an urban oasis immediately behind the New York Public Library, on 5th Avenue between 41st and 42nd Streets. It was a nice place for a respite in the middle of a hectic business day, well-manicured with mature trees and plenty of diversions to take the stress level down a notch or two.

No such luck today.

Would Lancer really have called the SEC to blow the whistle on Feinberg? Or was it someone else, perhaps Sasquatch, now that he had gone rogue, or Mal, or someone else at Broadway Life in advance of dumping the lawsuit on Smyth Johnston? What did it mean for him? Would he somehow be dragged into the investigation abyss, only now had he gone from SEC witness to suspect? Being on the wrong end of an SEC witch-hunt was the last thing he needed as he contemplated his exit from the business. Not quite the soft landing he was hoping for as he called it a career.

There was only one way to find out what was going on: call Jack Bonfiglio. A known quantity was better than an unknown quantity.

He dialed Bonfiglio's number as he took refuge on a bench in Bryant Park.

"Bonfiglio here. Hello Chip." He had placed Chip into the address book on his cell phone.

There would be no small talk from Chip.

"I wanted to talk with you further about how I might be able to help you out. The last time we met you had suggested a couple of possibilities. I've thought a lot more about things since then."

"I don't think I need your help, at least not at this point."

"Okay. Does that mean the inquiry is fading or that you have more information than before to move it forward?"

"Obviously, I can't speak in detail. But, you can assume it's the latter. The inquiry has made huge progress in the last two weeks. Thanks to a recent whistleblower—the guy told me everything. He told me about Feinberg, Zeus in specific detail, who else was involved at Smyth Johnston...and yes, you were on the list of those mentioned. I have more information than I could ever have hoped for, from you or anyone."

The anonymous call. The call from Lancer. Sasquatch was right.

Chip felt an uneasy feeling overcome him, as he noticed he was breathing hard. In an instant, not only had his potential role, formal or informal, in helping Jack and the SEC vanished. Now he saw the potential of his being on the wrong side of the inquiry. Namely, he might, as a salesman at Smyth Johnston who worked on Zeus, be considered complicit in whatever wrongdoing the inquiry eventually might discover.

"I thought I was your guy. Now you don't need me?"

"Right now we don't need you. We have enough information to proceed. Be careful, Chip. This could get ugly for anyone in its path. The SEC is chomping at the bit to make a strong statement about the regulators paying attention to Wall Street. Lots of pressure has been brought to bear from D.C."

The stakes had suddenly been elevated, well beyond his comfort zone. An SEC matter under inquiry into the credit derivatives market could be a runaway train once it gained ample weight. He could readily become collateral damage, road kill, in its path. No one—Jack or the SEC, Feinberg, Lancer, Mal, Broadway Life, or the political system in D.C.—would give a second thought to throwing him under the train.

As he ambled back to the office, Chip imagined himself, somber-faced with one hand up in the air, being sworn in before a Congressional subcommittee. Bad visual.

This was bad. This was very bad.

$ $ $

With broad-based fear strangling the market, what everyone anticipated materialized: wholesale firings or others taking themselves out in a Jonestown-like mass suicide. It was Wall Street theater of epic proportion. The disgorgement of Wall Street talent that had begun was a predictable culling of the herd. The engorgement of talent that had taken place in years past during the boom phase of the credit derivatives cycle was of an equal order of magnitude. It seemed like a form of corporate bulimia playing out before everyone's eyes on a daily basis. Absent selective strategic personnel, mostly management, the bloodletting was indiscriminately efficient.

No longer were there discussions of exit packages, walk-away payments or the like. It was more of a "don't let the door hit your worthless ass on the way out" situation, with each pink slip recipient knowing they had lost any and all leverage in the equation. Dead pools were being circulated on most trading floors, subject of course to the daily revisions necessary to account for the fallen comrades from the previous day. There is little decorum on a trading floor, especially one with businesses on the cusp of a meltdown.

"Fuck me," Chip yelled into his phone before pounding the handset into his desk until it shattered.

He kept repeating himself, until storming off the desk not knowing what else to do. The screens were all red, no longer just the debt markets, but now also including the equity and commodity markets. Except for U.S. treasuries, all other asset prices were falling. The Dow Jones had plummeted close to 800 points over the last three days following sell-offs of 300 points multiple times previously that same month. It had the feel of precisely the meltdown many had feared.

In truth, Chip wasn't too worried about what would happen to the bank, instead focusing more on his personal account. Like many, he had lost over 40 percent of his net worth, and it stung. Were the bank to go down, it would make his life easier, in some respects, except for the million dollars, and falling, of unvested Smyth Johnston shares he still owned.

At least, he thought, he wasn't working for a commercial bank. They were in real trouble, having shelled out billions of dollars in loan commitments. Originally thought to be customer-friendly, loss leader "trust me we will never use these but need them for regulatory capital purposes" loans, now, in the middle of the crisis, every single client was drawing them down. The desperate search for liquidity, private or through the fed, was on. He had heard nothing from Compliance, Legal, Feinberg, or Kerr, about either the tapes or the lawsuit over the last two weeks. Chip had been coming to the office wondering when he'd get escorted to HR, or have to do something about the lawsuit. Neither had happened so he just kept sitting at his desk following the market meltdown.

With no deal flow, much less motivation, Chip sat for hours and days on end considering how it would end for him and hosts of others in credit derivatives. How had the bull market of the last 20 years, with its explosive growth in credit derivatives and the shadow banking system, seized up so quickly? In fact, it was bleeding profusely, as if a financial hemophiliac. At the root of the bleeding were the recent market disruption events involving industry giants Lehman Brothers and AIG. Together, the two represented well over 100 years of market leadership and operating history. To fathom both collapsing in the span of the same month, let alone on consecutive days, underscore their magnitude in the annals of financial market history.

Chip began to reconstruct each event in his mind.

Lehman had filed for Chapter 11 on September 15. At the heart of its collapse, similar to Bear Stearns earlier in the year, was the subprime mortgage market as well as the use of what turned out to be excessive leverage. As did the two Bear Stearns hedge funds, Lehman had borrowed 31 times its capital to finance its housing-related assets. Such a leverage ratio meant those assets would only have to depreciate by three percent for Lehman's assets to be less than its liabilities. In other words, it was only a hair trigger away from technical bankruptcy.

After years of accumulating these assets, either by choice or because they were unable to distribute them on the back of their robust fee-generating securitization business, large losses had begun to snowball due to the ongoing crisis that had emerged earlier in 2008 in the subprime mortgage market. In their second fiscal quarter alone Lehman reported losses of nearly three billion, necessitating the sale of six billion in assets to assuage its lenders.

The rout was on, with the firm's stock losing 70 percent of its value by the middle of 2008. Despite multiple suitors—including the likes of Bank of America and Barclays—expressing interest in the purchase of Lehman, by September 13, 2008, all such interest had evaporated. In a last ditch effort to stave off the collapse, the New York Federal Reserve, led by then-president Timothy Geithner, called a meeting to explore the emergency liquidation of Lehman's assets.

Not to be outdone, the very next day AIG—a Fortune 15 company—narrowly averted collapsing into bankruptcy at the hands of its own exposure to the subprime mortgage market. Chip readily seized upon the parallels with Lehman and Bear Stearns.

Same shit, different day, he thought. Through its AIG Financial Products division, headquartered in London for favorable regulatory reasons, the firm entered into credit default swaps totaling an eye-popping $441 billion worth of securities originally rated triple-A. That amount made it one of the largest investors in the credit default swap market. Of those $441 billion, roughly $60 billion was backed by subprime mortgages. AIG was able to amass this enormous notional exposure by negotiating the ability to not post initial collateral with its trading counterparties, as long as it maintained its high credit rating. It was the equivalent of a person not having to come up with a down payment for a house as long as their credit score was above 700.

Reeling from the news of the day before, the market efficiently began the inevitable comparison between AIG's subprime exposures and those of now bankrupt Lehman. The findings were not inspiring. To the contrary, it was found that AIG's valuations were in many cases two times those used by Lehman. Investor confidence, as illustrated by the 60 percent drop in AIG's stock price at the stock market's opening earlier that morning, was hit in the head with a sledgehammer.

A liquidity squeeze arising from forced asset sales at AIG was in full stride.

The crisis hit terminal velocity when later that day Moody's and S&P downgraded AIG's credit rating. The downgrade, as per their contractual obligations under the near half-trillion in swap agreements, resulted in AIG having to deposit collateral of more than $10 billion to its counterparties and other creditors (leverage providers). With bankruptcy all but certain; and the catastrophic collapse of Lehman, then the largest in U.S. history; and the global economy hanging in the balance, the New York Federal Reserve was authorized by its Board of Governors to create an $85 billion liquidity facility backed by the assets of AIG to avoid such a systemic collapse.

In the immediate aftermath, the other shadow banking system participants scrambled to come to grips with their subprime exposures to avert a Bear Stearns, Lehman, or AIG-style collapse. No one was immune to the meltdown unfolding, with the rumor mill—much of which was at the hands of headline-seeking media sensationalism—churning at full throttle as gasoline was poured onto the raging fire. A high-stakes game of poker was at full play on the public relations front as participants jockeyed for positions of comparative strength.

What was fact, what was fiction, no one knew. It was unchartered territory, a market circumstance with far-reaching ramifications not witnessed since the Great Depression of 1929.

Everyone seemed to have a theory as to the precipitating cause(s) of the meltdown. Chip had heard most of them, ranging from a sinister Wall Street cabal, to simple bad luck, to bad risk management. While the competing theories abounded, Chip concluded that the underlying cause of the meltdown was inescapably the result of certain business practices fomented under the shadow banking system. These included the excessive use of leverage, regarded widely as the sacred cow of finance, permissible off-balance-sheet accounting, insufficient risk management, and the failure to recognize what might happen, as it did, when illiquidity grips the market.

Chip was startled from his musings when a colleague nicknamed Donut Boy interrupted him. Donut Boy had earned his moniker for being approximately 90 pounds overweight, yet another manifestation of how Wall Street's lifestyle can wreak havoc.

"Hey, Chip, what's your view?" he asked, using his signature vapid question. Donut Boy had the habit of wasting hours walking around the trading floor asking random people their views on whatever happened to be his topic du jour. Chip was just about to answer, My view is that you're fucking blocking my view of that smoking-hot trading assistant, before catching himself and choosing something obvious.

"Well, Bob, things in my client base aren't looking all that good. More sellers than buyers. My view is that we're in for a world of hurt."

Chip turned back to the computer screen, signaling the end of conversation. After Donut Boy had walked off, Chip was left wondering why the guy had come over.

$ $ $

"Another day in paradise," Chip declared by force of habit as he walked in the door of his house later that night.

His wife was sitting at the kitchen table reading, with a glass of Chablis.

"Guess I don't need to ask how your day was."

"Yeah, don't."

Chip had chosen to go to the Blarney Stone by himself after work, for a cordial eight beers before taking the car service home. He'd have to remember to call a cab in the morning, as his car was still at the train station. At least, in his drunken, irritable state, he had had the presence of mind not to get behind the wheel to drive home from the train station.

"What a nightmare."

"What now?" she asked, her familiarity having now bred contempt toward his tales of office woes.

"Just about everything, Market melting down, dealing with Kerr, Karros, and the rest of the nice Wall Street people...a client, Mal, sued us today...could it possibly get any worse? Wait, yes it could. I might be getting named in an SEC inquiry."

"I'm glad the kids are already in bed, so they don't have to see their father in this kind of shape."

"What do you think I should do? I can't walk in and quit; and, mind you, we're down a lot of money in the past week, so you have to stop spending. I don't need any more stress."

"Spend money? It's only on the necessities. You know that."

"Really, how in the fuck is a $350 dollar haircut from some Eurotrash a necessity, dare I ask?"

"I'm going to bed. It's no use talking to you."

As she was walking upstairs, Chip yelled, "Hey, how about some sex tonight?"

Chip heard his wife's footsteps ascending the stairs, and nothing else. Left alone in the kitchen, he walked to the fridge and popped open a can of Budweiser, then turned on Sports Center in hope of taking his mind off work. It didn't work. He continued to fixate on the events of the week, the continued and escalating market meltdown, Lehman and AIG, Mal's lawsuit, the anonymous SEC caller, and his diminishing bank account.

Rather than an imminent retirement, how long would he now have to work? And would he even have a choice? He could get fired any day. He was in a survival race, with his personal and work lives having spun out of control.

Too much to digest as he cracked open another Budweiser.

$ $ $

The next morning Michael Feinberg was waiting outside Kerr's office. He had been there for 10 minutes after being summoned by Kerr's secretary. He was pissed off for a number of reasons, not the least of which was waiting for 10 minutes while Kerr was on his phone. Didn't that asshole know he had better things to do, like make money?

"Yes, Sir," Feinberg said, sarcastically, as he finally got the wave and walked into Kerr's office. He could be sarcastic with Kerr, knowing that virtually every trading book on the floor was hemorrhaging money, except for his.

Over the course of the past 18 months, Feinberg, in contrarian anticipation of a potential market disruption event, had been selling the market short, especially subprime mortgages. As everyone else continued to pile into the market, he had quietly switched his book to being mostly naked short, using deals like Zeus. Under this strategy, Feinberg paid a negotiated premium to his trading counterparties. If the credit market went up, i.e., was bullish, he'd just lose the premium he paid. If the market went down, the value of his side of the deal went up, and he made money.

To be fair, as smart as Feinberg was, neither he nor anyone could have anticipated the velocity at which the credit markets turned bearish.

Nor would anyone have intuitively thought he was paying a premium to protect a credit portfolio to which he had no actual exposure. Most investors, not to mention the salespeople at Smyth Johnston, thought there was another party on the front end to whom Feinberg was selling protection or already owned the risk and that Feinberg was making money on the spread between what he received and paid. That had been the typical strategy used by Feinberg and his credit derivatives trading peers. Going naked short in this size would be the equivalent of buying insurance on the Empire State building without owning it. The difference being that in the derivatives world Feinberg didn't need to own the building to buy insurance on it. Instead of having an insurable interest he simply needed to have a directional view on the credit market.

Nor did he feel the need to reveal to investors his motivations in entering the transaction. Feinberg let investors draw their own conclusions, provided that the offering documents passed muster legally. If investors believed Feinberg was up to something, more specifically going naked short, they didn't have to buy the deal.

With Zeus having degraded immensely in recent months, Feinberg's book was now showing more than half a billion dollars of gains. With a historical payout ratio of 4 percent on average of the gains in his book, he was looking at a $25 million bonus. Not bad for a year's work, he thought, as he smiled at the completely stressed out Kerr. Maybe Kerr was right. Making that kind of money without the management bullshit was better.

Kerr knew that the year was going to be poor for the bank, and that Feinberg's bonus windfall would translate into many other traders and salesmen receiving little if anything in their annual envelopes. But that was a problem for January and February. Right now he had more pressing issues to deal with, namely whether the bank would make it to January or go the way of Lehman Brothers.

"I have to hand it to you, Michael. I'm glad you made the call and went short. You're saving the bank right now."

"Sometimes you get lucky and make the right calls."

"Don't give me that bullshit. You make the right call almost every time. Now I need you to do me a favor."

"Yes?"

"The entire bank is down about two billion year over year as of close of business yesterday. We're getting close to hitting our minimum liquidity provisions... I have regulators from the Fed, Treasury, and European Central Bank crawling up my ass. Stein is looking at me to figure out spots where we can show some profit, so we don't hit any triggers. We're not a Lehman situation, well not yet at least...but we don't need any bad PR in the midst of the current media witch hunt. Information and results have to be well managed. We don't need to give anyone a reason to make a run on the bank."

"Okay..."

"So, I have you at more than 25 bucks on the table, using your payout ratio of the past... If we get taken over by the feds, or worse forced into Chapter 11, guess how much you're going to get?"

"Duncan, what do you want?"

"You need to tweak the correlation assumptions on your book and then sell them to Risk Management as well as Product Control. You need to squeeze at least another $200 million of extra P&L. I need your book to be at around $750 million. I have a few other places to find some money as well."

"So, you're telling me to cook the books?"

"No, I'm telling you to reconsider your assumptions. Nobody is looking at hedges right now. Everyone is focused on the books that are in the red and what's in there."

"That's pretty dubious. People can go to jail for that kind of shit. You remember Enron, right?"

"Michael, Enron was outright fraud, an accounting subterfuge of egregious proportion. This is nothing like that. With new products, as you well know, there are no right answers as to your assumptions. Assumptions are untested in reality, green if you will. There are only subjective degrees of conservatism. No regulator or accountant can play God here; the Street is one step ahead of them. That creates the loopholes, the latitude we have with assumptions. Find a way to justify it. It'll be fine. The storm will blow over sooner or later. But we need a way to make it through now."

"I want to think about it."

Feinberg was a shrewd trader, his predatory instincts telling him that he had the upper hand, with time being in short supply for Kerr.

"We don't have the time, Michael. The fuse is lit and the bank is sitting at the end of it."

"Okay, fine, but I want a written directive from you."

"I can't do that. Don't get cute with me."

"Then no deal, I'll take my chances if or when the shit hits the fan. If the bank goes bankrupt, I'll recover

$10 million or so anyway. Not a bad outcome, much better than going to prison for fraud."

"Michael, be reasonable. Look at the big picture…I gave you this opportunity and have been your biggest advocate from day one. And stop using the word 'fraud'."

"C'mon Duncan. It was you who told me countless number of times in this office during bonus time that a trader is only as good as the P&L in his trading book. Remember '03? The firm really fucked me then, and now you're asking me to look at the big picture? That's bullshit."

"You need to do this, Michael."

"Write it down. I'm not taking a fall for this or getting dragged into an SEC investigation."

Duncan stopped for a minute to consider his alternatives.

He wanted to run the entire bank one day. It had been his dream since being a young associate some 20 years ago. If he didn't do something about the bleeding, at worst there'd be no bank to run, and at best his division would have blood-stained hands. If he got through the storm, he'd be a virtual lock for the job, with the current CEO preparing to punch the retirement clock. Stein, the CFO, was also vying for the top job. But if he could hit his P&L targets, or in the current circumstance limit the losses while holding the regulators at bay, he was sure he'd get the nod from the board. If he gave Feinberg the written order and everything recovered, nothing would be found out, and he'd be fine. If he didn't, the bank could go the way of Lehman and his dream of sitting in the CEO's office would be shattered.

"Fine, Michael, you win, but you have to keep this between us, and when things recover you return the note," Kerr said, and took a piece of blank paper on which he scribbled: "This is to confirm that I have authorized the re-evaluation of correlation models in Michael Feinberg's book. Signed, *Duncan Kerr*."

"That's not enough. I want it to say, 'This is to confirm that I have authorized the re-evaluation of correlation models in Michael Feinberg's book in order to source additional P&L'."

Again, Kerr had his back to the wall and relented.

"Thank you very much, Duncan. Let's talk about my deal going to 6 percent or you promoting me to global head of trading." Feinberg smiled, sensing victory.

"So you're going to retrade me right on the spot, Michael?"

"I'm sure Stein will like Exhibit A in my hand. If I give it to him, he'll take it to the board, get the nod, and then install me in this office."

"Michael, you're not ready for that level of seniority. You have no idea what goes on here in management. You'd be miserable. Be happy you can trade credit and make a mint. You don't want to deal with all this bullshit, at least not yet. It takes some time, some seasoning, to be groomed into a role like mine. You're a star trader. To be in this role you have to earn the respect of others around you; that can only happen over time. Besides, you didn't even earn your first job here. Deborah Goodman convinced me to hire you, as you should know."

"Maybe I do, maybe I don't. You're not the only ambitious guy here. I like optionality, as I know you can appreciate," Feinberg said, as he abruptly walked out of the office, leaving Kerr speechless—no small feat.

Kerr knew Feinberg would tweak the numbers, particularly because it would give him more leverage come bonus time. But he worried what would happen to the note, and the fact that it could be used by Feinberg or someone else if it fell into the wrong hands.

$ $ $

Jean-Pierre Bonet, global head of Credit Sales at Smyth Johnston, was, like so many of his peers across the Street, given the unenviable task of axman. Given his predisposition for avoiding controversy it was a task he hated but also one he recognized, ironically, as necessary to preserve his own survival. Kill or be killed. Fire or be fired.

Those deemed to be nonessential to the immediate well-being of the firm had already been culled. Foremost on the list were sales managers who, in more flush times, were considered bull market heroes, visionaries, and business architects of sorts, who propelled firms like Smyth Johnston to expand their footprint in the world of global finance. In less benign market conditions, let alone the current Armageddon Day meltdown, their value proposition was transformed from critical to expendable, an unnecessary luxury that needed to be eradicated. In a world where there is nothing to sell, Sales becomes acutely vulnerable.

Bonet surveyed his list. Many of his top managers were on it. He had personally hired most of them five or more years ago, Joey Karros being among them.

"Joey, this is beyond ugly. There is no task I loathe more than having to fire my guys. But, Duncan has made the decision to make cuts—lots of cuts, and you're one of them. I'm sorry."

"I'm being shown the door?" Karros plainly asked.

"Yes."

"Why?"

"We need to consolidate desks. And we've decided to go with Jim for all credit sales. And the Zeus or Broadway Life situation didn't reflect well on you. And your sales numbers are really down, so we decided to go another direction. You're not alone, as you can see."

Bonet held up his list, as if to assure Karros he wasn't the lone victim.

"Can I speak to Duncan? I have a long relationship with him."

"I'm afraid not. There is no appeal process here. Duncan told me he's in the bunker dealing with the media, that the firings are an unfortunate part of the PR dance the Street has to do to avoid getting slaughtered as the cause of the meltdown. You know, blame it on the evil bankers bullshit."

"I get it. Someone has to be the scapegoat to make everyone feel better. What about Trading, are they getting whacked as well?"

"A fair question. Yes and no. They're getting whacked to a far lesser extent. If books are melting down, you have to keep more traders around to figure out what exactly is in the books, and how to reposition the books, liquidate, or restructure them, right?"

"I guess so. What about Feinberg?"

"Feinberg is definitely staying. Duncan tells me his book is way up—especially over the last six months."

"The question is, why is it up so much and at whose expense? The answer: my clients. Did Feinberg have a role in who from Sales gets nuked?"

"I'd say yes. Duncan and Feinberg are very close or, at least, Duncan respects Feinberg's money-making talent. He needs Feinberg's P&L to salvage anything this year. Duncan wants to run this place." Bonet paused, and for the first time in a long time, Karros was speechless.

"Joey, again, I'm sorry it ends this way. I may be joining you in a day or two, right after I have to fire all my guys. That's not so great either. Wall Street is not a place for feelings."

Karros left Bonet's office, taking note of the next victim waiting outside. The two simply looked at one another, tacitly acknowledging the unfolding death march, as Bonet sat behind his desk waiting to swing the axe much like a game show host insincerely offering a losing contestant some parting gifts.

Karros was dismayed, his ego in denial. Had Feinberg put him on the list? He wasn't sure and never would be. As he walked over to HR—on another floor of the building—to receive his official pink slip and sign the various termination papers, he felt a numbness that overcame him. His career aspirations, those wistful dreams of the moneyed life that began back in the Staten Island days of his youth, had come to a halt. He had made more money than he ever imagined possible over his 18-year Wall Street journey. It was a journey that singularly consumed him, had come to define who he was, how success was defined—and now it was over, possibly forever. His world had been rocked. He was a master of the universe who had fallen back to earth.

One-dimensional dreams crash the hardest.

$ $ $

Feinberg had seen what others didn't see, or didn't want to see, in the credit markets of late. He saw the abundant patterns of reckless lending, both in consumer and corporate credit; an untenable culture of entitlement that had usurped personal and financial responsibility; and, most insidiously, he had seen how Fannie Mae and Freddie Mac, buttressed by the multitrillion dollar securitization business, had become a dangerous alliance between ideological Washington politics and Wall Street greed.

To Feinberg and few others, it was a bad recipe, he saw all of this as a fait accompli that would eventually precipitate a market meltdown. There was too much leverage, a simple over-reliance on "other people's money" in the financial system. Defaults would materialize sooner than later. He had bet on sooner, and in big size, taking the other side of the trade. The consumption-based bubble, with housing at its core, had burst. The explosion was loud and painful for those in its wake.

As he began to wrap up his day he looked at his P&L report and smiled, noticing that he had made $50 million, his best trading day ever. Because of the skillful repositioning of his book, Zeus, one of several deals that he had sold short, was itself showing a mark-to-market gain of $500 million. This gain, in painful financial symmetry, corresponded to an aggregate client mark-to-market loss of $500 million. What a business, he thought to himself. He was making money out of nothing, literally, other than a credit view.

For Feinberg, it was a banner day in all respects. Massive P&L was emerging in his book, the sales force was being held at bay, Kerr was in a trap, and his high-priced divorce lawyer had called to tell him not to worry about Franny or her lawyer.

He thought, in a rare introspective moment, of the ephemeral nature that had come to characterize his life. From the P&L that fluctuated wildly on a daily basis, to the credit derivatives products that generated the P&L itself, to his business relationships with other traders, salesmen, management, and, finally, to his personal relationships with his father and soon to be ex-wife; none of it had any sense of permanence.

Wall Street fame and fortune had indeed come at a high personal cost. It was a cost he had never fully considered enough to grasp its impact. Making money was his entire framework, the surrogate God that dominated his life. It was how he kept score, identified with himself, and benchmarked his personal sense of self-worth. All he needed to do was sprinkle a little money at any given situation, and all would be healed.

Franny would not be home tonight, as she had not been for many weeks. Maybe he would call for some company tonight. He made little distinction between marriage and paying for company. It was a variation of the same trade to him: both required cash. At least, he thought to himself, the call girl was a controlled expense while marriage, at least to Franny and, sadly enough, to her mother by extension, was akin to writing an open check—anything but controlled.

Bad optionality.

PART II

Death and Life

October 2008 to April 2009

Chapter 12
Day of comeuppance

Tuesday, October 14, 2008
1:00 A.M.

The Peninsula

After taking Detective Rodriguez to the security camera system, the manager of the luxury hotel returned to his computer. The security camera system was simple. There were four cameras: one on the street in front of the hotel, one above the front door inside the lobby, and two offering slightly different angles toward the back of the lobby.

The system saved the images from all cameras in time sequence, so Rodriguez could view all the pictures simultaneously. He was looking for any clues to the identity of the assumed killer of "Jack Jones."

He moved the timeline cursor back to 10:30. The cameras recorded no sound. A man entered the hotel at 10:37 wearing clothes similar to the body upstairs. The man went to the counter, prepaid his bill in cash, and took the key. The man went in the direction of the elevator and stood in front of it.

As the elevator door opened, someone wearing a dark, military-looking, knee-length coat and a large brimmed hat concealing their face appeared on the tape. Rodriguez couldn't tell whether it was a man or a woman. The cloaked figure managed to get into the elevator just before the door slammed shut. Where did he come from? The receptionist couldn't see the elevator bank from behind the counter.

Here's the killer, Rodriguez thought.

"Hi Victor," one of his Forensics guys said as he walked into the surveillance room.

"Good evening, Jay."

"Got something?"

"The potential killer, but first tell me what you got upstairs?"

Jay took out his notebook and flipped through entries.

"Who is it?" Rodriguez asked impatiently.

"The DL says Michael Feinberg, and he was 32 years old," Jay said, showing the victim's wallet. "He looks older than he is. In any case, one gunshot wound to the head. Not up close, as there's not gunpowder residue on the wound. No weapon has been found, but based on the width of the entrance hole it was a .38. No casing, so probably a revolver, or the killer picked it up."

Jay continued browsing his notes.

"Based on the blood splatters, he was standing at the time of impact, but not much else to say. After the shot, he fell to where we found him. The coroner will issue his own report, of course, but our preliminary inspection found no other injuries. So Feinberg hadn't struggled or been assaulted before the shooting."

"Fingerprints?"

"A lot. Working on lifting them, but I don't expect much from them."

"Why not?"

"Well, look at that video. The potential killer is wearing gloves. In the scenario, where the twosome entered the room together, the killer didn't have to touch anything. Feinberg probably opened the door and the killer followed him in, and pulled the gun as Feinberg ran to the other side of the room."

"Wouldn't he try to escape? Get away?"

"The shooter is clearly much bigger than Feinberg. If he was blocking the doorway, Feinberg only had the suite to protect himself in. Let's not forget, he wasn't expecting an intruder. Our ballistics expert suggests the entry point of the gunshot wound being on the side of the head, from 20 feet, approximately."

"Lot of speculation," Rodriguez said. "Shoe prints?"

"The victim had nice leather-soled shoes, and we've eliminated all the prints left by the police. It's difficult to say if something was left behind by a cleaner, but we found a print of Nike sneakers just inside the doorway."

Surveying the tape more closely, it was impossible to identify the brand of sneaker the person heading into the elevator was using.

"Size ten," Jay offered.

"What about a phone?"

"We found a Blackberry in Feinberg's pocket but don't have anything more. The keypad was locked. I tried the codes 0000 and 1234, but neither worked. We'll have to wait until we get it to the phone guys. After that it won't take long."

Rodriguez called his investigator at the precinct to request background information on Feinberg.

A few minutes later, the investigator called back to inform him that Feinberg was a senior trader at Smyth Johnston. He had a second home in Southampton in addition to his SoHo loft—both paid for with cash. He was married to a Francine Goodman. No children. No police record. MIT graduate. No flights had been reserved under Francine Goodman's name for today or the next day.

Southampton was a couple of hours drive away. Rodriguez didn't want to go there, not at this hour, to find Mrs. Feinberg. Hopefully she was at the loft in SoHo. The detective felt it was more and more probable the killer was someone in Feinberg's inner circle. The wife had to be one of the suspects; her husband was clearly unfaithful. Maybe she knew and finally had had enough.

The plan of investigation began to take shape. He had a starting point. He would deliver the news to the wife in person, while at the same time gauging her initial reaction. Body language was invaluable in situations like this.

In the morning, he would investigate the victim's movements in greater detail, then visit his office. The market meltdown could also be a motive, clearly.

Sergeant O'Roarke walked in. "There are a number of TV cameras out there. They want to talk to the detective in charge."

"Tell them to go away," Rodriguez said, irritated that the media vultures had already learned of the crime. The paparazzi had instantaneous access to the police blotters, courtesy of the internet.

Jay laughed out loud while O'Roarke simply grinned.

"Okay, tell them we have nothing to say at this stage of the investigation. We'll make a statement as soon as we get a lieutenant here."

$ $ $

No one had been at the loft in SoHo. Nor did anyone answer the phone at the Southampton beach house.

Arriving at the residence of Michael Feinberg's mother-in-law, Rodriguez knocked on the wooden door, one of four, on the sixth floor of the building on Park Avenue and 65th Street. He noted how remarkably quiet the building was, only to realize the time was 4:30 in the morning. Even New York had moments of tranquility. That was about to end.

Rodriguez had called Franny Goodman, whose cell number had been provided by Forensics after successfully unlocking the victim's Blackberry. Apologizing for the timing, he refused to tell her the reason for his call other than it was urgent. She had said that she was at her mother's apartment.

An older woman opened the door, introducing herself as Deborah Goodman.

"What has happened? Franny woke me up."

Rodriguez was welcomed into the apartment, where he found Franny sitting at the kitchen table. She looked worried.

"I have some terrible news. Your husband is dead."

"What?" she said. "I talked with him earlier today. It can't be."

"I'm sorry."

"How? Why?" Franny asked, naturally stunned by the news.

Her reaction seemed normal under the circumstance.

"He was a victim of a homicide a few hours ago, around midnight."

"Who did it... Oh, my God," Franny said, as tears began streaming down her cheeks.

"We'll find your husband's killer, in time. Do you have any ideas or thoughts that could be helpful to us?"

Franny shook her head. "No... No idea."

"What about you, Mrs. Goodman?" Rodriguez turned to the mother-in-law.

"No one directly comes to mind. But he wasn't a very well-liked person at his office."

"What do you mean?"

"He was a hard-edged trader at Smyth Johnston Securities and, as you may know, one person's win is another's loss. The last few months have been difficult in the financial industry."

Rodriguez turned back to the wife. "How was your marriage?"

"Not very good."

"How so?"

"He was starting divorce proceedings."

"Why?"

"He told me that our life together no longer satisfied him."

Rodriguez surveyed the apartment. Despite its Park Avenue location, it was far from lavish. Mrs. Goodman explained to him that she had moved into the apartment after collecting the life insurance proceeds following her husband's death several years ago. It was a new start for her, a departure from her suburban New Jersey life, a new sense of freedom, and a desire to live a more glamorous Manhattan lifestyle. Living on Park Avenue was an important statement for her to make.

"Where did the homicide happen?" the mother-in-law asked. "At the loft in SoHo? Franny and Michael had agreed that she would live in the Hamptons and Michael in SoHo."

"No," the detective said. The information was probably already in the news now, so there was no point in hiding it. "At The Peninsula hotel."

"How did he die?" Franny asked.

"He was shot. He died instantly."

There was no need to elaborate.

$ $ $

Detective Rodriguez and his partner, Detective Bush, convened at 8 a.m. at a coffee shop on the same block as Smyth Johnston. Rodriguez was tired, having slept on a couch in his office after he finished with Franny and Deborah Goodman. There was no reason to make the 45-minute trip to his home at that hour.

"How did it go with the wife?" Bush asked.

"It's never easy to break this kind of news to family members, let alone a spouse. Mrs. Feinberg went through the expected shock and hysterics, then seemed to settle down faster than what I thought should've been the case. Set aside the fact that I got the sense her marriage was not in good shape. Her mother was there, it was actually at her mother's home on Park Avenue where Mrs. Feinberg was spending most of her time. Her mother was emotional, but her emotions seemed more directed at her daughter's reaction," replied Rodriguez.

"Interesting how she got herself under control so fast," observed Bush.

"Well, I'm not sure what to make of it at this point."

"With that type of strange reaction, it makes you wonder. Did she love him, did she hate him, was she using him for the money? There are almost endless possibilities. You always hear about the off-the-chart divorce rates and other marital issues with the Wall Street crowd. Something about money being the root of all evil."

"Hard to say. By definition she has to be a suspect. I also picked up a lot of information about Feinberg's reputation at work. Not a well-liked guy, to put it mildly, according to the mother-in-law."

"Okay. Not well-liked. That can mean a lot of things."

"Oddly enough, remember that assault case a couple months ago, involving that big English guy? Guess who the victim was?"

"That's right, Feinberg. Looks like we have our second suspect. So why did the mother-in-law think the victim was so disliked?"

"She didn't know anything specifically, although she did say that he had a reputation for doing deals that made him a lot more money than his peers."

"Does that mean he screwed everyone he did deals with? Or does it mean he was just smarter than everyone else? I guess that's what we need to find out when we go to the bank."

Rodriguez proceeded to debrief Bush on other developments over the course of the night. Police officers had checked the SoHo apartment, finding nothing of interest other than its extravagance. None of the hotel guests had heard gunshots, or anything else that might be helpful. Forensics had found a 9 p.m. call to the escort service. Apart from that, along with plenty of email traffic, there was nothing striking.

"I managed to get the name of his boss from Mrs. Feinberg. Duncan Kerr is his name. A serious player in Wall Street circles."

"Sounds like our first appointment. Let's hope he's in town today."

"Yep. I also called my friend, Jack Bonfiglio, from the SEC earlier this morning. I used to work with him a long time ago. When I ran into him heading home one day, he told me he was in the middle of an SEC matter under inquiry with credit derivatives. He told me Feinberg was one of the key persons of interest in their inquiry, after I broke the news to him on the call today. He wasn't happy. He said he was getting close to having a case to pursue, with a whistleblower, the whole nine yards."

"Interesting to know. Maybe that gives us another angle to pursue here. At the least, it strengthens the possibility of it being a work-related inside job. Okay, let's figure out the game plan for the morning at Smyth Johnston," Bush stated.

"I see several on the dance card. Feinberg's boss, Duncan Kerr, strikes me as the logical first stop. Then I see this Nigel Woodley, who had the assault case with Feinberg as next, then his boss as well."

The pair walked into the lobby of Smyth Johnston's offices on 47th Street, where they explained the purpose of their visit to security and were immediately shown the elevator bank leading up to Michael Feinberg's former office.

"Can I help you?" asked the receptionist.

"We're here to see a Duncan Kerr. It's a private matter."

"I'm not sure if Mr. Kerr is in today. Let me check with his secretary. May I let him know who is here?"

"Detective Victor Rodriguez from the New York Police Department."

The receptionist phoned Kerr's secretary, speaking in hushed tones.

"Mr. Kerr's secretary will be with you shortly. Please have a seat."

No sooner had they seated themselves in the plush leather chairs when Duncan Kerr's administrative assistant appeared. Sensing the seriousness behind the police's unexpected visit, she escorted the detectives into Kerr's office overlooking the trading floor. Both instantly noticed the enormous size of the trading floor and the legions of younger, well-dressed people in a high-energy state of orchestrated chaos, as they peered out the glass-sided office.

"Good Morning. I'm Duncan Kerr. What can I help you with this morning?"

Rodriguez, the senior of the two NYPD officers, proceeded. "Mr. Kerr, I'm here to inform you of the death of one of your employees. I need to ask you and others here some questions as they relate to the investigation that has now been opened."

Kerr sank in his chair. "Who is it?"

"The victim's name is Michael Feinberg. We understand that he reported directly to you."

"Yes, to answer your question, he reported to me on a global basis, but he had a local reporting line here in New York. He is…was…one of the bank's superstars."

Kerr paused, then he asked, "How did he die?"

"Gunshot."

"Did he…?"

"We don't know yet. That's what we're investigating. How was he doing at work?"

"His book was up big on the year, to the tune of half a billion in P&L. His profits are vital to the bank's performance this year, every year for that matter. You may have seen in the news that there are some issues in other areas of the financial markets… Losses have spiraled to heights never seen before." Kerr rambled, instinctively reaching for the phone to take action.

Rodriguez was taken aback by Kerr's money-centric reaction to the news. One of his employees had died, yet he was focused on the financial ramifications it might have on his division and his own career. It was as if Kerr was a money automaton, devoid of all compassion, motivated singularly by his naked self-interest.

Or was the rambling response a sign of nervousness? Was Kerr trying to hide something?

"Put the phone down, Mr. Kerr. We need to talk with you privately before anyone else here becomes aware of this. Once we get done with you, we're going to need to speak to others Feinberg had frequent contact with here at the bank."

"I understand, provided that you understand what's going on in the markets today. I can't put the trading floor on hold in the middle of a market meltdown. The Street is bleeding money. My people need to be in their seats."

"Mr. Kerr, don't talk to me about blood. I saw enough of Mr. Feinberg's last night. You'll need to cooperate with us here and now. If not, we'll subpoena every person on that floor out there for questioning, and do it downtown. I can make this very difficult for you. This is an investigation, and your firm is in the middle of it."

"Okay, okay. What do you need?"

"We're going to need a place to question some of your employees. We have some names already, but will need to get additional ones from you. We need to know everything you can tell us about Feinberg's relationships at the bank. Who were his friends, did he have enemies, who were his closest colleagues, whom did he work with the most, what was his reputation… His HR file, anything that could be of interest. I'm sure you understand."

"How would you like to start?"

"Let's start with your relationship with Mr. Feinberg."

This time Kerr was staring right at Rodriguez' eyes.

"As I said, Michael was a superstar. He made loads of money for the bank year after year. That includes this year when everyone else is losing money due to what is happening now. He is as sharp as they come, and his trading instincts are as good as I have ever seen. He is a Six Sigma event. You can assume he got paid according to his talent. No chance was this bank going to let him get poached by the competition."

"Sorry, what is a Six Sigma event? And just how much money was Mr. Feinberg getting paid?"

"Six standard deviations from the mean. A very rare intelligence. A true superstar. And, well, he was on track this year for a total payout of as much as $25 million. His book, as we speak, is up half a billion, and climbing."

"Twenty-five million dollars?"

"Yes, twenty-five million."

Rodriguez glanced over at his colleague Bush, who looked equally stunned by this figure. Neither had any feel, much less ability, to grasp this level of compensation, leaving one another with the same immediate reaction: why would someone about to get paid $25 million put a gun to his own head?

"When you say *total payout,* what do you mean?"

"Total payout is a combination of base salary and bonus. Wall Street is all about the bonus. Base salary is really a subsistence wage. Bonuses are typically not guaranteed compensation, unless the employee is new or has an extenuating circumstance that would compel the bank to give an existing employee an agreed upon or formulaic, performance-based bonus. Either way, a bonus never gets paid if the performance doesn't justify the payout. Perform or perish—a brutally fair proposition. There are no handouts on the Street. And, sometimes, for other reasons, a bonus doesn't get paid even if the performance justifies it. This year, for example, there will be lots of good performers whose bonuses get cut or eliminated due to the world blowing up. There is a lot of discretion on the part of managers in the process. We call it optionality in this business."

"So how much was his salary, this subsistence wage?"

"Two hundred thousand."

"I see. So he had a lot riding on his bonus to say the least. Mr. Feinberg was a wealthy man."

"Yes. I would say he was personally worth as much as $100 million."

"As a 32-year-old?"

Rodriguez was trying not to get blinded by the dazzling success of Mr. Feinberg. Envy, a natural sentiment, stirred his animal spirits. The disparity between his 90 grand income to that of Mr. Feinberg was overwhelming. The math was simple: he could work almost 300 years to equal what Feinberg was making in that one year.

"How would you describe your relationship with Mr. Feinberg?"

"I would characterize our relationship as respectful. I can tell you that a talent like this does not come around often. He was a whiz-kid, and I could depend on him to make a lot of money for the firm every year. I hired him seven or so years ago."

"Respectful" was an odd choice of words, Rodriguez thought.

"I've heard Mr. Feinberg was not well liked by his colleagues. Is that true?"

"Well liked, I'm not sure about that. I would say someone as successful as Michael probably had created much envy on the floor and probably some ill will based on his trading style."

Rodriguez blushed, having just felt that envy.

"Trading style? What do you mean?"

"Michael liked to win, and often did. He was ambitious, brash, and smarter than anyone out there. I'm sure he rubbed many with whom he interacted the wrong way."

"Would that include some of the other people here, or just people he dealt with outside of the bank?"

"You'll need to talk with them, but it probably includes internal and external people. As to internal people, you might want to start with some of my salesmen. There's always a natural level of tension with a trader, particularly one as successful as Michael. That's just the way it works with Sales and Trading. And, keep in mind that virtually every person you see here is a Type A personality. Not a lot of laid back people in this business."

Kerr hesitated for a minute, "You also may or may not be aware of the assault case that Michael was involved in a few months ago."

"Yes, we are. I was actually the detective on the case. Mr. Woodley is one of the people I would like to talk to. And his bosses."

"Well, as a result of that incident, Mr. Woodley is no longer employed by the bank, but I can call his former manager in here. There was an incident involving a particular transaction."

"Who in particular?"

"His name is Chip Smith. Should I have my secretary get him?"

"Yes, please."

Minutes later, Kerr's secretary returned, alone.

"Chip Smith does not seem to be here today, and no one knows where he is. He's not picking up his cell phone either. Tracy Maxwell said she's been trying to reach him all morning."

$ $ $

Chip opened his eyes, wearily.

Everything was blurry as he started to feel the pain and the cold asphalt he was lying on. He noticed himself shaking, as he tried to figure out where he was. He had no idea.

His sense of smell promptly kicked into overdrive, detecting the rancid scent of days-old, rotting garbage surrounding him. He mustered the energy to place himself in a sitting position, hoping to gather himself as he stared at the piles of garbage stacked up everywhere against the tight brick walls. It was cold, with no direct sunlight. What the hell had happened to him? Why was he waking up in an alley behind a dumpster, feeling like death warmed over?

He next noticed he was wearing a military-style dark green jacket, something he didn't own, and a pair of sneakers. He only wore sneakers during sports. He was also wearing a large brimmed hat. Chip stood up, using the dumpster as a crutch. His legs were weak as he struggled to get his eyes focused. He saw a street up ahead, at the end of the alley.

As he walked toward the street, he tried to retrace his steps from the night before. His last recollection was the Blarney Stone. He had no idea what had happened after that.

The street was vibrant, with shops and people everywhere. A sign told him it was Fourth Avenue. Cars swooshed by him, the noise pounding his head like a sledgehammer.

"Excuse me," stopping a passer-by. "Where am I?"

"Fourth Avenue," replied the woman, not stopping to chat to a random, disheveled stranger.

"Manhattan?" Chip didn't recognize his surroundings.

The woman smiled. "No, Brooklyn."

Chip felt something heavy in his coat pocket and, curiously, pulled it out.

"Gun!" the woman screamed. "Look out! This nutcase has a gun!"

People scurried around, rushing into shops for refuge. Fifty yards away a police car hit the lights, accelerating just short of Chip. Two uniformed officers jumped out of the car, with their guns pointed directly at Chip.

"Drop the gun or I'll shoot," one of the officers calmly yelled.

Chip did not understand anything, but obeyed.

"On the ground! Now!"

Chip did as told. One of the officers approached him, pressing his knee into Chip's back as he jerked his hands behind his back. The steel handcuffs felt cold, as did the sidewalk he was lying face down on.

"Who the hell are you?"

"Charles Smith"

"Why do you have a gun?"

"I have no idea," Chip replied, as he was forced into the backseat of the police car.

$ $ $

Duncan Kerr knew he had limited time to address the trading floor about the tragedy—local news channels were already covering it. Michael Feinberg was high profile on Wall Street. His absence on the floor was also conspicuous to those around him, as it was to him, and he knew the media would soon be devouring this story— in Smyth Johnston's offices, outside the building, anywhere they could get an angle. They were already circling the wagons of Wall Street to cover the market meltdown. Now a murder was being added to the sensationalistic mix. The most creative minds in Hollywood would be hard-pressed to orchestrate such a media frenzy.

The last thing his Sales and Trading personnel needed at this point was another shockwave, as the market disruption was causing more than enough trouble on its own. He had no choice but to make the announcement.

Kerr went to the middle of the trading floor, where he eventually got everyone's attention, no small feat, and proceeded to deliver the next shockwave. One of the government bond traders had given him the hoot, a microphone that was heard throughout the trading floor.

"It is my regrettable task to advise all of you of a terrible tragedy involving one of our colleagues. Last night Michael Feinberg was found dead. The police are conducting a homicide investigation into the matter. Some of you will be asked to speak with them as they proceed with the investigation in the coming days. I can't and will not elaborate any further. This is a great loss to our firm and I would ask that each of you be respectful of the situation and do your utmost to help with the many challenges this will impose on his trading desk. For the time being, I'm asking Vasily Bure to assume Michael's responsibilities."

As Kerr walked back to his office, the trading floor, as if in suspended animation, re-erupted into its more characteristic state of perpetual chaos. While shockwaves were nothing new on a trading floor, this one was of a new type. The reaction on the floor spanned the gamut of emotions. Fear, sadness, consternation, and heightened panic, particularly among those on Feinberg's desk, gripped the floor.

Kerr sank into his chair, digesting the enormity of the announcement he had just made to the hundreds of Smyth Johnston employees. Bure stood up. He looked around to see the remainder of his colleagues, all of whom had ashen looks on their faces.

"What the fuck?" said Bure, who was prone to little if any emotion. People didn't call him Dr. Doom for the hell of it. Kerr's announcement knocked him off his dispassionate feet. He stood there, catatonic for a few minutes, gathering himself.

He turned to his immediate right, where Peter Baum sat with his head in his hands.

"Peter, we must talk immediately. The book is way up. Grab Jorge. We need to set up triage on how to manage through this, or we get crushed like a ripe melon. Game over."

Vasily Bure was highly similar to his now-deceased boss, Michael Feinberg. He wanted Wall Street riches and he wanted it now. He was there to extract as much money out of the system as he could. If doing so meant crossing that squiggly thin line that separated proper from improper conduct, he would think nothing of it. In this respect he was the perfect Feinberg operative. Win at any cost, with money being the way to keep score.

He saw the opportunity to play the hero, now foisted into a new circumstance.

$ $ $

Later that afternoon, Detective Bush had made contact with Sasquatch, who agreed to meet with him at his home in Long Island. Hoping to avoid the onslaught of rush hour traffic, he went back to the precinct and sequestered a police car. As long as he got through the Queens Midtown Tunnel by two, he would probably avoid the dreaded gridlock of the Long Island Expressway, sometimes called the "World's Longest Parking Lot." He could always find a place to have a coffee if he arrived early. Besides, that would give him the opportunity to organize his thoughts about his interview.

He arrived without incident at Nigel Woodley's home with ample time to spare.

As he drove around the neighborhood, he immediately noticed the quality of the homes with their well-manicured lawns. He could tell this was a neighborhood of mostly professional types—bankers, lawyers, doctors, and accountants. It was far different than his blue-collar neighborhood back in Queens.

Bush rang the doorbell.

"Hello Mr. Woodley. I'm interested in speaking to you about your relationship with Michael Feinberg. We understand you had frequent interaction with him at Smyth Johnston."

"What an asshole."

"I'm aware of the assault charge that was filed and then dropped by Mr. Feinberg."

"That's right. He dropped the charge, which was total bullshit, after he got me fired. I wish I had assaulted him. He deserves much worse than that."

Bush wondered if they had found their guy.

"Let me cut you off there. He got much worse than that—he was found dead this morning in his suite at The Peninsula hotel. I'm here as part of the homicide investigation. We're talking to many persons of interest, which includes you."

"I see," Sasquatch said, toning down his antipathy toward Feinberg as he considered whether or not he needed a lawyer.

"Let's get back to your relationship with Mr. Feinberg, how you interacted with him…"

"Okay. Yes, I had frequent interaction with Feinberg in my role in Sales. To be more accurate, my interaction was more so with his Trading colleagues. Feinberg was very senior to me so my direct exposure was limited. The Sales desk I was part of was involved with a lot of his team's deals."

"What were your impressions of Feinberg?"

"His business approach was eye-opening to me, to say the least. I guess that explains the so-called assault. His job was to maximize the P&L for his book, while mine was to ensure he does so in a way that is fair and lucrative for my client. Competing interests that make for a tenuous balance. The problem is that he didn't really care about anything other than his P&L on any given trade. He would think nothing of screwing a client, because that client was someone else's problem. As a salesperson, you don't survive if you allow your client to get screwed. Making money, however he could, was a zero-sum game to him. Salespeople lose almost every time in that game."

"So he was more aggressive than most?" asked Bush.

"He was very aggressive, more than most. But it really goes beyond that with me, and I'm sure the same holds true with many others who had to deal with him. The bigger issue is a simple matter of trust, or lack thereof, with the guy."

"So you and others didn't trust him, even though he was a big money-maker for the bank?"

"Nope. I wouldn't trust the guy as far as I could throw him. Nor would I trust many of the sidekicks on his desk. Some of these guys are rotten to the core. It's as if Feinberg hired a bunch of people who bought into a perverse value system that condoned, not condemned, scumbag behavior.

"Money became the lone governor of their behavior. The money became the justification for everything they did. And keep in mind a lot of the people on Feinberg's desk come from different countries where the ability to make money on a scale like Wall Street doesn't exist. Their mindset is that they're here to take from the system—this is their opportunity to rob the bank so to speak. Their version of the American Dream, I guess.

"When I joined Smyth Johnston I heard a story about Feinberg and his savages during 9/11, that Tuesday afternoon Feinberg had his people calling around Sales to make sure the counterparties on his trades, the clients—some of whom were in the World Trade Center—were still operating, to find out what his exposure to them might be. Or who knows, maybe he was trying to short their stock to grotesquely profit on the circumstance. Think about it. While I was trying to figure out how many of my friends and clients who worked in the Twin Towers were still alive, he was thinking about money. Look, I understand the need for risk management, but the cavalier way they went about it is as telling as it gets in terms of their behavior."

Sasquatch paused for a moment, knowing he had peeled the onion way back.

"I don't want to give you the wrong impression, that everyone acts like this. They don't. I dealt with lots of different trading desks, bankers, and others who operate with integrity and aren't on a scorched-earth quest for money. The fact that Feinberg's desk is full of comparatively younger traders, many of whom seem to brashly make a mockery of the system only adds to the negative feelings people have toward them."

Bush was starting to think Sasquatch wasn't the killer. The demeanor, the candor didn't seem to fit that of a killer. He decided to push another button.

"Tell me about Feinberg's team, what are they like?"

"The foreign legion, you mean?"

"Lots of foreign folks I gather."

"I too am a foreigner—English. My comment is about nothing other than behavior and decorum. Behavior is a choice and at a point, despite cultural and circumstantial differences, there is proper and improper behavior that transcends these differences. Whether you're Swedish, Mexican, Greek, Asian, Indian, Russian, English, Jewish, we all have a choice on how we conduct ourselves. They just seem to have no respect for the opportunity they have in being here and even less interest in playing the game according to the proper rules of decorum or integrity. The issue, as I said before, is that some people are more vulnerable than others to having their value systems subverted."

"We see it every day as police officers."

"Yes, but there is a lot of money at stake every day on Wall Street. I trust you have a sense of Feinberg's compensation."

"We do. He was making Major League baseball superstar money, like A-Rod or others on the Yankees. Tell me more about the assault incident."

"That's pretty simple. On a recent deal one of my clients felt he had been ripped off by Feinberg, and I took a lot of heat. Rather than not let Feinberg hear about it, I confronted him with it. Feinberg claimed I physically intimidated him and had me thrown out of the building and taken downtown. He dropped the charge after having me fired. I guess he thought he was letting me off easy."

"And where were you last night?"

"Right here. My wife and some neighbors were here with me."

"Okay. We can verify that later. So, that's it for now. Who else should we speak with?"

"You have a lot of people who dealt with Feinberg. His trading desk, others from Sales, his local boss, external clients...take your pick."

"Specific names please."

"Sure. As to his trading desk, I already mentioned Vasily Bure, Jorge Soto, and Peter Baum. Sales people might include my colleague, Chip Smith, and Joey Karros."

"You mentioned external clients. Who?"

"One of my clients, make that former client, comes to mind. His name is Mal McMahon. He's fresh off of getting fucked by Feinberg on a deal. I can give you his number, but he may already be fired. If so, I know he lives in Rye...in a house he can no longer afford."

Bush was pleased with the discussion. It was time to head back into Manhattan to meet with Rodriguez, whom he decided to call with an update en route.

"My meeting with Woodley went well. I don't see him as having any role in this thing."

"I think we may have found our guy," Rodriguez replied. "He's being detained in Brooklyn, where he was picked up earlier today. Meet me there."

$ $ $

Chip sat down in the interrogation room, handcuffed, his inexplicable hangover still in full bloom. Having been told he was at a detention center in Brooklyn, he remained utterly perplexed as if in a hallucinogenic out-of-body experience.

The first detective had questioned him, though without much success. Chip hadn't been able to tell him anything of consequence. He told him what he had remembered—not a lot. The police informed him he was being detained as a prime suspect in the murder of Michael Feinberg.

After another 20 minutes he was returned to Holding, where he would be taken through a battery of tests. Fingerprints were taken; some tape had been used to take a sample from his hands, chin, and under his nose. The inside of his cheek was swept with a cotton swab. A hair sample was taken.

He was undressed and given an undignified cavity search. His clothes were sent to Forensics. His new clothes were a gray T-shirt, socks, and orange overalls. In the span of fewer than 24 hours, he had gone from sitting at Smyth Johnston, clad in a nice suit, to this sad, befuddled state.

Not exactly the romantic vision of riding off into the sunset of his Wall Street career. This was not the ending he had scripted for himself.

As he sat in his detention cell, for what seemed like an eternity, a Hispanic-looking policeman eventually entered the room. Hanging from his neck, an ID card read Victor Rodriguez.

The man sat down, reading him his Miranda rights.

Chip didn't think he needed a lawyer. Something had gone wrong, but he hadn't killed Feinberg. He didn't think much of it. Some mistake had been made. It would somehow be corrected.

"I don't think I need a lawyer."

Rodriguez looked at him in silence, and then asked. "Are you sure?"

Chip nodded.

"Let's go back through your day yesterday."

They started from the time Chip woke up at his home on Long Island and took the train to work.

Chip told Rodriguez how he had been following the nose-diving financial markets, the blood on the computer screens, and how he freaked out to the point of smashing his phone on the desk. Ultimately, he told Rodriguez, he had to get off the trading floor, heading late afternoon to the Blarney Stone by himself.

"Do you normally drink by yourself?"

"Never. This was an exception, born out of a feeling of hopelessness as I saw my retirement funds getting wiped out, yesterday at a rate greater than most. You have to understand, a lot of bankers work in tough conditions in hope of making a lot of money—fast—so that they can do something else with their lives, with financial security. Seeing all of that threatened is not easy."

Rodriguez didn't say anything for a while. For a moment, he actually felt sympathy for the distraught, confused banker.

"I understand a large part of your net worth is tied to Smyth Johnston shares," he said hoping to keep Chip talking.

"That's true. Last winter, they were worth about four million."

"What about now?"

"I haven't seen the market today as I sit here in my orange suit. Yesterday it was around two million, and plummeting."

"So you've lost half. Can't you just sell?"

"No sir, I can't. These are mostly tied up in restricted shares for multiple years. All I can do is watch the train wreck."

"You blamed Michael Feinberg as one of the reasons for the financial crisis. At least two people, Joey Karros and Tracy Maxwell, also told us you had from time to time made threatening comments about Feinberg."

"I wasn't serious."

"Is that so? You told me that you left at three o'clock to go to a bar. What's its name again?"

"Blarney Stone," Chip said.

"What brand of beer do you drink there?" Rodriguez was testing Chip, using the thinly-veiled police tactic of getting a suspect to verify the consistency of the information they provided.

"Budweiser."

"What did you drink yesterday?"

"Budweiser."

Stay consistent, Chip thought. Don't fall into the trap.

"How many beers did you have?"

"I'm not sure. Maybe four."

"The bartender remembered six, and at a fast pace."

"Then I guess so."

"Did the fact that Joey Karros got fired have any impact on your behavior?"

"I doubt it."

Rodriguez paused.

"Why not? He was your boss. You'd think that would have an impact."

"Perhaps to a degree."

"Your wife told me that you have been in an aggressive mood most of the time when you come home. A lot of ranting about your job and how Feinberg has caused a lot of your problems…"

Chip looked at Rodriguez, realizing the cops had already managed to speak with his wife in the last couple hours?

"Feinberg was an asshole. I didn't like him. I will not tell you otherwise. But I still didn't kill him. Remember, I told you I'm trying to get on with my life. No reason for me to do this, even if I were inclined to do so. You have to understand that my world is cratering at exactly the wrong time, in a parallel universe with the markets. To see so much of your life's work cratering uncontrollably is painful."

"I understand that you had frequent interaction with Mr. Feinberg. Can you elaborate on that."

"That's correct, along with lots of others whom he screwed on deals. Looks like he got screwed this time. Poetic justice, you might say. I know that sounds harsh on my part. I apologize for that, but you need to understand just how disliked Feinberg and some of his sidekicks are. I'm not the only one who found him deeply offensive. I'm sure of that fact."

"And what was it that made him so offensive to you?"

"Where do I start? Well, it wasn't the mere fact that he was anathema to any salesman or client by his deceitful tactics. It wasn't the fact that you knew you weren't getting the whole story when working on one of his deals. On that point—his lack of transparency on deals—there was a joke among Sales that if you did a deal with Feinberg, you, or worse yet your client, had just been fucked. And it wasn't the fact that the guy would do anything in his power to see to it that you got screwed come comp time if you didn't help his desk, no matter the circumstance. I could go on forever."

"Go ahead," as Rodriquez had begun to form a less-than-sanguine view of not only the deceased, but Wall Street more generally. He was surprised at Chip's tone. There was some serious hatred. Enough for a murder

"At a more philosophical level," Chip continued, "he embodied something much worse."

"He embodied a behavioral malaise, or devolution if you will, that has transformed parts of this business into its current toxic state. There was a time, not too long ago, when people, myself included, would pursue a career on Wall Street for a number of well-intended factors. Don't get me wrong, the money was foremost among those factors. But there were other reasons as well, namely being surrounded by business-savvy and intelligent people, the competitiveness of the business, the innovative spirit, and the overall high standards of performance—including proper behavioral conduct—expected of those in the game. There was an implicit sense of decorum to the business, a respect for the system, and those in the system, that has been lost lately."

"And you feel Feinberg had something to do with that change?" asked Rodriguez.

"Feinberg and his type, yes."

"His type?"

"His type being those who can't see beyond the scope of the current trade. Or maybe it's that they don't care to see beyond the scope of the current trade and P&L...meaning profit...of their book. It's created a winner-take-all mentality. Gone is the decorum, gone is the notion of doing the right thing for the firm or client. It's all about them. Many of these types, like Feinberg, were so successful—in terms of P&L—that they could leverage, or, more precisely, rig, the system to avoid the checks and balances that might otherwise have curtailed some of this punk behavior. Left largely unchecked, they hijacked the system knowing they could get away with virtually anything."

"Getting away with anything wouldn't include illegal actions would it?" asked Rodriguez.

"Good question. No, I have no reason to suggest illegal conduct whatsoever with Feinberg or others like him. But understand that they operate in the largely unregulated over-the-counter derivatives marketplace where the rules, contractual terms, and market practices were being developed in real time for the past 10 years. It's their toxic behavior, stopping short of illegal, that has transformed the business culture. Making matters worse, they feel as if it's their entitlement to act this way. It pisses a lot of the otherwise decent people off that these guys, a small minority, have corrupted the system to their advantage."

Chip kept at what must certainly have seemed to the detective to be a bitter diatribe from a disgruntled banker.

Rodriguez was pleased that Chip continued to talk freely. "Okay, let's go back to yesterday; do you remember the rest of the evening events?"

"I do not."

"How, then, can you say that you did not kill him."

Chip was silent.

"For your information, we've searched your home, and confiscated your computer and phone. Speaking of your phone, you sent a number of photos to your home email around 2 p.m. yesterday."

"I believed I was about to get fired. I wanted to save some personal stuff because the bank would have taken my phone immediately. Like they did with Karros."

"So you were afraid of being fired."

"Well, yes. Karros had been. Why not me? This is all a terrible misunderstanding…"

"Do you know where Feinberg lived?"

"Southampton. He took a helicopter to work. But he had another place in SoHo."

"You know where it is?"

Chip nodded. "Yes. I've never been inside, but one time after a meeting downtown we dropped him off there."

"Going back to the events, so you're telling me your last recollection of yesterday was at the Blarney Stone?"

Chip smiled.

"Yes. I wish I could tell you more. Maybe your forensics guys will tell you there was a trace of drugs in my blood. That's what I feel like."

Rodriguez looked coolly at Chip, turning up the heat on him.

"Mr. Smith, you do not remember or you don't want to remember?"

"I would tell you, if I only knew more. I don't."

"Michael Feinberg was shot in The Peninsula hotel last night. We have video of a man going to the hotel. His outfit is the same on tape as the one you were arrested in. Fiber studies support the finding. The hotel suite revealed identical shoeprints of the same size Nike sneakers you were wearing. Your hands as well as nasal passages contained gunpowder residue that indicate you had shot a firearm within the previous 24 hours before your arrest. We found five hair samples in the suite that match your DNA. The escape route in the staircase had a Kleenex that also matches your DNA."

Chip was silent.

"What do you think now?" the detective asked.

"I think I should get a lawyer."

"That would be smart. We have enough evidence to prosecute you as is," Rodriguez said.

Chapter 13
Bad math

Wednesday, October 15, 2008
10:15 A.M.

Lower Manhattan Detention Facility

Dwight Gordon, Esquire, introduced himself to Chip as he sat down in the detention cell.

He was high-priced and as experienced a criminal defense attorney as there was in New York. Part of a large, pedigreed Manhattan law firm, he had been involved in cases spanning the gamut of white collar crimes, including murder. His firm had clout, a track record of successful defense work, and a support structure of friendly police investigators, junior lawyers, paralegals, and anyone else who could help win cases.

Dispensing his first counsel, he immediately told Chip to remain silent during further police questioning until he had ample time to look into the matter. The media was already, in its unquenchable thirst to sensationalize, labeling the case "The Wall Street Bloodbath." The seasoned lawyer knew he had to act with alacrity before his client got railroaded in the court of public opinion, as the media profited wildly. He harkened back to the Preppy Murder case of the 1980s.

At first blush Gordon felt the case lacked the type of theatrical conflict that sold newspapers. An ordinary citizen couldn't really decide who to support in a banker vs. banker case; it was similar, he felt, to black-on-black gang violence, though higher profile and certainly more topical given the current state of the financial markets. The sympathy factor was missing.

Gordon reminded his client not to talk to anyone until instructed to do so by him. He would be building the case over the coming days, assuring Chip that someone from his firm, if not him, would be visiting him each day.

The short, heavy man had his battle-scarred brown leather briefcase with him. He dug out a bundle of papers. He looked over his reading glasses at Chip in his overalls.

"Apart from the obvious, how's it going?"

"How's it going? I've spent a night in jail, wondering when I'm ever getting released for this trumped-up bullshit against me."

"Unfortunately, we can't get bail because as of now we're looking at murder two. I haven't requested it as it's not worth it yet," Gordon explained. "It wasn't very wise that you talked to the police yesterday without us. But looking at the entirety of the case, it didn't cause too much damage. The situation is, frankly, pretty difficult regardless."

"I can't say anything further than what I've already said. What about the blood tests? Was I drugged? If so, by whom, and was I therefore set up?"

"Whether it was intentional or not, the police did not do the blood test. The breathalyzer gave a zero at 11:00. Maybe that's why they thought it might've been unnecessary. Maybe we can use that in your defense."

"But, if…"

"Mr. Smith," Gordon interjected. "The police investigation is not yet complete, but quite frankly the situation is difficult unless we can use the botched blood test to create a reasonable doubt. Or maybe something else emerges that saves the day. However, failing that, the evidence I see today is that you will likely be convicted of second-degree murder, which means a 10-25 year sentence. So that you know New York State law has limited scope for first-degree murder, typically involving only cases with multiple victims, torture, or the victim being a police officer, judge, prosecutor, or prison guard."

Chip looked quietly at his lawyer.

"So you do not believe in the possibility that I am innocent."

"Of course I do. But hard evidence is difficult to refute. There are other possibilities to pursue. If we can verify your memory loss, we can get it reduced to intentional manslaughter. Or if we can get psychological tests to show you were deemed to have been seriously stressed, temporary insanity of a sort, leading to the offense. In light of all the evidence, it seems difficult to overcome murder two. If I could convince the DA to believe that we have a realistic chance at the state of stress, we could plea bargain. Then you'd get maybe 12 years, with the possibility of parole at 8. If you end up in court, the sentence is probably somewhere around 20."

Chip counted quickly. After 8 years, he would be a little less than 50, while after 20 years he would be over 60. Sixty sounded like bad math to him. Maybe, despite believing in his innocence, he should take the plea bargain.

"Is the evidence really that air tight?"

"So it seems."

"Seems? I didn't ask that. If I'm the killer, let's go ahead and plead guilty. If not, then let's not."

Gordon shuffled his papers. "There's one small detail that didn't quite fit the whole picture."

"What?"

"Your phone was located near the Blarney Stone bar, when you got a phone call at 7:33 p.m."

"What call?"

"Someone called you from a phone booth next to Central Park. The call lasted 17 seconds, according to the phone records."

"Who called?"

"We don't know. We went to the public phone but there was nothing there…"

Chip closed his eyes.

Blarney Stone's toilet. It was familiar. He remembered the harsh urinal. But a phone call—nothing.

Absolutely nothing, until he remembered a sharp pain in the upper arm that hit him as he stood at the urinal.

"Something happened in the bathroom there," Chip said. "I don't know what, but you should check out the clothes. I've never owned such a jacket or hat, and I never use Nike sneakers. I'm an Adidas guy."

$ $ $

Dwight Gordon and his legal staff had been canvassing any and all colleagues of Chip who might shed light on the accused, his personality, his relationship with Michael Feinberg. He was looking for anything that might help in his defense of a case where the evidence appeared overwhelmingly stacked against his client. Uncovering nothing of consequence as of yet, he called Sasquatch.

"Mr. Woodley, I'm Dwight Gordon. My firm is representing your friend Chip Smith in the Michael Feinberg murder case. I would appreciate being able to ask you some questions about Mr. Smith."

"Of course. I'm glad you called. I have as much time as you need."

"My staff has uncovered a great deal of information about the sales-trading relationship, specific friction between you and Feinberg, more specifically the incident culminating in your firing, Mr. Smith's relationship with Mr. Feinberg, and much more."

"Okay, so you know what an asshole Feinberg was to his colleagues, clients, and even wife."

"You can assume we are aware of most of this, yes. We are also aware of the wealth of evidence stacked against your friend—the threatening language, the matching clothing on the night of the murder, a Kleenex found in the hotel stairwell with Mr. Smith's DNA on it. I must say it does not look promising. So, what makes you believe your friend did not kill Mr. Feinberg?"

"I don't know how to explain all of this other than to comment on him as a friend. Chip was not alone in the threatening language. Hell, I assaulted the guy, or so it was falsely alleged. Feinberg pissed off a ton of people in our business circles."

"We don't need to cover any of that. My staff has a thick file on Feinberg at this point."

"I'm sure you do. I do not believe Chip killed Feinberg. First, he was typically pretty calm in the face of adversity. While he may make comments, maybe even threatening comments about someone, he would do so mostly to provide comic relief, to lower everyone's stress level, or to build consensus within his team. You might also consider he was looking forward to checking out of the Wall Street game as soon as possible. He had made enough money and was looking forward to a new life post-Wall Street. None of this makes sense to me, and I knew the guy as well as anyone. I worked with him, drank with him, commuted with him…he is not the killer. I don't care what the circumstantial evidence looks like."

The conversation continued for the better part of an hour and a half, when Gordon decided he had accomplished his goals.

"Mr. Woodley, thank you. I'll likely be back in touch."

Chapter 14
Anatomy of a meltdown

Wednesday, October 29, 2008
2:30 P.M.

A Coffee Shop
SoHo, New York City

Sasquatch pulled open the door to the coffee shop in SoHo. His wife, Kelly, had wanted to come into the city. He agreed, reluctantly, the pain of his sudden departure from Smyth Johnston still fresh as if an open wound in the healing process. He knew he couldn't avoid his less-than-triumphant return to Manhattan forever; and he was making an effort, for the first time in years, to please his wife. It had been months since his friend Chip had driven him home in the Smyth Johnston town car.

In that span of time, he had gone from being fired for cause, to being a suspect in the murder of Michael Feinberg, only to be quickly exonerated, to having spoken at length with Chip's attorney, to having visited his friend who was still considered the prime suspect and remained in a detention center in Manhattan. As if this personal malaise weren't enough, he couldn't escape the fixation on the financial market meltdown that had escalated to proportions never imagined possible. He didn't have all the answers for the cause of the meltdown but he knew much more than the average guy reading the sensationalized local New York papers. He tried his best to ignore the news, despite its direct relationship to his life and his fragile bank account. Like many, he knew that the whole thing—the bailouts, political posturing, banker scapegoating—were out of control. Sometimes, reflecting on a sage piece of advice imparted to him from Chip, the best way to deal with a problem was by not dealing with it.

They were having dinner later that day on East 4th Street in the Village at one of Kelly's favorite restaurants in Little India. Sasquatch was fine with it, especially given that it was on the relatively inexpensive side of things. Kelly understood the ex-banker lifestyle; places like Nobu and other stratospherically-expensive restaurants were out of the question.

A mid-afternoon caffeine jolt, some browsing around lower Manhattan, then dinner. Quality time with the wife.

Being in the city again, Sasquatch found it impossible to disassociate his thoughts from his friend Chip. He had visited him two days ago. Feinberg's murder impacted Chip enormously, particularly as its prime suspect. If not front page news, the story remained prominent in the tabloids. He wanted to help his friend, however possible, refusing to accept that he was capable of murder. His conversation with Dwight Gordon led him to begin an investigation of his own, making calls or visiting anyone he felt might help in exonerating Chip. He had recently spoken to Bob Lancer, the bartender at the Blarney Stone, Mal, and Tracy, while also attempting to speak, to no avail, to Detective Bush and Duncan Kerr. Sasquatch had not told his wife that he had actually chosen this coffee shop so that he could speak to Goldberg's widow, who, surprisingly, had agreed to meet with him. Franny had told him that the only reason she would meet with him was that she needed to ask a favor of him.

"What are you having?" Chip asked his wife.

"Just a latte, I think. What are you thinking?"

"Same for me."

As the two sat down for their relaxed coffee, a novel concept for them, Sasquatch spotted a woman sitting alone at a table across the café.

The wife became interested, as her husband continued to glance at the woman.

"Do you know who that is?"

He nodded his head, affirmatively.

"It's Feinberg's widow. I saw her a few times at Smyth Johnston functions. If you're okay with it, I need to talk with her."

"Who do you think you are, Magnum PI or something?"

Kelly was poking fun at her husband, then realized the importance of this to him.

"You should, but be careful. You're stepping into the middle of a murder investigation."

Sasquatch walked over to Franny Goodman, stopping in front of her table.

"Hi Franny, I'm Nigel Woodley. We spoke on the phone yesterday. Thanks for meeting with me."

Franny looked at him, with a somewhat vacant, distressed look, a look of emotional despair.

"Please have a seat."

"My wife is with me, so I won't bother you long. I'm sorry about Michael."

"Well…" she said. "Thank you. Did you know that Michael was divorcing me?"

Sasquatch shook his head, feeling sorrow for her while also recalling her deceased husband's unfaithful ways.

"He manipulated me into signing a revised prenuptial agreement, in effect robbing me of the assets. Now I have to sue his estate to keep the assets from being deemed part of a divorce in progress. Not very pleasant business for a widow."

Franny continued. "And, also not very pleasant is this photo. It's the one you texted to me, right after Michael claimed you assaulted him and had him fired."

Sasquatch nodded, remorseful at having sent the photo, particularly in the current circumstance.

"Is it him in the photo? This isn't some Photoshop job? I need to bring closure to it, though I always knew it was him but never had the courage to confront the truth."

"Yes it's him. Chip Smith sent it to me the night he took it, and I was there in the hotel lobby at the time. I am sorry."

"I had bad thoughts many times of doing him harm myself, as I'm sure many across Wall Street have had. I know what it's like."

"Thoughts are one thing…"

"I…"

"It's okay," Sasquatch said calmly, hoping to keep her emotions in check.

"It just weighs on me so hard. I'm not supposed to talk about this; it's just wrong. I was just a small part of it, not once did I think there was anything wrong," Franny said, succumbing to her emotions.

After the better part of 10 minutes, Sasquatch felt he had gleaned as much information as he had hoped.

"Thank you. I'll leave you alone. Once again I'm sorry for your loss."

Sasquatch returned to his wife. She could see the cell phone shaking in his hand, that her husband was obviously anxious.

He needed to make a call, stepping outside.

"Mr. Gordon, it's Nigel Woodley. We spoke fairly recently. I'm Chip Smith's friend."

$ $ $

Sitting in his office at the SEC, Jack Bonfiglio needed some time to collect himself after what had been an intense two weeks since Michael Feinberg was found shot to death. He still didn't know what the impact of the NYPD investigation would be on his efforts.

The matter under inquiry had become immensely more interesting for Bonfiglio since the call from Rodriguez the morning after the murder. As was procedure, he had asked his forensic accountants to do countless background checks on any wire transfers, bank withdrawals, or anything of interest with Feinberg's bank accounts before and after the night of the murder.

An $8 million transfer had taken place shortly after the murder, to a Cayman Islands account.

He was tired and decided it was time to leave for his home in Queens.

Upon his arrival his wife, Samantha, was still awake, lying in the same bed they had shared for the entirety of their 16-year marriage.

"How was your day? You seem preoccupied, more so than usual. Is everything okay?"

She had barely seen her husband that week, with midnight being the earliest he'd arrived home. Bonfiglio, unbuttoning his shirt and preparing himself for bed, mustered a response.

"My day was interesting, to say the least. Detective Rodriguez called me again to give me more background on the Feinberg case. One of my potential informants is still being held as the prime suspect."

While she knew Jack took his work seriously, Samantha knew the Wall Street banker angle of this investigation held particular interest to her husband. She had heard him bemoan his existence as a SEC investigator before. His past ambition of becoming a banker, more specifically the chance of leaving his blue collar caste in Queens and turning his life into something "bigger" was no secret to her. To his credit, Jack didn't play the self-pity card too often, but she knew his unrealized ambition remained an inextricable part of his psyche.

"Wow, so what's going to happen?"

"In addition to all the work we had done, we got an anonymous tip about Feinberg and his business practices...very damning. Just would have needed to verify a few facts and we could've nailed the guy big time, possibly sending it to the FBI for a criminal investigation."

"I know you'll never look at it this way because it interferes with your work, but maybe this guy being found dead is a form of justice served. There's one less asshole banker out there doing bad things to people. You know that's what most people think of the Wall Street crowd. I mean, look at the financial press lately—they say Wall Street has single-handedly caused the mess the world is in. If it was up to them, Feinberg and all his colleagues should be lynched in Central Park. Despite some of the media sensationalism to sell papers and ads on TV, I tend to believe what I'm hearing. They can't be that wrong."

"Justice served is a little harsh considering this guy's head was literally blown off. By the way, he was married, but no kids at least. So think about that. And the circumstances surrounding the market meltdown are a lot more complex than simply blaming the bankers. Since working on this credit derivatives case, I've learned quite a bit about those products as well as the causes of the meltdown. It'll shock you just how widespread the causes are in actuality."

"Okay, try me—unless you're dead tired and ready to sleep."

She was more than a disinterested spouse. Before retiring to take care of their two sons, Samantha Bonfiglio had been a mid-level lawyer in the district attorney's office. It was there that she and Jack had met in the 1980s.

Jack asked her to give him a minute, walked downstairs to grab a file from his briefcase and returned to his bedside discussion.

"You see this? This is a brief of the inquiry thus far, extracted from literally thousands of pages of information collected since I began working on this 18 months ago. You sure you really want to go through this?"

"I'll let you know if it gets too much. Just try to hit the high points. This should be pretty interesting though. I guess you can't believe everything you read in the *Post* on see on TV."

Jack was tired but knew Samantha's observations would be helpful to him, possibly offering a new perspective.

"To start with, there is no doubt in my mind that Wall Street is a contributor to the meltdown. But the seeds of the meltdown have been germinating for decades, many decades in fact. You can trace its origins back to FDR and the New Deal in the 1930s, when Fannie Mae was established as a means to facilitate liquidity and lending among banks."

"So the politicians are at the root of this?"

"You'll see soon enough—the story has only begun," Jack smiled. "The historical record is clear; politicians have had an unmistakable role in legislating the meltdown. Simply trace their role in the housing market. FDR got the ball rolling with Fannie Mae. Johnson's Great Society reforms made Fannie Mae a government-sponsored entity or a GSE in '68. This status gave them the authority to issue mortgage-backed securities, essentially creating the ability for the banks to sell their loans. In '70, Nixon chartered Freddie Mac as a GSE to compete with Fannie Mae. All this activity—to note, bipartisan in nature—intended to make the housing market function more smoothly for all, individuals and lending institutions alike. Are you with me thus far?"

"I am, although this isn't the most exciting conversation between husband and wife. What about all those sexy derivatives?"

"You asked. Bear with me as this is where it gets more interesting. In 1977 President Carter signed into law the Community Reinvestment Act. The original intent of the act was to encourage banks to promote home ownership by lending more in so-called underserved communities. On the face of it, not a bad objective."

"What do they call it when banks avoid lending in certain areas? Isn't it the same thing insurance companies always get accused of?"

"*Redlining*, or drawing a red line around low-income communities and limiting the amount of business done in those zones. Anyway, with the Community Reinvestment Act came greater scrutiny of banks to make sure they were lending more to low- and middle-income communities. This put banks in the precarious position of complying with the act and a host of other anti-discriminatory lending legislation, while at the same time resisting imprudent lending practices."

"It's starting to sound like Big Brother and George Orwell."

"Big Brother's definitely involved in the housing market at this stage. But here is where the unintended consequences begin to surface. The fact that Big Brother laid the framework for housing market oversight enabled aggressive community organization groups such as ACORN to put more pressure on banks. And these activist groups used intimidation and other tactics—bank lobby protests, demonstrations outside of bankers' homes, you name it, they did it—all to force more lending in poor communities. Any resistance was summarily met with accusations of racism, as a lightning rod. You know, when in doubt throw the race card."

"Isn't that like some of the greenmail cases you've been involved with before?"

"It is similar. As you can imagine, ACORN began to inundate the courts with lawsuits alleging noncompliance against countless banks. Cutting to the chase, the litigation eventually coerced the banks into increasingly making loans that didn't otherwise meet their credit standards. In a great irony, Fannie Mae and Freddie Mac—the government creations—initially wanted nothing to do with these loans. It wasn't until the mid-'90s when the Clinton administration encouraged them to increase the percentage of these loans in their portfolios."

"Aha, these were the subprime loans, correct?"

"Yep. This is the birth of the subprime mortgage market. Soon enough ACORN and other like-minded groups, aided by the Clinton administration's pro-home-ownership strategy—the hallmarks of which included looser credit standards and subprime lending quotas—and Congressional Democrats had driven subprime loans into every pocket within the banking system, well beyond the original scope of the Community Reinvestment Act."

"It's not hard to see how this story is now playing out."

"The political jousting continued for years. Back and forth it went among the politicians, some clamoring about the prospect of systemic risk and the dire need for heightened internal risk management of Fannie Mae and Freddie Mac while still others denied such a prospect. Remember Barney Frank back in 2003 denying that there was a problem? I seem to recall him saying the federal government had done too little in pushing the affordable housing agenda. And he wasn't alone in the political denials.

"In the mid-2000s, there was much more talk of systemic risk to the financial system. Virtually every politician, Greenspan and others in the Washington complex, had their own spin on the topic. As the Washington complex continued its partisan tug-of-war, the subprime loans, also referred to as high-risk or affordability loans depending upon one's political bent, represented 60 percent of foreclosures by April 2007. In September 2007, President Bush called on Congress to pass legislation aimed at strengthening regulation and internal risk management practices at Fannie Mae and Freddie Mac, underscoring the urgency of doing so. Congress failed to act, and the rout was on. The housing bubble began to burst. Foreclosures turned into defaults and the portfolios of Fannie Mae and Freddie Mac collapsed, sparking contagion and the current meltdown."

Jack's wife had been listening, intently so, as she looked at the clock, which read 12:45 a.m.

"If I were to summarize what you just went through, I'd have to say the politicians set the table for the meltdown, and Wall Street cleared the table by spreading the contagion from the subprime market into the broader capital markets. Does that do the story justice?"

"I'm impressed. This stuff can get pretty dull when you're not in the middle of it, or making a living from it. I will say it makes for an interesting paradox when you've spent as much time as I have thinking about it. You have the political proponents of 'social engineering and social justice' married to the free-market capitalists of Wall Street. The politicians wanted the votes from those rewarded with affordable housing, while the bankers wanted the enormous fees associated with the billions of dollars from deals tied to the mortgage market. The twin forces of power and money bridging the worlds of Wall Street and politics—on the grandest of scales."

Jack continued.

"But the blame game can be cast with an even wider net. There were many other groups who fanned the fire of the meltdown. Take for example the rating agencies. Virtually all of the deals that were sold by the banks into the capital markets were rated by one, two, sometimes as many as three rating agencies. Did they get it so categorically wrong or were they in it for the enormous fees they earned by rating the deals? You have the mortgage brokers, the fast-money guys with no skin in the game, just moving mortgages from one party to another and pocketing handsome middle-man fees. You have the defaulted borrowers themselves who, like crack addicts, took the money to live lifestyles they couldn't afford. Many of them claim they were duped by their mortgage providers. That just doesn't hold water in the court of common sense. It's a lack of personal responsibility and accountability on the individual level, all part of the entitlement culture that has developed in this country. What about the investors, who were complacent, relying on the rating agencies to bless the deals. And last, certainly not least, you have the media and its penchant for sensationalistic spin-doctoring for the purpose of advancing a thinly-veiled political agenda and improving their ratings. Add it all up and you have what some are quickly calling the worst financial crisis since the Great Depression of the 1930s, perhaps ever, given its basis in the housing market. Had enough of my meanderings yet?"

Jack looked over at his wife only to notice she had heard enough and fallen asleep. He rolled over and turned off the lamp by his side of the bed. Gathering his thoughts before nodding off, he had a sense of contentment that his life was pretty good, on balance, at least when compared to what he had uncovered over the course of the inquiry. It was not a wholesome snapshot of humanity.

Jack loved his wife and she loved him. They had common interests, mutual respect for one another and the bond of two children whom they both loved unconditionally. Their life together rested on a solid foundation, a foundation capable of sustaining them through the certain struggles that life indiscriminately doles out. Sure the Bonfiglio family lifestyle evidenced some of the comfortable trappings of the American good life. But it paled in comparison to the lifestyles a few miles away across the East River in Manhattan or to those in Washington.

If not money, power, and control, he had simplicity of life.

Chapter 15
The Hamptons, revisited

Friday, November 14, 2008
12:15 P.M.

The Southampton Beach House
Long Island, New York

Deborah Goodman had chosen to celebrate her 60th birthday with Franny at the Hamptons beach house. For each of them the house exuded a strange aura about it, still digesting the reality that Michael would never again be present.

Joining the two was Duncan Kerr, no stranger himself to the Hamptons. He had brought a gift for Deborah, a bracelet from Tiffany's valued at $10,000. He seemed pleased, in a positive frame of mind. In the lone month since Feinberg's death, the bank, unlike a cadre of its peers, had survived the meltdown largely due, coincidentally, to the credit derivatives desk. Though Smyth Johnston wasn't quite out of the danger zone, Kerr felt as though it had weathered the worst the meltdown had to offer. The next few years would be painful, but an implosion had been averted. Vasily Bure had done an admirable job in managing the book amidst the meltdown. For his part, Kerr had been appointed successor to the retiring CEO for his adept handling of the crisis.

As the three sat on the enclosed deck overlooking the Atlantic, Kerr raised his glass of champagne, offering a silent toast to the occasion.

Deborah smiled, as Franny sat, stoically, in the same room of the beach house Michael enjoyed most. It was possibly the only place she found her husband capable of relaxation, however short-lived it may have been.

"What is it?" the mother asked.

"Do you remember Sasquatch from the bank?"

"Of course I do," Kerr said. "He was fired for assaulting…" He didn't finish the sentence.

"Well," Franny said with concern. "He's one of the best friends of Charles Smith."

"So," Kerr said.

"I saw him at a café in SoHo recently. He offered me his condolences."

Kerr responded. "If he's bothering you, get a restraining order. It's not difficult."

Franny shook her head.

"What if he knows something, or—even worse—finds something out? He's been digging around, trying to help his friend out. He told me that he's convinced Chip Smith is not the killer."

"What would he find out?" Kerr asked. "The case is solved. Smith is awaiting trial and sentencing. The police informed us they believe the case is closed."

"But," Franny said. "What if he finds out that I made that call from the phone booth."

"How could he do that?" the mother scoffed.

Kerr looked at Deborah. "I told you we shouldn't have involved her."

"But someone had to make that phone call to distract Smith in the bar's bathroom," Deborah snapped.

"Franny, I'm sorry you got involved. We needed your help."

"I wish you would've told me what you were going to do."

Franny, crying, buried her face in her hands, stunned by the fact she had been duped by her own mother. While suspicious, she had agreed to make the phone call never once entertaining the most painful of betrayals or the thought of her mother co-conspiring to murder her husband. She had confirmed her worst fear.

"Franny, there is nothing to worry about. You don't have to feel guilty about any of this. It was not your idea. Don't worry. The end result is the most important thing. Duncan suggested it, and I went along. Everybody is better off now that Michael is gone. You, me, and Duncan."

"Everyone calm down. Let's have more champagne," Deborah continued, in an attempt to steer the conversation in another direction.

Detectives Rodriguez and Bush abruptly appeared on the other side of the French doors. With them were numerous other members of the NYPD; it was a rude interruption to the trio's intended celebration.

Dwight Gordon, on the heels of the recent phone call from Sasquatch outside the SoHo coffee house, had notified Rodriguez of a potential break in the investigation. Rodriguez had been staking out the beach house, including having it wiretapped. All he needed was the right opportunity for someone to speak into the flower. He now had it.

"Deborah Goodman and Duncan Kerr, you are being arrested on suspicion of the murder of Michael Feinberg. You have the right to remain silent. Anything you say or do…"

"On what basis? This is preposterous," Kerr insisted.

Rodriguez wasn't confused by the question, continuing to read the two their Miranda rights until the end.

"We have your discussion here on wiretap."

Deborah needed a second to put it together.

"Franny, you betrayed your mother? After all I've done for you…"

"You didn't think I'd notice that you stole $8 million from my husband's account?"

Rodriguez had informed her about the missing funds, as had been originally discovered by Bonfiglio.

The police took Deborah and Kerr from the table, placing them in handcuffs.

Alone with Rodriguez, Franny was lost in the conflicted, torturous thought of having returned the favor of betraying her mother in exchange for clemency as part of a plea bargain.

Her husband was dead. Her mother was a co-conspirator in his death. Ultimately, she provided the means by which to solve the murder. Though she would face no jail time herself, she had erected her own prison, an emotional prison she would have to live with the rest of her life.

Epilogue

Wednesday, April 15, 2009
9:14 A.M.

Mal McMahon's Driveway
Rye, New York

Chip, Sasquatch, and Mal, all three of whom had now joined the ranks of the unemployed, had previously decided to get together for a round of golf once the weather cooperated. What else were they to do in the aftermath of their career Armageddon?

Sasquatch picked Chip up on Long Island, where the two had agreed to make the drive to see Mal in Rye. Today's golf would be different than their outing in Pebble Beach. There would be no caddies, no majestic views of the rocky northern California coastline. Instead, they would be teeing it up together at a municipal course minutes up the road from Mal's house.

Mal had relinquished his membership at the prestigious Westchester Country Club, as had many of its other members. The waiting list had disappeared almost overnight.

"Any interest in your house, Mal? By the way, it's beautiful," Chip politely asked his former client as he saw the prominently displayed Sotheby's "For Sale" sign on the two-acre cascading lawn.

"Funny. There aren't any dumbasses left to pony up $2.5 million for a house in this environment. I'm stuck in my own mess, crapped in my bed you might say. I know it. I guess this is the hangover I have to live with. Maybe I'll just turn in the keys when the market value dips below the note—play the personal bankruptcy game."

"Solid act of personal responsibility," Sasquatch joined in.

"Yep. I was talking to a neighbor the other day, unemployed neighbor that is, who said he had a 100 percent loan-to-value mortgage and really was going to mail the keys to the bank. And I quote him, he said he 'was getting even with the evil bank.' How's that for personal responsibility? A well-educated guy living in Rye, and he's thinking that way."

"What did you say to him?"

"Nothing; I was so offended, I just walked away mid-conversation. He's bitter at the bank for giving him a plate of money, 100 percent of the market value, and the bank is evil. This is what it has come to…anyway, what's up with you guys in your new world order?"

"I'm enjoying being unemployed for the first time in 20 years. Granted, I've only been at this for a few months. For now I'm content chasing my kids around— school, soccer, dance, T-ball, other activities, and looking for daily projects to occupy myself while not driving the wife crazy. I have to tell you, this Mr. Mom bit is fun but it's actually a lot of work, not that I'll concede that point with my wife. Basically, the key for me is to feel busy, productive, and enthusiastic one day at a time. It's immediate gratification. What my plan is beyond the here and now, I have no clue. We're all living with the same crucible. It certainly won't be what I used to do—no one is hiring and won't be for a long time."

"Pretty much the same thing with me," added Sasquatch. "The Wall Street pot of gold, the dream, is gone. In my case, it's probably gone forever with Feinberg having engineered my firing. Even if there were jobs out there, I was fired for cause which means my résumé gets deposited into the circular file 99 out of 100 times. I will have to keep doing the real estate thing for the time being. Tenants haven't been that bad. Some folks have left, but there are still enough of them left that I make some money. However, there will be no Disneyland vacations for the Woodley family."

"Well, lads, all variations on the same theme for the three of us and thousands of others. Very challenging times."

"It's hard to see how this plays out for everyone. Some will reinvent themselves in a personal lifestyle makeover. Some will desperately, out of force of habit, search for a job, any job, in an effort to sustain their unsustainable lifestyles. Some will kick the can down the road, buying time under the blind faith that something will change for the better eventually," Chip conjectured.

"So, what happened to Karros?"

"He's probably still hanging out in Monmouth County, staring at his own statue, wondering what the fuck happened to him. He's the kind of guy, however, who will reinvent himself somewhere, in some capacity. Maybe he becomes a New Jersey congressman. The guy has the political acumen, and he probably has enough cash to bankroll a decent campaign. Who knows, maybe he finagles his way onto the Greek negotiation team with the EU bailout when Greece finally blows up."

"And Bure?"

"Living the dream, on his selfish terms no doubt. You're lucky you're not seeing deals from him. He makes Feinberg look good. Boy, don't I miss it."

"Tracy? How do you spell collateral damage? Timing is everything in this crazy business."

"I actually spoke to her the other day. Get this. She's in night school at Columbia business school, still working at Smyth Johnston. She's running a team of three in derivative sales. She's the new me I guess you could say."

"What a twisted script this has all become. How many times did we tell her that one day this could all be hers. Looks like her wish has come true."

The three paused, seizing on the mildly comical nature of it all. Success on Wall Street was a thin line, often dominated, as they so often mused over the course of their now former careers, by circumstances outside of anyone's control. Indeed, it often felt like a random walk.

"Yep, she's the boss of three, overseeing an empire with no products to sell. I wonder if she's read about the 'winner's curse' at B-school yet."

$ $ $

The three had gathered in the no-frills clubhouse. It was minutes before their 11:07 tee time, enough for a nostalgic chug, a social, of their Budweiser tallboys. It was as if the cans of beer held in each of their hands symbolized the only remaining constant in their radically transformed lives.

Minutes later they found themselves standing on the tee box on hole number one, smiling, and feeling better by having had a cathartic, existential Wall Street post-mortem.

The conversation, as expected, soon turned to Feinberg.

"So dude, how did it all go down?" Mal asked the other two.

"Franny Goodman was the weak link. But without Sasquatch, the weak link never would have been solved, and I'd be in Sing Sing up here in Westchester now— and not playing golf."

Sasquatch grinned with self-satisfaction.

"Thank my wife. She's the one who wanted to go into the city. Otherwise, I would have never set up that meeting with Franny at the coffee shop."

"Yes, thank your wife. And I'm thankful that the random walk doesn't always lead to bad outcomes, now that I'm out of jail that is."

"Your theory about bad things happening to good people may yet be disproven."

"Gladly," Chip conceded.

$ $ $

Victor Rodriguez sat in his precinct office in Manhattan. He was on the phone with Jack Bonfiglio, recounting NYPD's work to his old friend.

Duncan Kerr and Deborah Goodman thought they had hatched the infallible plan to kill Feinberg. As it turned out in their interrogations, both had accused one another, unconvincingly so. Their alliance unraveled during their desperate attempts at mutual self-preservation.

During a search of Kerr's home, a tattered note was found. It was the note he had written to Michael Feinberg about P&L recognition. It was damning evidence of the threat Feinberg posed to Kerr's power and ambition of becoming the next CEO of Smyth Johnston.

Deborah Goodman's motive was accessing the money her daughter would get. That amount, estimated to be $100 million, would pass to Franny as per Michael's will. He was worth multiples more to Franny in death than divorce, thanks to his marital sleight of hand with the pre-nup. By extension, Deborah would presumably be in better financial stead as well, so she had calculated. She was badly in debt, with the 65th Street apartment likely having to be put up for sale within the year. She had become the victim of her profligate, gold digger Manhattan lifestyle. Her maternal instinct further compelled her to protect her only child from the deceitful ways of her husband. Money and blood.

Kerr had found out from Tracy Maxwell that Chip could be found at the Blarney Stone early on the night of the murder. Kerr had been there, ready to follow Chip into the bathroom. Upon being alerted by a text message, Franny called Chip from the phone booth. When Chip, well-lubricated by the many beers, was concentrating on looking for his phone, Kerr stuck the needle into his upper arm. Posing as his friend, he dragged Chip out of the bar, citing alcohol as the problem, to the sidewalk where Deborah Goodman was waiting in a rental car.

Deborah had purchased the clothing to be used in the murder. After following Feinberg to the hotel, Kerr's contract killer shot Feinberg, searched him and, as per the directive from Kerr, found the incriminating note about P&L stashed in a briefcase. In the hotel stairwell, the killer planted a Kleenex which had been used to wipe the unconscious Chip's nose earlier in the evening. Following the shooting, the killer met Kerr and Goodman in their car, where he handed over his clothing, a cotton swab of the gunpowder residue, and the murder weapon itself. While being driven to Brooklyn, Chip was changed into the killer's clothing, his nose and eyes swiped with traces of gunpowder, and the gun placed in his coat pocket. He would be left, near lifeless, resting next to a dumpster, in a secluded alley. When combined with alcohol, the Rohypnol, better known as a roofie, injected in him by Kerr several hours prior, would assure Chip was going nowhere until sometime the next morning. Even after waking up, the drug would likely cause severe disorientation and memory loss. It was the perfect choice for the perfect crime.

At the time Chip was formally exonerated, Victor Rodriguez apologized for the miscarriage of justice and the four-week jail time.

In the final result, Detective Rodriguez concluded with his friend Jack Bonfiglio that, as it always does, the day of comeuppance had arrived for all involved. To each of the law enforcement officers, it was reaffirming, tragic consequences notwithstanding, that bad behavior never prevails. Duncan Kerr was felled by his unquenchable ambition for power and hierarchical stature. Deborah Goodman was felled by her shallow pursuit of ill-begotten riches and would have to live each day knowing she was the cause of her estrangement with her only child. Both would be spending much if not all of their remaining time disgraced and incarcerated.

Franny, dragged into the net of her mother's wrongdoing, was left to live with having blown the whistle on her own mother in exchange for her freedom. She would also be the beneficiary of much of her now-deceased husband's fortune, which Jack Bonfiglio was told by the SEC accountants amounted to $115 million, even more than had been suspected. Whether she would do something positive with the money or remain a slave to the superficial, hedonistic lifestyle to which she had grown accustomed remained an open question. Michael Feinberg, deceased at age 32, stands as a symbol of a young, at times misdirected, life turned bad, a life deprived of fulfilling its promise of potential greatness defined in terms other than money.

All told it was yet another morality tale, the human drama, replete with its many human frailties, acted out on the stage of Wall Street. It was a tale of money, power, and control—that unholy Trinity found episodically throughout history—corrupting an otherwise necessary and productive business culture. It was a tale of bad behavior becoming a tyranny of the few.

$ $ $

Sasquatch ordered three more Budweisers as they sat, contentedly, at the muni course bar.

"As odd as it sounds, but, 'To Feinberg.'"

"And to Franny and Sasquatch," Chip added. "I knew there was a reason I hired you."

"You hired and fired me, to be clear. Thank you, for both."

They took a long sip.

"The bank has offered me three million in compensatory damages." Chip said.

"Afraid of a lawsuit?"

"I guess. My lawyer called me with the news while we were on the course."

"Bargain it to four, at least. They'll take it for sure.'

"Gordon's law firm is taking care of it," Chip grinned.

"He can earn his exorbitant legal fee. I propose we use the money to go on a trip. My treat," Chip suggested.

"I would be okay with that." Mal said.

"Fishing or golf?" Chip asked.

"Pebble Beach, golf. We've been fishing with you before—no thanks," Sasquatch smiled.

"And let's bring the wives this time."

Glossary of Terms and Acronyms

Asset-Backed Security ("ABS") – a financial instrument whose value and payments are derived from and backed by a specific pool of assets.

Alternative Assets – an investment product other than stocks, bonds, or real estate, including certain financial derivatives and hard assets.

Basis Point ("bp") – equal to one hundredth of a percentage point. It is used as a unit of measurement where percentage differences are less than 1 percent.

Correlation Risk – the probability of loss to an investment from the difference in price movement of two or more assets.

Collateralized Debt Obligation (CDO) – a type of an asset-backed security which is backed by debt obligations (bonds and loans).

Credit Default Swap (CDS) – a financial derivative where the seller agrees to compensate the buyer upon a company's default or other specified event.

Credit Derivative – various instruments and techniques that transfer the credit risk of an underlying loan or bond from one party to another.

CFTC (Commodity Futures Trading Commission) – a federal agency charged with overseeing the futures and options market.

Default Correlation – the interdependence of default between two companies.

Derivative – an instrument whose price is derived from one or more underlying assets.

FASB (Financial Accounting Standards Board) – an independent body responsible for establishing and interpreting Generally Accepted Accounting Principles.

Gaussian Copula – a mathematical tool that uses correlation coefficients to calculate interdependence of returns of two or more assets. It has been applied to many areas within finance.

Leverage – a technique to multiply gains and losses by borrowing money.

LIBOR (London Interbank Offered Rate) – the interest rate leading banks in London charge each other; the primary benchmark for short term global interest rates.

Liquidity/Illiquidity Risk – a loss arising from either a) not having enough cash available, b) the sale of assets at less than their fair value, or c) the inability to sell an asset due to a lack of buyers.

Mark-to-Market – accounting for the "fair value" of an asset or liability based on the current market price.

Mortgage-Backed Securities (MBS) – an asset-backed security based on a portfolio of mortgage loans.

Notional Amount – the face or nominal amount that is used to calculate payments made on an instrument.

OECD (Organization of Economic Cooperation and Development) – an international economic organization of 34 countries to stimulate global trade.

Over-the-Counter Derivative (OTC) – a derivative traded directly between two parties that does not go through an exchange.

Positive Carry – the profit from an investment whose return is higher than the cost of borrowing money.

P&L – a catch-all term for Profit and Loss, or net income.

Securitization – the pooling of debt instruments such as mortgages, auto loans, credit card debt or bonds and loans, and selling securities backed by such instruments to various investors.

Subprime Mortgage – a type of mortgage granted to individuals with poor credit histories (with no ability to qualify for a conventional mortgage), usually having a high and adjustable interest rate.

Synthetic CDO – a collateralized debt obligation that is backed by credit default swaps rather than bonds or loans.

Tranche – a piece or portion of a collateralized debt obligation having a distinct risk profile; a tranche is created to more effectively appeal to varying investor risk preferences.